THE
BOOKSTORE
MURDERS

THE BOOKSTORE MURDERS

BY

MARCY HEIDISH

Dolan & Associates, Publishers

THE BOOKSTORE MURDERS
Copyright © 2015 by Marcy Heidish

Published previously as *The Torching*
Printing History
First Printing, 1992, Simon & Schuster ISBN 0671743759
Republication 2008, Dolan & Associates, Publisher
ISBN: 978-0-9792404-4-7

LIBRARY OF CONGRESS CATALOGING-IN-PUBLICATION DATA
Heidish, Marcy.
    The Bookstore Murders
    p. cm.
    ISBN:978-0-9905262-2-3
    I. Title
Library of Congress Control Number: 2015932586

Lines quoted with permission from the poem "You, Andrew Marvell," by Archibald MacLeish in *New and Collected Poems*, published by Houghton Mifflin, 1976.
....
Revision & Retitle

For Upton Brady

At first you will not know what it means
And you may never know
And we may never tell you.
Those sudden flashes in your soul
Like lambent lightning on snowy clouds at midnight
When the moon is full.
Sometimes they come in solitude
Or sometimes you sit with your friend
And all at once a silence falls on speech
And his eyes, without a flicker, glow at you.
You two have seen the Secret together,
He sees it in you and you in him
And there you sit, thrilling,
Lest the Mystery stand before you
And strike you dead with a splendor like the sun's.
Be brave, all souls who have such visions.
As your body is alive, as mine is dead,
You're catching a little whiff of the ether
Reserved for God himself.

> Faith Matheny's Epitaph
> *Spoon River Anthology*
> Edgar Lee Masters

PROLOGUE

Fluke.

Nightmare, coincidence. So I explained it away at the time and so I tried to believe.

Moments before, it seemed, I was reading in bed, held within a ring of lamplight on the quilt. Now the light was out, the room was cold and there were rustlings in the dark. The sounds drew nearer. Something grazed my cheek: a hand, a sleeve like a frozen wing.

I twisted away. I raised my head — and saw them, all at once. Ranged about the room, they stood: a dim frieze of figures. Their faces were hard as flat pale stones, their eyes deep and lightless. Slowly, they began to shift and move again, cloaks rustling, steps deliberate, as if part of some grim dance. In their hands, torches flared; shadows streamed across the walls as the figures pressed around me. I saw a spinning ring of fire and then only smoke — veils of smoke clinging to my face; I could not breathe. The sheets were taking flame.

From somewhere beyond, there came a sudden jolt of sound, high and thin, a ceaseless call. I grabbed at this sound, as if at a rope, and let it pull me from the bed, the room, till I was plunging forward through the dark — and found myself in the upstairs hall.

I leaned against a wall and ran my hand over my face. I was awake. I wasn't burned. Faint morning light filtered through the lace curtains. The hall clock read five forty-five. Everything looked safe and sane: the gate-legged table, the blue rug. Still, below me, came that high taut shriek: it seemed to flatten out across the floor, as if the house itself were screaming.

Snatching at the banister, I ran downstairs into the bookstore, one floor below. The shop's smoke alarms were going off: all of them, ranged about the spacious rooms, and I streaked through, scanning shelves.

Nothing. Nowhere.

And still, that banshee wail went on. My ears ached, my head ached, the fillings in my teeth ached. Climbing a ladder, I groped for the ceiling and wrenched the batteries from those screaming plastic disks, the one in HISTORY, the one in ART, in WORLD RELIGIONS, TRAVEL ... Silence: stunning, perfect, sweet. I took a breath. In the quiet shop, I could hear my pulse. Warily, I moved back through the store, past every shelf. Still, I found nothing amiss, nothing to show what had set off the alarms.

At the desk in the main room, I let the batteries roll from my fingers; brand-new batteries. For a moment, the bookcases blurred before my eyes. Still shaking, I turned to climb the stairs to my apartment; the banister seemed to skid beneath my hand. I remembered the dream then, that frieze of torchlit figures ... At the landing I hesitated, then forced myself to the bedroom door.

I looked into the room. Peach-colored light lay across the quilt. The clock's tick made the calm metallic sound of someone knitting. On the nightstand, beneath the lamp's glass shade, a book lay open, my place marked. From beneath the bed, one small face peered: the face of Red, my marmalade-colored cat.

There was no sign that anyone had been here. Any one but me.

Fluke, nightmare, coincidence. I muttered those words like a prayer until I believed them — for a while. Now, though, after everything that's happened, those smart words have slipped away and I need others. I need to tell this story through and listen, myself, to what it says; perhaps then I will understand it. I should be able to do that much, as I am by trade a storyteller and, moreover, a handler of stories, a dealer in stories.

I am practiced at untangling plot lines. I think I have an eye for character, an ear for the internal syntax of a story. Of course, all this applies to tales that are pressed and folded, neat as linen napkins, within the covers of bound books: other people's books. This story is not neat or folded or finished, and it's mine. I'm not sure if I can decipher that: a story, half-scrawled on the air, involving my own life.

I'll call this story a book then. Instantly, it becomes more manageable. Downstairs in the shop, I'd shelve it where? No categories spring to mind. MISCELLANY, then, for the record; just in case.

Those last words have a faintly ominous sound, but I should be used to that. I've made a moderate living from ominous sounds. As a novelist in the genre of Historical Horror, I "do" Ominous, and Ominous never bothered me before. It used to feel quite ordinary and, at book-signings, it seems, I looked "too ordinary" as well. I remember a woman staring, aghast, at my bright silk blouse and miniskirt, then asking if I *really* was the author. "I only wear black when I work," I snapped. The woman looked relieved. No wonder, considering the book she was buying. It was my first novel, based on that all-American dysfunctional family, the Donners: a clan of Western pioneers who got through a bad winter, quite simply, by cannibalizing one another. My next subject was Lizzie Borden, the nineteenth-century ax-murderer; and my latest, unfinished, is about a lesser-known colonial woman with a hidden life. I have this last novel's synopsis, written for the publisher:

> *The Torching*, by Alice Grey, is the story of a woman possessed. In 1738, it was said, the Devil roamed the town of Maidstone, Maryland. Evangeline Smith, midwife and nurse, was at first seen as a ministering angel — until her secret life came to light. It begins with the shocking discovery of the eyes, gouged out and collected by Evangeline for supernatural rituals, and ends with the fall of an American heroine....

Even as I wrote this, I knew something didn't quite fit. I went ahead with the novel even so, encouraged by my agent, but even after the manuscript had been accepted, I felt some hesitation. I had been rereading a source book, the night of that scare; the night of the smoke alarms. It was unlike me to analyze. I have never known exactly what drew me to these tales: tales like strange houses, built on history's darker floor plans. I didn't particularly want to know, either. Analysis, I believed, killed inspiration. Certainly I would not be analyzing this new story if it weren't happening to this shop. My shop; our shop. Kate's shop.

Weatherell's Rare & Used Books was my grandmother's store. She founded it here in Georgetown before this neighborhood was restored, renovated, and chic. Once a slum in the northwest section of the nation's capital, Georgetown now resembles a quaint Federal village, with real estate worth multimillions. But when the bookstore opened, Weatherell's was just an old clapboard house on a street of old clapboard houses in a rundown part of Washington.

Kate Ryan Weatherell, a young widow, had a Celtic love of words and a shrewd Yankee way with money; both talents served the shop, as did Kate herself. As a child, I remember playing amid crates of books, and riding up from the cellar in the creaking dumbwaiter. I remember, too, the smell of old leather, old paper, creosote and glue, as my grandmother restored antique volumes — tall, straight-spined Kate, with her elegant hands that seemed to float among the bookshelves.

I thought of her even when I was away at my parents' summer place on the Maine coast; Kate was always more real to me than my parents, who left me often in her care. In Maine, I'd sit on a sun-warmed dock, swinging my legs over the water, and the lilt of my grandmother's words would come back to me: her voice half-singing, half-murmuring the poetry she would never quite write. And then there was the summer I came home to her and Weatherell's to stay; the August I was sixteen and my parents were killed in a boating accident during a squall on Perkins Cove. My brothers went to college; I came back alone.

I came back to these sheltering eaves and sloping floors, the dormer windows and odd-shaped rooms, where my quirky, strong, magical grandmother waited. She taught me how to run the store, and between-times, I began writing upstairs in the garret, where I'd slept as a child, and wept as a teenager, and laughed again with Kate. I've been running the shop since her death, seven years ago. I was twenty-five then, and felt old; she was eighty and felt young.

Now, when I open the shop in the mornings, I think of her. I think of another morning when I was a child and my grandmother led me deep into the shelves, commanding me to listen. I thought she wanted me to listen to her voice, but she said nothing for a long time. She wanted me to listen to the books themselves. *Here, here, is where the power is,* she said at last, *not in names, money, politics, but here* — her hand cupped my chin — *here, in the words, the stories.* She smelled of cigarettes and rose water; her blue gaze held mine.

I recall that now, as I begin the telling of this strange new story — to myself. If something is affecting this bookshop, I want to know what it is, what it's called, what it does, and I want it out where I can see it. I want to find what is not apparent now; this interests me. As a reader and an appraiser of books, I always look for what the writer *doesn't* show; that, too, shapes the story.

This is true in all narratives, those we read and those we live. One occurs to me from girlhood. Once, with a group of Washington schoolchildren, I was invited to the White House to meet the First Lady. We were to be entertained by a tall Boy Scout dressed in full regalia, who would start a fire for us by rubbing two sticks together.

Young, expectant, we sat with our eyes on this hero. He grasped the sticks and flicked them together like batons. Nothing happened. He ground the sticks together; still nothing. He tried again, his face reddening — not a spark. Abruptly, the Boy Scout burst into tears. A servant with matches was hastily summoned and, off to one side, kindled one stick. The Scout grabbed it and spun around. Dutifully, we all applauded. The First Lady smiled. The White House photographer swiftly snapped a picture. I have it still: beaming woman, clapping children, glowing flame.

Missing from the photo, but part of the picture: failure, tears, servant, matches. And yet. they were present, just beyond the frame. What lies beyond the logical frame — that is what I'll look for in this story: the story of our shop, these last few weeks. It begins, I believe, with the open book beneath my lamp, that night of false alarms and vivid dreams.

It begins with invisible fire.

■

PART ONE

NOVEMBER 1, 1991

« 1 »

*C*andles. I stared into a blaze of them; sixty-five of them. "What is it, a shrine? A public burning?"

Everyone else laughed. I was transfixed by those tiny, frantic flames dancing above an enormous cake made in the shape of a book. A tome, in fact. A Russian novel on hormones, Shakespeare on steroids; "bound" in mocha icing, the thing even had a spine. I couldn't find the right words to say. Obscene, I thought. "Amazing," I finally managed.

It was Weatherell's sixty-fifth birthday and we were celebrating with an open house, which I'd envisioned as a fairly sane occasion: wine and cheese and nothing dramatic. I didn't expect that cake to appear, nor did I expect my reaction to the candles. Normally, I like them and have always lit them by the dozens in church, but these flames made me uneasy. Suddenly, then, I recalled my dream — like a flashcube, its odd light burst before me. I leaned over to blow out the candles, but immediately, as if to stave off some catastrophe, urgent hands held me back.

"Wish!" my guests commanded.

I hesitated.

Call it prescient, call it perverse: something somber brushed me — something I must wish *against*. It would not surface, refusing to name itself. I dismissed it, politely but firmly, as a wrong number.

"We'll all wish," I said. "This is a group shrine."

Suddenly hushed, we bowed our heads. Encircling the cake were neighbors, customers, "regulars," friends, local shopkeepers, members of our writers' group, and some local glitterati, who seem to know, uncannily, where there will be press. And, to my astonishment, there was press. How did they get here? I lowered my eyes again; the hush deepened. As one, we leaned forward, just as the door burst open. Chill autumn air swirled toward us, extinguishing half the candles. Across the threshold leapt a gorilla, waving red balloons and belting out a song that I have completely, unforgivably, repressed.

Perhaps it was only "Happy Birthday."

Day of arrivals.

Day of omens.

A day unusual for Weatherell's: a respected shop, a bit of a landmark, but relentlessly shabby and old-fashioned. In my grandmother's day, books were delivered personally, on bicycles, all over Georgetown. Before holidays, the shop took its regulars' gift lists, made selections, and wrapped each one. The deliveries are gone now, along with special wrapping, but we still make selections for patrons and our patrons still care about books — and put up with Weatherell's dust and dinginess.

It's a quiet store on a quiet street, where the sidewalk is uneven and the roots of old trees push up through the cement and birdsong drifts overhead. Past the shop, nannies wheel prams and street people push carts; a homeless woman named Dinah sleeps in our lit doorway, between the two bay windows, and has become a friend. Once a farmhouse, Weatherell 's slumps and sprawls on several levels, branching into several rooms. It is decidedly not chic, not pop, not wow, no literary in-spot, but so it seemed that fizzy birthday, the Feast of All Souls — and all manner of souls kept arriving.

There was general chaos. There was a rhythmic rise and fall of voices, and the flash of many faces, and the splash of more balloons breaking loose, bouncing high, skimming the ceiling. Crumbs dropped. Flashbulbs flared; the door chimed repeatedly. Roses arrived from the corner pharmacist, and champagne from the Jesuits of Holy Trinity. More ice was winched up on the dumb-waiter, and as the party unfurled like some great trick paper hat, the cash register churned and the phone rang on the Civil War desk in the corner: my grandmother's old command post.

I loved this desk, and could still see Kate's head bent over it; whenever I sat there, I thought of her. I'd logged in thousands of hours leaning on that seasoned wood, taking orders, placing orders, reading, dreaming, and consuming quantities of tuna fish: my remedy for a tendency to low blood sugar. Now, rather than drift about the shop, I chose to stand behind the desk and watch the party. That massive oak-wood slab was, I confess, a bulwark against chaos.

My unease with parties had been with me since childhood; I was the daughter of two painters who were always "having people in." Before my parents got the studio in Maine, I remember, I'd crouch on the stairs of the Georgetown house, watching parties swirl below, observing clothes, kisses, killer-looks — while my two older brothers threw spitballs down into the guests' drinks. Now I found myself observing this party with that old, odd detachment.

As I watched, the shop's lights flickered. It was so brief, I thought I had imagined it; then the lights wavered again. Old house, faulty wiring, I reasoned, but the wiring, I knew, was fine. Suddenly, amid this bright gathering, I recalled that hush around the cake. *Wish, make a wish.* Again I felt a vague sense of something unnamed moving like a pickpocket through a crowd. *Make a wish* ... I wished the bookstore would not blow a fuse. I wished I would stop translating electronics into my fiction genre.

I had just convinced myself the lights had not flickered when they flickered once more — and went out. There was an instant of surprised silence in the shop. I came out from around the desk, and immediately the lights were back on. Dinah looked at me, then at the air, with that incandescent violet gaze of hers. Then she ran a hand through her rough, ginger-colored hair and drew her several sweaters tight about her. The hum of voices had resumed, and with it laughter, music.

Only I remained still, listening . . . for what? I glanced through the large main room into the next one, not quite knowing what I expected to see — and, of course, saw nothing. There was only a faint chill, like a fine winter rain, and then that, too, was gone. The door was chiming and someone was waving and, from the great desk, the phone was ringing again.

I grabbed the receiver, wanting instant contact with Real Life. "Weatherell's Rare Books." Listening, I sighed. "No, we don't carry video games . . . no, not even *rare* video games . . . no, not even *used* video games ... " I tried to keep the edge of irritation from my voice, and failed. "We sell books, y'know — *books?*"

The caller's sign-off was lost in the approaching music duo: two strolling players, a lute/trumpet combo, doing something they called Dixieland Renaissance. I hoped they wouldn't shatter any windows. The lute player, Gerald Shane, was a member of our writers' workshop — otherwise I might have stuffed a rag in his friend's horn. Gerald smiled at me. "Alice, you look like a seraph."

"A *what*?" I shouted over the din.

"A seraph," he shouted back. "A *tomboy* seraph."

"Great. A celestial cross-dresser."

Something was getting on my nerves. Maybe it was the noise or the lights or the crowd, or the wino urinating in WORLD RELIGIONS. Maybe it was aftershock from my dream the night before, or maybe it was just the phone, ringing once again.

"Weatherell's Rare Books," I snapped into the receiver, my voice less than seraphic. "No, I'm sorry, that title's not in yet, I'll be sure to call you ... "

"You do that." Over the desk, a man leaned toward me. "Why don't I just find a phone booth ... "

He leaned closer, kissing me full on the mouth.

"Your name?" I looked up at him.

"Truman Capote." Jake Randolph stepped behind the desk with me. He has always been bold, cloaking this in his Virginia drawl. The boldness is what drew me first. It took me months to like the drawl and that was years ago. He had just shelved his law degree then, breaking family tradition, to spend his time flying planes — small ones, for a charter company based here at National Airport. The Irish in him, he said, rebelled. He is Irish on his mother's side, sandy-haired, with light eyes like my grandmother's, and a gift for words like her: powerful, but not quite realized.

For five years, Jake has been working on an ambitious novel: the story of a pilot from a Southern family who shelved his law degree to fly small planes for a charter company at National Airport, a pilot with a gift for words ... Jake. If he'd stay out of the sky, out of those Beechcrafts, he'd finish his novel; then he might own the bookstore he says he's always wanted. Instead, between flights, he helps out here, and we go on with our "arrangement," living separately, never quite attached, never quite apart. It's an arrangement that suits me, though I know he'd like to change it; we tend to know what the other is thinking.

"You're worried about the lights," he was saying now.

I nodded. "And the smoke alarms. Something — "

"I'll check the wiring later."

"I just *had* it checked, I — "

The phone rang again; he grabbed it.

"Neiman Marcus," he said into the receiver.

"*Jake.*"

"Women's Lingerie. Brassieres. May I help you?"

I grabbed the phone.

"Weatherell's Rare Bras — oh *God.*" I hung up.

And amid the laughter, I forgot the lights and the chill and the dream; forgot them for a while. Then, past the crowd, past the cake, something else jarred me: the door had flown open again, as if on its own.

Day of arrivals, day of omens.

The arrival, this time, came in the form of two deliverymen, kicking the door open, suddenly, swiftly, as if to make a mass arrest. Moments later, they lurched in, staggering under three large crates, before I could direct them around back, to the cellar door. And then I recognized the seal on the crates. They hit the floor with a solid *thunk,* and as soon as I'd signed for them, I'd forgotten the party — I was slicing through tape, prying up lids with such haste, my knife slashed the wood; I winced at the thought of marring even the vessel of this expected treasure. A dark rich smell of leather rose toward me and now, within the crates, I glimpsed dark rich bindings on very old, very fine books. For a moment, I simply inhaled.

"This is it," I said, more to myself than anyone. "The Bishop's Bonanza."

So it was. An actual unfolding Antiquities Event. The crates held a coveted find. My friend and assistant, Edwina Cassidy, had bid against a dozen buyers for this prize: the theological library of a famed Episcopal bishop, retired, reclusive, and recently deceased. Negotiations were conducted only by phone. The family had sent a list of titles, photos, data, and two samples; these last by courier. The books, all first editions, were bound in tooled leather, with hand-sewn spines and marbleized end papers. Collected during a long, honored life in the Church, these volumes were suddenly ours.

Everyone encircled the crates, stamped with the bishop's seal. There was a hush. My guests seemed like awestruck children, gazing, not quite daring to touch; small wonder. I lifted out one book, then another, then more — books the color of oak leaves and aged brandy and rich swift winter dusks; books that exuded a scent of boxwood and a sense of echoing cathedrals, ancient light-drenched stone, chime of bells across a field, holy smell of beeswax candles, arches soaring over sacred space. Like some enchanted doorway, this open crate seemed to draw us toward a distant, misted time, and hold us there in silence.

"They *are* magnificent." Edwina Cassidy knelt beside me then, her voice relieved. "These phone auctions . . ."

We exchanged a knowing glance. That auction had made us both nervous, but she'd managed it well and, as always, I was grateful for Eddie. Like Jake, it seemed she'd always been here and we'd always been friends, though it had taken time to know her. At first, there had been a kind of smoky reserve around her, a studied elegance; something opaque about this handsome, dark-haired woman who had joined the shop's writing group. Gradually, though, I saw her kindness, her shyness — and her keen eye that took in everything.

She'd read everything, too; had taught writing, and, at thirty-five, was starting her first novel, a mystery. We'd talked about that, I remember, and then about expensive lingerie: a mutual weakness. "A *strength*," she had corrected me. We soon discovered we read the same fiction and haunted the same sacred groves: lace stores, bookstores, cathedrals. As I came to know Eddie, I saw her sense of humor; she was a sharp mimic of critics and authors, a teller of funny, trenchant stories.

Quiet and ladylike in public, considerate of our customers, she could always get me laughing in the back room, over her innumerable cigarettes. Now, over the bishop's crates, she winked at me. A photographer from the *Post* snapped our picture.

"Could you both *lean* over the books?" he asked.

"Lower . . ."

Eddie and I exchanged glances. The camera flashed again.

"Appropriate." The photographer nodded at the cross-shaped slash I'd made on the crate. "Can we get a close-up, girls?"

"Certainly," said a masculine voice.

Into the picture stepped a figure that set the cameras off again. Tall and elegant, he slid in like a hot knife through wax. Wherever he went, Andrew Hastings appeared like that: well-known author, Washington personality, smiling down on books and women, pressing his long fingers together.

"Magnificent indeed," he said. "And perfect timing." He gazed down into the crates as if into a well, and whistled softly. "Quite an anniversary gift."

"Not a gift," Eddie reminded him. "We paid."

"And not three for nine ninety-nine," I added.

Andrew Hastings clutched his chest, reeling backward in mock horror. "Don't shock me. Don't tell me — the reverend clergy have ceased to make donations? Bishops? Our *Most* Reverends?"

"This one ceased. In all senses of the word." I moved toward Andrew. Far taller than I, he reached down to kiss my cheek. "Ah, I've done it all wrong." He kissed my hand instead. "Alice. Anniversary blessings. Kate would be proud."

I'd known Andrew for years. He'd frequented the shop when I was living with my grandmother and he was a graduate student in literature. An odd, gangly, diabetic young man then, he'd had few friends. Now, some fifteen years later, he was dapper and polished; no longer odd, but delightfully eccentric. "ANDREW HASTINGS," his bio might read, "is the author of three 'instant classics' hailed by the critics as 'jewels,' each about the inter-section of religion with modem life."

He ritualized everything, from a meal to a meeting, but no one complained because he was so unabashedly charming. "President of a prestigious writers' work-shop" — ours — "he lives with his wife" ... hardly ever, she is often at their country home; still, never a murmur of scandal. Andrew seemed somehow celibate, a kind of taller, handsomer, at-large Thomas Merton. No wonder, now, that Andrew was immediately entranced by the bishop's books.

"Gems," he said, studying them.

"Dynamite." said the gorilla, leaning forward.

We all looked up. The gorilla removed his head, revealing Brad Stein within, another member of our writers' group. "BRAD STEIN, popular author of a dozen spy thrillers" ... cranked them out, mostly for paperback. Lately, he verged on plump, his clothes pleasantly rumpled; an interesting contrast with Andrew. "Vice president of a prestigious writers' group" ... he wasn't literary and didn't pretend to be. Perhaps that was what had drawn me to him, seven or eight years ago now, when we were briefly — what? I never quite knew. Afterward, we remained friends; at least in my mind. Now Brad glanced away from me.

"Got to get out of this suit," he said. "Don't sell all those books before I get back." He disappeared in the direction of Weatherell's single rest room. I think Brad was the only one missing when, before that crush of guests and reporters, Eddie and I began to examine the bishop's books.

I opened the first: *Elements of Doctrine.* I shut it again, swiftly, before anyone else could see. Taking it to the Civil War desk, I started over.

Elements of Doctrine.

Breasts.

Thighs.

Buttocks.

I took a breath and kept turning pages. In photos and drawing, with brief, racy captions, each page, every page held hard- and soft-core pornography. I stared. This was a joke, had to be, one of a kind, a prank. I returned to the crates. Eddie, a book open in her hand, looked up, her face ashen. I glanced over her shoulder. *Selected Divines*: different breasts, different buttocks. Different camera angles. The basics, just the same.

"Oh God," she whispered.

"Andrew?" My voice was steely. I could hear him rapidly flipping pages in another book.

"*Egad.*" Andrew glanced at me, then back to the page. "Yes, indeed. *The Reflective Soul* is definitely into leather."

I snatched another volume from the crate and opened it at random. Jake gazed over my shoulder. "*Life As Contemplation* — ooh baby."

"Covers as *covers.*" Eddie was opening more books, faster now. "*The Complete Works of the Bishop of* — " Her eyes widened; the book fell shut in her hand. "I don't understand, the samples were perfect."

"*These* are perfect." Andrew had begun to laugh, to my surprise. I'd assumed, somehow, he'd be offended. "It's the perfect irony, the perfect satire. Erasmus would have adored it."

"Erasmus isn't on our mailing list," I snapped.

"*Who* will buy them?" Eddie looked stricken.

"Oh, you'll have buyers." Andrew nodded toward the approaching press, then at the door. "Here's one now. I'll lay a wager on it."

Brad, his gorilla suit discarded, stepped back into the room.

"What's wrong?"

We stared at him; then suddenly, darkly giddy, we were laughing.

"What'd I say?" Brad looked at us.

"I think ... " For an instant, I thought the lights flickered again.

"See that?" I turned to Jake.

"What?"

"I think . . . I definitely need some air."

"Out back?"

I nodded. "Come get me . . .?"

"Tomorrow? Two hours?"

I flashed him a look. "Ten minutes."

The door from shop to cellar locked automatically when shut, and we could never get it open from below. It was another of this old house's quirks, often irritating, but just now it suited me. It suited me to get locked out of my own party. Quite likely, my circuits were overloading.

Moving through the crowd, I reached the shop's back stairs. For a moment, I turned, watching the knot of people around the crates, and beyond them, in widening ripples of color, the party. Then I opened the cellar door, moved quickly down the narrow flight of steps, across the cellar and out the door. I was gone maybe three minutes, Jake said later, when he heard a scream from the alley behind the shop. I was there, just outside the door, when he ran out to me, and though I heard him, I did not turn or move. He touched my shoulder — and then he saw what held my gaze.

It was a cat.

Not mine. Not any cat I recognized.

The animal was dead. Its mouth seemed frozen open in a howl. Its gray fur looked smooth and oddly untouched. The outstretched paws had stiffened; for a moment, I'd thought the cat was yawning as it woke. Except for one detail: the cat's eyes were gone. Blood and clear fluid ran from the deep sockets, and there, beside the head, were two pale spheres.

The yellow irises seemed to stare beyond us.

That evening, after the store had been swept and the cat removed and the new books stowed away — after it was all done with, I walked through the empty shop alone. The batteries were back in the smoke alarms. The display windows were lit, casting amber pools back into the store. I stood there, looking at my grandmother's oak bookcases. Their shelves spread evenly, like branches of some great symmetrical tree, unfurling into a million word-filled leaves. Nothing stirred the air around them now.

For a moment, I thought again of the dark-cloaked figures of my dream. I thought of alarms and flickering lights and cat's eyes in the alley. Then I turned and climbed the stairs to the second floor.

Fluke.

Coincidence, nightmare.

Such explanations were still possible.

■

« 2 »

Jake stayed with me that night. Whenever he was there, I tended to sleep deeply, dreamlessly, but that night, even in Jake's arms, I dreamed.

I saw a story writing itself out: my story of Evangeline. Within the borders of white paper, I saw the words appear in straight black lines, and the images unreel again.

Thatched roofs; slate roofs.

Mud streets, deep wheel ruts. Stab of church spire against sky.

Morning light: Small town lifted into brightness, lifted across centuries into life and motion, once again. Flash of cloaks and carts; people running, calling out. A crowd gathering, moving now past fences, doorways, toward one house: Evangeline Smith's. Running now himself, the priest reaches her doorway — and stops short.

Evangeline stands by the fireplace and the wide room narrows in around her. At her feet lies the body of a man, dead upon the hearthstone, his eye sockets empty, dark, dried blood on his face.

The crowd presses in behind the priest. Kneeling by the body, he murmurs a prayer, but from the onlookers, a sharp breath rises. On the stool are three glass jars. Regarding them, the priest himself draws back.

The jars are filled with floating colored spheres, like pebbles. But not pebbles. Eyes. Animal eyes, several sizes, trailing veins and sinew in blood-tinged brine. Rolling, turning, some appear to stare out crazily, as if through a reddish mist; others, bruised and purplish, are scarcely recognizable. In the last jar, in fresh brine, are two spheres: blue-gray human eyes, trailing fleshy tendrils.

Hands rise, making the sign of the cross and the circle against evil. The crowd draws back from Evangeline. Mid-wife and apothecary, she has sat with them at sickbed and childbed. Perhaps she has blighted them as well.

The priest turns to her.

"This — your work?"

There is only her fierce silence.

"You do not deny it?" The priest's hand sweeps from corpse to jars.

Hissing, catlike, she spits at him.

"Evangeline Smith, you are under suspicion of murder and sorcery. May God have mercy on your soul."

She is confined by the Town Watch to her house, until court and council can convene, for they'll not have her in the jail.

"Burn her, burn her now," the crowd begins to chant.

"Nay." The priest holds up his hand. "History shall remember us as fair-minded folk. We are not Puritans, not another Salem. We stand on our faith — and wait."

As the crowd disperses, Evangeline stands at the window. She will stand here many nights, many days. She will wait, but not for rescue now. Her Master, who

had promised her all things, has abandoned her at the
last. She will wait, instead, for a night which she foresees,
when the crowd shall come again, with firebrands and
torches ...

I shifted in Jake's arms.

The dream shifted with me,

Once again, within borders of white paper, the typed
words appeared in straight black lines — and broke off.

My own hand reached in, crumpling paper, border,
words.

I could see for certain now, the story was wrong and
must be changed. Something lay beyond, just outside the
frame. And there was some urgency about it.

The next afternoon, I was among books and shelves again
— not in my shop but in a library, where something else
lay beyond the picture, just outside the frame.

Somehow, I knew that's how it would be. I knew it as
I left the shop in Eddie's care and walked along the C&0
Canal. Beside me on the water, leaves floated, their
colors muted ochers and rusts, and around me, the air
held a faint autumn mist. I loved this walk and Red made
it many times to a small jewel of a library, once a stately
Georgetown mansion. Romantic, voluptuous paintings
swept across its walls, but its books were history, not art.

The place always magnetized me — particularly
upstairs, in Special Collections. These rooms were always
bathed in amber light; steeped, it seemed, like tea, in
centuries of forgotten words. There was a faded Persian
rug, a rolltop desk, a few ancient fusty chairs, and, rising
beyond, the inner sanctum: the stacks, protected by a
shimmering steel-mesh grille. On the desk, pleasantly
disordered, an ancient glass inkwell weighted down a
stack of wrinkled papers; from a distance, they looked like

a pile of handkerchiefs to iron. A Wedgwood cup held another pile of documents in place. Mr. Archer, the angel of Special Collections, knew where and what everything was. I wondered where he was, himself, today.

Suddenly, at the room's glass-paned door, a large pair of eyes appeared: eyes like gooseberries, like grapes. Mrs. Lind pushed the door open. A large, middle-aged British woman, she always seemed somehow slightly damp. Her cropped gray-brown hair was always rumpled, her blouse escaping from her skirt, her manner harried, worried, kindly, alert. Despite that, she was precise and efficient, taking questions, turning with a squinch of rubberized heel, then reappearing with surprising speed, deftly balancing columns of heavy tomes.

"Oh dear," she would say when thanked, "I hope they're right." They always were, though she was fairly new at the library, having retired the year before from "the foreign service." I supposed that meant a post in America, where she confessed she had lived most of her adult life. There was little time to talk with her, though, as she was constantly at someone's service, and did research for many of our workshop's writers.

Brad, Andrew, and Jake spoke highly of her; she was one of those women who is always called "a gem." Fiercely protective of the privacy of "her writers," she was circumspect with those she did not know as well, including me. In any case, I had always worked with Mr. Archer, another friend we had in common. Mrs. Lind was devoted to him; so was I.

"Oh dear," she was saying now. "Mr. Archer isn't in again."

I sighed.

"He took the last two days off." She added, "Personal business."

That was why he'd missed the party, I realized. A friend to Weatherell's and its workshop, he was a bit of a poet, after the style of Horace. I wondered if his personal business was verse or research.

"I don't know where he is today ... "

I sighed again, wanting to swear. Instead, I held up a key to the stacks. "It's okay, he slipped me one."

"I didn't see that." Mrs. Lind averted her enormous eyes. "I'll be up later, call if you need ..." Her voice faded down the stairwell.

The kind of help I needed, however, could come only from Mr. Archer. I looked at his desk again, as if somehow a glance could make him appear. Elderly, with a reedlike voice, he was a wisp of a man, thin as a stream of his own pipe smoke. Now I listened for his step, in the needlepoint slippers he wore at work, but I heard nothing. I listened for Trask, his white rabbit, who slept by the desk and sometimes bounded through the stacks. On several quiet afternoons, I'd heard Trask, across the room, lapping from his water bowl. This afternoon, however, there was only the silence and the tea-colored light.

"This is not a good time," I said aloud to the desk.

I envisioned Mr. Archer squinting up at me.

You've decided to reopen Evangeline's case?

"Don't say 'I told you so.' "

Merely hoping so.

"You knew I hadn't gone deep enough."

I knew you would.

He was too polite to say otherwise. I remembered how courteous he'd been, through all my research forays here. He was one of the few who didn't find my looks incongruous with my writing. I recalled a sketch he made of me once: it shows a woman outlined before the stacks' mesh grille, a small-boned woman, fragile-looking, in her thirties, with a halo of curly hair. In the dim light, her ivory blouse appears to glow. Her hand, raised, looks like a pale leaf blown against a gate. But he'd also caught the sturdy denim skirt, the argyle socks, the pencil stuck behind one ear. Mr. Archer, I always felt, understood me. And, I suspected, he understood Evangeline Smith. In search of her now, I unlocked the stacks.

The shelves rose up, hedgelike, around me. The light was dimmer here, dimmer still as I went on. I was moving down the aisles, down the centuries; past CIVIL WAR, past REVOLUTION, toward COLONIAL, in the Maryland section. Only Mr. Archer would have books on a place like Maidstone, a small town in southern Maryland, on the Patuxent River; an insignificant town now, a producer of cheap pottery. In 1738, however, it had been a thriving port, with big tobacco money, a powerful Town Council, and a rich Anglican church, which planted other missions. Maidstone: proud, prosperous — then faded, forgotten.

It was here, amid these dim shelves, that I had first glimpsed the town, shimmering like an emergent island, bright with cloaks and carts — and characters. Before this, I had written about well-known figures: those who carried darkness, who drew the Shadow. For this next novel, I'd wanted someone obscure. Mr. Archer had guided me to this section, where I had discovered Evangeline Smith. As I read about her, I remember feeling an almost imperceptible click, like a key turning in a lock.

Evangeline herself seemed to step forward into this amber light: a woman of thirty, just two years my junior, and, like me, unmarried. She was a woman with a profession, apothecary-midwife, and a woman with an intriguing background. Born of English settlers in Bermuda, educated by her father, she had grown up on the island with unusual freedom, swimming in the gemlike waters, wading out to reefs, running on stretches of peach-colored sand.

At fourteen, however, she had to leave it all behind. Evangeline's mother was killed in a carriage accident, and in his grief, Mr. Smith moved his apothecary shop to Maryland; Baltimore first, then after some trouble, helping slaves escape, to Maidstone. Trained in his craft, Evangeline had carried on her father's work after his death, and, at twenty-one, she was ministering to the town of Maidstone, replacing the old midwife. The young woman was skilled, much-loved — or so it appeared on the surface. Beneath that surface, according to official sources, there lay something else: darkness again, the summoning of the Shadow. My own stock-in-trade.

I'd been struck by the parallels between Evangeline's life and my own, but what hooked me was that darkness, that evil which eventually broke through this story. I wasn't interested in a pretty tale, some luminous happy ending. Young enough, deep enough, my life had been shaped by wreckage in a cove. I knew the stark edges of true tales, the sudden irrationality of darkness, and the way it twisted stories, skewing them forever.

And yet, from the beginning, I'd felt something was not quite right with this official story of Evangeline Smith. Everything looked perfect; too perfect, perhaps. The reports of Council and Church, signed with a roster of respected names, had condemned Evangeline. This condemnation, moreover, had been corroborated by records left by a councilman, a warden, and a priest.

Even so, I'd spotted inconsistencies. Various sources conflicted on key points, certain facts did not tally. Mr. Archer, I knew, had wanted me to probe deeper; for some reason, I had resisted. Passing through these shelves now, I knew why. I'd wanted the sensational story, the Wow Ending, the dark thrill — and for these, I had cheated my sources, and my story. Here in the stacks, I saw that clearly. "The Torching *is the story of a woman possessed* ... " I was no longer sure.

Angry now, I moved deeper into the shelves. I was angry at myself, at having to start over, and all the while I knew I deserved this. Back to step one: the step Mr. Archer had urged me to take. I was looking for an obscure journal, kept by an obscure contemporary of Evangeline's: *Peagram's Diary*. Mr. Archer found Peagram keen and reliable, more precise than the official records. Fool that I was, I'd politely scanned this source, then put it back. Now I meant to study it and other documents Mr. Archer had collected for me long before, and saved.

I was getting closer to the right shelf: close to Peagram's log, and other monographs. Deep in the stacks, the light was shifting; odd, pale light, lying in icelike patches on the floor, and it was cold back here, growing colder still. Chilled, I squinted at the narrow spines of these old books — there, under my hand, was *Peagram's Diary*. Gently, as with heirloom lace, I drew it from the shelf. Now more titles leapt to sight, some of the others I'd wanted. My hand reached out again.

That was when I thought the floor tilted. I paused, straightening up. Perhaps I'd only lost my balance, leaning over. I waited an instant. The floor was stable. I was clear-headed. The heavy bookcase itself was tilting — suddenly, sharply, it veered toward me. I threw my weight against it. Faster now it came, pelting me with books; in a rush, they fell like bricks around me. I pushed back once more but the bookcase seemed a great wall shaken by some secret earthquake. Books, more books fell faster, as if hurled, and then the case was plunging forward. I dropped low, ran, then dived clear of the shelves just as they crashed down against the museum's north wall. The room shook, the building shook; the stacks' grille quivered as if electrified.

I stood there, staring at it. My hands still clasped three books. A trickle of sweat ran down my spine. For several moments, I could not seem to move.

"Oh *dear*." Mrs. Lind's voice wavered behind me. Slowly, I turned.

"What *happened*?" Mrs. Lind's eyes were on the bookshelf.

I shook my head. The crash had knocked vocabulary from my mind.

"Oh my ..." The librarian's face was stricken. She cleared her throat." Maybe...maybe it was the work-men, they were supposed to come, I think, this week, they ...."

There was a silence. I gripped my books.

"I didn't see anyone," I said finally. ∎

« 3 »

And I didn't. "No one."

I rinsed a head of lettuce and glanced up at Jake.

"This bookshelf ..." Slicing radishes, he raised an eyebrow. "This huge bookcase leaned, lunged, crashed — all by itself?"

"Yes."

"This heavy piece of furniture ... attached ...?"

"It seemed — " I broke off and there was a silence in my apartment over the bookstore. Jake and I were cooking dinner; he'd come as soon as I'd called. Outside now, the dusk was turning my small kitchen bright. Light touched the dried herbs, hung like exotic birds in many-hued bunches. The stained-glass lamp, swinging overhead, spilled wine-colored squares across copper pots, and through the dormered window came the sounds of east-end Georgetown — a child's call, the tap of a door knocker, the bark of a dog. Common sounds. Peaceful sounds; village sounds, in this urban village. For a moment, one might have mistaken it for a small English town, far from Washington's gleaming marble corridors and dim inner-city alleys. For a moment, one might have thought we were a peaceful couple, with peaceful lives, peacefully discussing furniture. What was wrong with this picture?

"Are you saying the bookcase had some sort of vengeful fit?" Jake tried again. "Or ... the library's haunted?"

"Neither," I said, after thinking a moment.

I reached for a string of garlic.

"Maybe you should wear it," Jake teased.

"You're *not* taking this seriously."

"I am, that's why I'm joking."

"Ah." I followed; I knew Jake.

"Maybe you should stay out of there."

"I can't."

Jake hung the string of garlic around my neck.

I looked up at him. For an instant, I felt like a scared child feigning bravery in the dark. I'd rather not see myself that way. I'd been on my own quite a while and I preferred to see myself as sturdy, strong, a survivor. I'd thought of myself as grown up since I was sixteen, and I didn't want Jake to notice this brief regression.

"Mr. Archer might know something." I tossed the salad with unusual vigor. "I'm going back tomorrow."

"*He'll* take this seriously?"

"He's got stuff, papers, for me, I was supposed to get them today." I diced chicken at my typing speed: puree.

"Al ... relax...."

My dicing speed jumped from puree to liquefy.

"Coincidence ... fluke ..." Through the dicing, I heard Jake repeating the words we'd used the night of the party.

"I'm not sure anymore."

"The bookcase was old, maybe off-balance. Maybe when you took the books out, it shifted."

I looked at Jake. "That thing was on a floor, not on a tightrope, and I swear, it got cold back there, the light changed...." Spoken, the words sounded slightly wacko; even to me. I finished off the chicken. "Okay. Accepting your premise, just for a second, what about the cat in the alley, yesterday?"

"Kids. Crazies. Druggies."

"Too simple." I shook my head.

"What the hell's wrong with 'simple'? I like 'simple' sometimes, why not?"

I thought for a minute. "Jake. I know Weird, I have a sense for it, you know that, and it's here someplace. I don't know why, but I think it's got to do with this book thing, this ... decision to rewrite the novel. I just can't see the connection yet."

Jake turned the flame up under the oil in the pan. "Well, we've been through this before, other books. And you always found the connection."

It was good to be reminded. Jake knew; he had flown me around on my research trips. We'd met, in fact, when I needed a pilot to fly me over Donner Pass and he had offered his services.

"Remember that airstrip?" he was saying now. "In the middle of Nevada, the desert? We were nowhere, I'd got us lost, didn't want to tell you — "

"And I knew and didn't care ... " I had hoped we could stay lost for quite a while. "That sky, just blazing — you picked up music on the cockpit radio, music from some-where." Old songs, dance music, and Jake had opened the plane's doors so we could hear it, so he could ask me to dance on the desert floor.

"After a while, all those stars." Jake drew me to him. "Those slow-dance songs."

We moved a few steps in the silent kitchen to that remembered music, in that remembered twilight, our lips brushing. Without letting me go, Jake reached over and turned off the stove's burner; then he untied my apron. I felt it slip off, and after a while it was just a slice of white amid my clothes on the floor.

It was later, from the bedroom, that we smelled the smoke. I was out of bed and on my feet before Jake could move. For an instant, I thought I was caught inside the dream again — then, naked, running for the stairs, I listened for the shop's smoke alarms.

Silence.

Nothing.

Turning, I climbed the stairs, and then I smelled the smoke again: thick, oily smoke, issuing from the kitchen, pluming above the pan on the stove. From the doorway, I saw a thin flame sway like a snake in the pan; an acrid smell filled the air.

Moments later, I heard Jake behind me. By that time, wearing only my apron, I was pouring baking soda, then water, onto the flame. Then, finally, I snatched up my skirt and threw it over all.

Jake's hands were on my shoulders. "It's out. You got it the first time, with the baking soda." He plucked my skirt from the stove. An inky mass swam in the pan. Jake looked at it a long time. "Funny," he said. "I know I turned it off."

"You did, I remember."

We looked at each other.

"A little too much Weird for one day," I said.

Jake held me out at arm's length. I was scarcely covered by the apron. "Nice outfit," he observed, untying the strings behind my back once more.

We skipped dinner that night.

~

Another night of disturbing dreams; these, I can't remember. Jake remembered something of those hours, though. He recalled waking around three in the morning, to hear me murmuring in my sleep. He leaned his head closer to mine and listened. "... colonies ... Maryland ... Maidstone...." My voice, he said, was soft and slow, drifting like milkweed on the dark. It sounded as if I were dreaming my way back into the library, back into the stacks. Jake whispered my name, rocking me against him, and still I slept; still I dreamed. "I can't find it.... Mr. Archer ... Mr. Archer ... ?"

■

« 4 »

Mr. Archer ..." Mrs. Lind's eyes filled. "We'd best go upstairs."

I felt an inner sinking. No one spoke. For a moment, Jake and I just stood there. Then, still silent, we climbed the library's steps.

The moment we entered Special Collections, I knew no one had been in there. The amber shades were drawn, the space awash in tea-colored light. Desk, shelves, rug — all seemed abruptly fixed in time, as in a tintype, and there was a stillness, tangible as settling dust.

We stood awkwardly by the desk, which seemed untouched since the day before. Mrs. Lind made a visible effort to summon her voice, as if from some far corner.

"Mr. Archer ...." She began to weep and the sound of her weeping filled the room like fine rain. It made me wish I were in the Fiji Islands or the Outer Hebrides. I didn't like this and I didn't want to cry and I didn't want to hear what seemed about to come.

"They found him last night." Mrs. Lind wiped her eyes. "At home, in bed — " She broke off.

"He'd been harmed?" My voice was sharp, abrupt.

"He'd been reading, the book was beside him. And then he just ... *died*. Two nights before, the police said, afterward. I hate to think of him like that, not, you know, *found*, right away."

"Heart attack?" I felt slapped.

"No, and not a stroke."

"They told you that?"

She nodded. "They said his heart, it just, well, stopped." Her tears fell on my hand. "He was never sick, perfect health. They said he was lying in bed, his eyes wide open as if he'd been startled, I don't know. They said his hands were gripping the mattress, they said ...." Her voice threaded away.

"No one broke in, stole anything?"

Mrs. Lind shook her head. "Nothing was disturbed, they had to break down the door, they ...." Again her voice cracked; she hurried from the room. "Excuse me, so sorry...."

Jake and I stayed. I don't know how long we stood like that in the tea-colored light, in that tintype of a room. Dust motes, caught in a shaft of sun, a rip in the shade, filtered to the floor. I saw the muscles shift in Jake's jaw. I tried not to think of Mr. Archer in his bed, staring, gripping the mattress. There was something else I was trying not to think about, something that seemed to circle me, just out of sight.

"Damn," I said aloud.

Suddenly, I was angry; angry as I was that night I'd stood by Perkins Cove, watching the bodies pulled from the water, caught in the flash of ambulance lights. My oldest brother, so much older, the hockey star, the tall one, the tough one — he had cried. All I had felt, in that moment, was rage: rage at this water I had always trusted, rage at my parents for letting it betray us; rage at them for leaving me. I'd stood hot and dry-eyed on that dock, as I stood here in the library now.

My gaze returned to Mr. Archer's desk. The anger began to abate. I touched the faded blotter and then, knowing he would want this, I tried the top drawer on the right. It stuck, then slid out. Within, as always, there were file cards, pens — and, as always when he left research for me, a long white envelope. I lifted the envelope, holding it flat across my palm, like a small prized tray. "Miss Alice," in feathery script, was written across the packet. Faintly stained, it bulged, making those two words uneven.

"Open it later, let's get out of here." Jake's voice was suddenly urgent, rough; I too felt a kind of panic, a rush to escape. What was wrong with me? With us? Some thought prowled my mind's edges again, circling closer now, like a thief at a fair. All at once, I caught it, held it, pinned it down. Mr. Archer had died the night before the bookshop party. He had died reading in bed — in bed, and in terror, at something untraceable. He had died the same night I woke in terror to shrilling alarms.

I turned to Jake, took a breath — and said nothing. We moved swiftly through the room and down the stairs and out into the autumn sunlight. Only there, on a bench by the canal, did I feel able to open the envelope. Jake watched as I ran a pencil under the fold and looked inside.

"Only one sheet ...."

Puzzled, I slit the sides of the envelope and opened out the bulging paper. For a moment, I just looked at it; my throat seemed to close. I dropped the sheet of paper on the bench.

The sheet was blank. On it were two round forms: paired, white-rimmed, with pinkish centers. They trailed a web of red-brown veins, stuck to the paper with clotted blood and congealed clear fluid.

Eyes. A white rabbit's eyes.
Trask's eyes.
From the first, I had no doubt.

■

« 5 »

" ... though he rests in peace, we mourn his loss ..."
Andrew Hastings, in command as ever, was somber
tonight. He looked out across the writers' group gathered
in Weatherell's back room. On a table next to him stood
two candles and one inkwell: this last from the library.

"... we have come together in honor of Thomas Trow-
bridge Archer: his gentle life, his love of words and history, his tireless support of writers ..."

It was to be an unquiet wake.

A wake, that is, to us. Our friend's ashes now reposed
in Baltimore, with most of his effects. Not a fleck of
library dust clung to his inkwell. Someone had committed
the sacrilege of cleaning it and now it looked quite new
and most unlike itself; its owner would have been
appalled. There were, however, other reminders of his
presence, and these were disquieting.

In front of me was Dinah, the homeless woman who
often slept in Weatherell's doorway; she had joined the
group some months before and brought in strong, disturbing, lucid prose, which she kept in a battered notebook.

Tonight, her notebook was closed. Head bent, hunched over, she wept silently; her layers of frayed sweaters trembled. Wool gloves turned in her fingers: a gift from Mr. Archer, who had befriended her.

Beside Dinah, face thrust into hands, was Gerald Shane, one of our young writers. Mr. Archer had befriended him, too. I stood watching from the doorway of the shop's cavernous back room. One of the oldest wings of the house, it had for years been used for storage and had never been redone. Water stains made cloudlike shapes across the ceiling, paint peeled from the walls, and our group of writers sat on folding chairs; we'd liked the rough-edged atmosphere, when we'd started out — but tonight, the room seemed merely depressing. Perhaps it was simply the occasion. Or the readings Andrew had begun.

> "And here face down beneath the sun
> And here upon earth's noonward height
> To feel the always coming on
> The always rising of the night ...."

Mr. Archer had loved this poem, and had recited it for many of us. Now, through its words, I could hear his reedy voice, and before me, the room seemed to blur. Others wiped their eyes, and Gerald plunged abruptly past me, through the doorway, lingering just beyond in the shop.

> "To feel creep up the curving east
> The earthly chill of dusk and slow
> Upon those underlands the vast
> And ever-climbing shadows grow ...."

Brad was reading a stanza now. His rough, warm, untutored voice, still tinged by Boston accents, made the words more poignant. He stood there, this great bear of a man, the slim book in his big hands, and somehow he seemed a pastor; a country pastor, as they used to be, soup stains and incense clinging to their cassocks, reading prayers at a grave, then stooping to tease the children. Once more, against my will, my eyes began to fill.

As a girl, to hold back tears, I'd learned to count stitches in whatever I was wearing. As a woman, to hold back tears, I'd learned to count faces, in whatever room I was. Eighty-something faces here tonight. A faithful group, I will say that, but quite different from its roots. We'd grown so large; too large, too well established, nationally known, a model for others. And, I think, smug.

I'd started this group ten years earlier. Along with me, those first few writers had been struggling. We'd all needed to draw from some well of belief, in ourselves and in our stories; all of us were stuck. And so, one night, I'd set out coffee in this room and named the new group "Writers' Bloc." We'd met for support, readings, camaraderie and conversation. We'd had some fine evenings; friendships, besides stories, emerged.

Ten years later, we'd retained the title. Ten years later, we were six times as large, and in the world's eyes, a success, a phenomenon. We had money, big names, a glossy national newsletter, clout with publishers, prizes to award to writing programs. We had acquired a computer and, most recently, a fax machine; this last took up space in my workroom upstairs.

We had also acquired other things: politics, intrigue, gossip, rivalries — "group dynamics." Retired from leadership, I had grown critical of where we were now. I wondered if we'd lost humility and patience, especially with the stragglers, the strugglers, the margins. Writers'

Bloc, in some ways, had become like any cushy club or neighborhood or parish. I missed our first poor years.

Lately, as I watched these meetings, I missed one scene that would float before me like a dreamscape, abruptly present, fully rendered, and so vivid I could almost feel its buoyant air.

It is seven years ago and, as a group, we are attending a wine festival at a small, struggling vineyard in Virginia's rolling hunt country. It is early September and still warm; the earth smells of sun and August and childhood, and there is enough breeze to swing a hammock. We are all wandering among the vines, heavy with deep-blue grapes; grapes the color of summer skies just before dawn, while the stars are still visible.

We all wear clothes that seem to change us: Lorna, in a big tilting straw hat, looks as if she could drift beneath a parasol; Brad is suddenly a farmer in his plaids; Andrew's simple denims seem to place him in an Amish buggy; and all the others, too, appear transformed by their bright shirts and baggy shorts and billowing shifts, by their purpled fingers.

With some of us, Andrew is picking fruit. He passes a large bunch to Lorna, who bites into a grape the size of a small egg; juice runs down her chin, her laugh is rich and long. She tosses the bunch of grapes like a ball to Brad, who leaps to catch it, clowning, face upturned, in his mouth, where he holds it gently like a dog with a bird, and the rest of us are laughing, sun-streaked, earth-stained, as we gather around a table to sample this year's first wine.

All the faces swing into a heightened clarity now, and a silence, pure and sweet and piercing, holds us. Hand to hand, we pass a long-stemmed glass, shimmering bright as blood. In that light, the glass is invisible; all I see is the wine and our many hands, long-fingered and short-

mottled and smooth, clumsy, deft, delicate, huge — hands
that tell the story ...

With a jolt, my attention returned to this room, this
meeting.

"He helped me,
Listened in the library .... "

Dinah was standing now, as Brad stepped down.
Thinking the poem was finished, I guessed, she began to
read from the notepad in her hand.

"In the nights, sometimes,
He let me stay, didn't say — "

"Thank you." Lorna had stood up to read another
stanza. "If you'd take your seat ...."

Polite words, in a voice that cut. Dinah, head bent,
sank into her chair. I looked at Lorna. A tall, stately
woman, her soft flowered skirts could not mute her hard
edges. "LORNA MART, author of three critically acclaimed novels" . . . had the stern face of a Russian icon, framed
by straight strict hair. "At work on a doctorate in English
Literature" ... she had a mind like a microwave oven, and
a smile that seemed stretched, simulating nurture.
"Active in the nationally prominent workshop Writers'
Bloc, she lives" ... happily unmarried, she says ... "in
Washington, D.C."

I watched Lorna begin to read. As usual, I struggled
not to dislike her. I tried to remember a time I had seen
her in a department store, trying on a hot-pink minidress.
As I gazed, startled, from another fitting room, Lorna had
struggled with the zipper till it broke; she'd burst into
silent tears and pressed a fist to her mouth. At times like
this, I reached for that image: Lorna, at forty, trying on

a secret image. Lorna, eyes straying, sometimes, to young men in our group. Lorna, her face severe now, as she read aloud:

"And strange at Ecbaton the trees
Take leaf by leaf the evening strange
The flooding dark about their knees
The mountains over Persia change ...."

Her voice softened as her eyes moved to Gerald, pacing past the door. In her flowing purple dress, she resembled a high priestess intoning those eerie words.

"... And evening vanish and no more
The low pale light across that land
Nor now the long light on the sea — "

Behind me, Gerald Shane paused. I turned in the doorway to watch him. Where had he come from, this brilliant blaze of a lost boy? No one knew, he never said. He lived in a tiny basement room filled with the birds and books he collected. He had money from somewhere, probably family. Gentle with the birds and brotherly with me, Gerald was always working off some inner anger, mostly by rowing on the river — his sanctuary was Kelly's Boat House.

With his own writing, he was savage. Off and on, at his request, I had read bits of exquisite stuff, but it was always discarded; I'd seen nothing lately. Why? Again I didn't know, but Gerald struck me as someone held under a bad spell. I'd begun to wonder exactly what that was. Something, someone, was draining his gift — and his spirit. Always frail, almost elfin, he was even thinner than he had been this summer, when he'd taken me for a boat ride on the river. His cheekbones protruded above

his straw-colored beard, and now, joining me in the doorway, his green eyes blazed, then abruptly filled. I handed
him the poem's last lines, which I was to read, and he
strode to the front of the room.

"And here, face downward in the sun,
To feel how swift, how secretly,
The shadow of the night comes on ...."

The room was still.

Brad stepped forward next, but Gerald did not move
aside.

"I propose a closing word," Brad began.

"I propose a closing *prayer.*" Gerald's voice swung,
whiplike, on the air. There was a tight silence; the room
seemed to contract.

"Thank you," Andrew said then, smoothing, conciliat-
ing. "Would you lead the prayer, Gerald?"

"*Silent* prayer." His intensity seemed to fill the room.
Moments passed; the tension remained.

"Amen," Andrew said finally, and the group appeared
to breathe again. Faces came back into focus: the courtly
silver-haired professor, the green-haired poetess, the
lawyer in pinstripes, the young mother nursing her baby.
Andrew stepped up to the table now and surveyed the
room, sensing the uneasiness tonight.

"This is difficult for us all," he began. I don't remember what else he said; something about survival as a
group, despite loss — in Andrew's words, it didn't sound
trite. I marveled, as always, at his poise, comparing him
in my mind with the young man he'd been. My grandmother had spoken kindly of Andrew, who spent hours in
the shop; I must be kind to him too, she'd said, he was
homesick. In those days, he'd still missed the house by
the lake in Chicago, where his mother taught piano and

his father, a brilliant poet, wrote and drank — and left them, to die a vagabond, a part-time odd-jobber.

My grandmother had hoped Andrew would build himself a life that walled out his father's shadow, and so he did. At Georgetown, the Jesuits became fathers to him. He began a respected teaching career, then married rich; very rich. Then came the books, the fame, reputation, awards — the new leadership of this group. And now he was calling the meeting back to order; I'd missed some transition. ". . . and now, briefly, business, announcements?"

Gerald, halfway down the aisle, spun around.

"I have one. 'Meeting adjourned.' "

"Hey — " Brad stood, protesting.

"*Excuse me.*" Gerald's voice shook. "A man has died. Our friend, one of us. We hold a memorial for him — and then we *do business?*"

"We all miss him, I do too." Andrew took control. "But I'm certain he'd want us to go on, that's our best tribute to him."

"And it's your evening, Gerald." Brad became genial again. "I know you've been waiting to discuss your work — "

"I *forfeit.*" Gerald moved abruptly, tears in his eyes. A chair crashed over as he walked out. Again, a tight silence enclosed us.

"Maybe we're all upset, more than we think." I spoke from the door. "Anyone else want to let things go just for tonight?" Lately, I'd been challenging the leaders — they tended to forget consensus.

Now there were murmurs of assent from the group, heads toward me; I saw some grateful glances. Then, for a moment, Brad, Lorna, and Andrew turned a collective gaze in my direction. In that moment, I saw something I didn't like. And then it was gone.

"All right." Andrew looked about the room. "Just one reminder. A week from tonight, no meeting — a book-signing instead, you've all received your invitations." He stepped aside.

Brad tried to add something, but Gerald, glaring, reappeared in the doorway. The two men eyed each other, and people began to shift in their seats, rising, reaching for coats. There was an odd, uneasy hum; the room's air felt sour. What was wrong with us? Our meetings were always so smooth, so professional.

Had Gerald stirred us up — or was it the death, or something else? We seemed like a big family about to fight, hard and nasty, as only families can. Knots of whispering members were forming; I began to snap off lights, and people moved out into the shop. There, too, I started flipping light switches. This bad evening needed to end. Now.

Hostesslike, I stood in the shop's doorway: "Good night, good night, see you soon " ... until, I thought, the last person had gone. Suddenly weary, I leaned against the shut door. Sometimes I didn't feel up to this. Sometimes I wished I could quit the group and all its dynamics. Sometimes I wished I could just stay upstairs and write, and often I missed my grandmother's crisp wisdom. What would she say? Most likely, *Go to bed.* I began to lock the door — and this time, I did hear a voice. It was not the voice of Kate Ryan Weatherell. I stood absolutely still at the front door.

"You traitor — I saw the manuscript." A voice in the next room.

Another voice whispered a query.

" — easy, on your *desk*, for God's sake," Gerald's voice replied.

There was a whispered protest.

"You were supposed to help me — *my* writing."

Another whispered response, unidentifiable.

"Played me like a fish, didn't you?" Gerald's voice again.

The whisper rose again in protest.

"You sucked the life out of my novel, then breathed it into y*ours* — plot, characters, even the one I based on *you* ... Oh no, you were clever ... *not* word for word, *of course*...."

The whispered answer seemed a hiss.

" — think I'm simpleminded? I know my own work." Gerald's voice stung. "And I know plagiarism. Anyone else would just expose you."

There was a sudden movement, a rustle, a step. Abruptly, I opened the front door, slammed it; opened it again, and rattled the coat tree. Instantly, the voices fell silent. I slammed the front door once more. Then, removing my shoes, I went in the other direction, through HISTORY, through the kitchenette, and, circuitously, into the back room. That would give the pair time to leave in privacy. I didn't care to know who Gerald was with, or why; this was one of those things I didn't want to find out.

Turning sharply, I disappeared into the back room. The candles had been left burning. Damn it, I thought. As if this weren't an old clapboard house; as if I weren't a little nervous, lately, about fire. I leaned over to blow out the candles and, between them, on the table, I saw an envelope. Someone must have left it there, forgotten; I leaned closer, then drew back. The writing on the envelope held my gaze. "Miss Alice," the feathery script read, in Mr. Archer's writing.

"Jake?" I said absurdly, knowing he wasn't there.

Forcing myself, I picked up the envelope, and before I could think, ripped it open. And then I found myself groping for a chair.

Here was the special research Mr. Archer had promised, all of it, orderly, intact. Attached, with one of his collar pins, was a brief note: "Good haul. Copies, in case you can't come for the originals. Blessings — TTA."

I didn't want to know how it got there.

■

« 6 »

Evangeline Smith was paging Alice Grey.

According to the concierge at the Bainbridge Hotel, there was a phone call for me from Ms. Smith; would I care to take it at the table?

We thought we'd heard the name wrong, first. We thought they had the name wrong, next. Coincidence, we thought, at last — but we hadn't, they didn't, it wasn't. They went to bring a phone to our table. It seemed to take a very long time. We sat and watched our tea get cold.

So much for diversion.

Teatime in the Back Court: palms and floral love seats, tiny jewel-like pastries, smoky tea; double Devon cream and scones, azaleas in autumn and a rippling piano. A few hours of respite, a segue to a bygone era, Edwardian of sorts — no farther back than that. And yet, the eighteenth century seemed to find us, tug us, pull us where I had not planned to go.

Every month, Eddie and I took two hours off and came here, leaving the store with our part-time clerk and Violetta, our cleaning woman, who was vague about stock, vague about such areas as kitchen and cellar, but was a whiz at the cash register. For us, these hours away were imperative, recharge time when, we swore, we would not talk shop. We would simply be women, friends, and we would talk about anything else. Today, however, Eddie was not talking; her old reserve had come over her like an almost imperceptible veil. For an instant, I thought I saw a flicker of pain in her eyes.

"Ed?" I glanced at her. She could not be pressed, even out of concern, I knew. It was just recently that she had spoken of her divorce, some years before, and a dark tunnel of time afterward, when it was hard to work and men didn't stay and her image of herself had frayed. Healing had come gradually but steadily, she'd said. Ever since I'd known her, she'd been whole and strong. And yet, now and then, that veil would fall between us.

"It's ... nothing ... major." Each word seemed plucked from her, light and quick, like notes from a lute string. Eddie took a sip of tea. Her jaw was taut, chin tilted; her back straight, not touching the cushions. For a moment, her handsome dark hair and eyes seemed hazed in cigarette smoke; her face seemed to hang before me like a portrait on a wall: "Woman in Quiet Desperation."

"I've been seeing this man ... " She paused. She never talked about her men; I never asked. "I've been seeing this man and writing this book, and not doing terribly well with either just now." She set down her cup. "The book's become a maze, and so has this ... relationship. I see the way out, the hole in the hedge, but I won't take it, I *won't* be alone." She lit another cigarette and smoked in silence; then her face grew wry. "And, just to help matters, Lorna's been grating on me, calling, making special orders, talking, talking, talking about *her* work, *her* words, *herself*. Talking about 'the burden of gift.' . . ."

I nodded. I knew.

"God, let's not do this." Eddie put out her cigarette and shifted some inner gear. "I'm depressing *myself*. Distract me, tell me about your book. You've delayed publication?"

"Just did it." This still sounded rather awesome. "You know, something about the story never felt right, just wouldn't fit. Evangeline, healer, midwife — with a sideline as murderer and sorceress. . . ."

"Some Jekyll-Hyde thing?" Eddie reached for a scone.

"That's how I *wanted* it to play." I poured my own tea. "Makes a better story, horror-wise." *Horror-Wise*? What had my writing done to my command of the English language? I started again. "Evangeline nursed runaway slaves, fed tramps, befriended the town simpleton. She got in trouble for it, too, I saw complaints to the Town Council. Does an evil person risk herself like that, do you think?"

"You're right. Something doesn't fit. Was she isolated, a man-hating spinster, anything like that?"

"Just the opposite. She ran a thriving business and had two suitors: Tom Kemp, the brewer, described as 'perpetually dishevelled and eager' — Evangeline 'spurned' him, he took it hard. Then there was the longer courtship of Luke Arnold, the potter; it was thought they would marry. He stayed loyal to her throughout the scandal and disappeared a few months after her death." I pushed back the plate of scones and drew from my bag *Peagram's Diary*. "It's all in here, some angel must have put this in the stacks."

Eddie scanned the title. "Daniel Peagram — who was that?"

"Landowner, church warden, bachelor, amateur historian, odd bird. Collected books, unusual for his times. Had
one slave he freed, Cass Tanner, who was then paid
wages, and hired out to others: the brewer, the potter, the
other warden. I think Tanner provided Peagram with
some of his information, but Peagram himself saw more
than most. His journal's a series of events, anecdotes,
vignettes of town life, unofficial life — all interspersed
with Peagram's own poetry."

"Any good?"

"The poetry's bad, the diary's terrific. Peagram was a
sharp observer; maybe he saw too much. Something
troubled him; he said he would 'die in sorrow.' "

"What did he say about Evangeline?" Eddie spread
blueberry preserves on a scone. I looked away. Suddenly
the berries resembled tiny eyes, congealing on pastry. I
wondered if I'd ever be able to eat preserves again.

"He didn't think Evangeline was guilty *or* evil. He
also notes a confession drafted for her — never signed, it
disappeared." I opened the diary. "Look at this entry, the
year she died."

Eddie read it aloud. " '... so much Goodness shone
from her, I am certain All they spake of her is False.
Such a Creature was no Murderess, no Sorceress, no
Mutilator of the Weak, whom she always Befriended....' "

"Subjective impressions aren't enough, of course."

"Still, that's pretty strong." Eddie, pouring more tea,
seemed thoroughly engaged now; the mystery writer in
her was hooked.

"Mr. Archer thought highly of this source...." I flipped
pages. "That last entry came after Evangeline was
accused of murdering Nick Rhoades." A date snapped into
focus. "Here's an entry made the day before the sexton,
Nick, was killed: '*March 10. — The Church Sexton, Nick,
poor simple Man, thrown down a drye Well again, by*

young Rowdies. Symilar event noted two months past. I pulled him out. Poor Nick all a-tremble. Frail, at thirty, he looks dwarfed and aged. He clutched to his Chest a large glass Boule with a Stopper, filled with strange round Objects which he then secreted in his Jerkyn. I know not what to make of this Last, save Nick means harm to None and 'tis a gentle Soul. I've seen him most tender wythe Animals, burying the dead Ones, after extracting a small Keepsake from them, as we would a Locke of Hair from a Beloved.'"

"Aha." Eddie and I leaned forward as one, so fast, so urgently, a waiter instantly appeared.

"More tea, I think." My voice was distracted. "And another order of scones and eyes."

The waiter paused only an instant. "Very good, madame."

He vanished. The piano played "Blue Moon." On the table, I spread more papers. These were Xeroxes, but you could see the originals were old, creased and stained. They looked as if they'd arrived in a seaborne bottle — not Mr. Archer's envelope.

"This one ..." I pointed. "From a contemporary ledger, kept by agents at Maidstone's port. They placed orders for people, imported articles from England in exchange for money, credit, hogsheads of tobacco."

We read through the old order.

2 glass jars, large, stoppered
2 glass vials, small, stoppered

Credit to Nicholas Rhoades, Sexton to All Souls Anglican Church. Rhoades's private account. 6 February, 1737.

"Aha," Eddie said again, and again, this seemed to summon the waiter, who appeared with teapots and fresh cups. Pouring the hot brew through small strainers, he politely ignored our nest of papers.

"Look at this," I said as he vanished. "A complaint to the Town Council from a Master Hoare, the next year —
"

"I didn't know there were Hoares in Maryland," Eddie mused.

" — a complaint about Nick trampling through Hoare's property the day of the murder. Hoare was so steamed, he wrote immediately. Described Nick in a sweat, running from the church, ranting about 'lovers' and 'desecrations.' He clutched a stoppered jar in one hand as he ran, fell down, got up, stumbled on. Master Hoare's conclusion: The sexton was drunk."

"*Fascinating.*" Eddie bit through a lemon wafer. "Master Hoare didn't get a good look at the jar." She set the wafer down. "Probably full of 'strange round objects.'"

"And speaking of Hoares — here's a double *piece de resistance.*"

The piano played "You Do Something to Me." Eddie and I leaned over the Xeroxes.

"First, a birth record." I spread out one of Mr. Archer's prizes. "From Maidstone's *Book of Possessions, Births, Deaths & Marriages.* I checked the deaths, last time around. I didn't think to check for births on the night of Nick's murder. But here: 'Born, March 11, 1738, Boy child, Ishmael, to Lily Jenkins, *unwedded* Mother of Three.' " I shifted papers. "Now compare that account with Pea-gram's, same outline, but filled in — different picture...." I read: " '*March 12, 1738. Born early this morning, a Boy child to Lily Jenkins, attended all Night by Mistress Evangeline Smith, Midwyfe. Lily Jenkins, unwedded and of ill repute, is not a member of any*

Church. At her request, the Midwyfe baptyzed the Child Ishmael, in case of his demyse. Faith Roper, tavern-keeper, upstanding, kind- hearted, who brings the Town much Revenue by shrewd Enterpryse, did witness to the Baptism, being Lily Jenkins's only Friend save the Midwyfe. One Warden of the Church did also witness.' "

We sat a moment in silence.

"Quite something," I said finally. "Look at the detail. Peagram must have been the church warden who witnessed. But if I don't misconstrue, someone kept his name off the official record ... his name, and Evangeline's."

"If I don't misconstrue," Eddie said, "this also implies Lily wasn't a Hoare — but a whore."

"And — " I tapped the paper. "Evangeline's alibi for Nick's murder."

"Amazing."

The piano played "Tea for Two."

"If Evangeline didn't kill Nick," I said, "who did? And if *she* didn't put those jars of eyes there ..." My voice trailed off as a jingling sound neared us, breaking our concentration.

Approaching was a hand-held signboard, hung with small bells — the hotel's paging system. Had I told the shop where we would be? Had I been that dutiful — that stupid?

"Ms. Grey?" The liveried man jingled the sign as he moved nearer; now I could see the words inscribed on the board: my name.

"Call for Ms. Grey ...?" the man's voice inquired politely of the wide bright room. I signaled to him and he approached smoothly. "Alice Grey, of Weatherell's?"

I nodded, feeling a prick of alarm.

"A call for you from Ms. Evangeline Smith."

We stared at the messenger.

"Long distance," he added.

"Understatement," I muttered.

And then we sat and waited while he brought the phone. We sat and tried to joke, but in the end we sat in silence. The phone was set before me on the table. I lifted the receiver.

"Yes?" My voice snagged on that one simple syllable. There was a pause. A voice came crackling through the line. I saw Eddie's eyes widen. "How did you ... find me?" I said finally.

The voice went on; I cut it off. "Violetta told you. Well, great — you scared the hell out of us, Hap."

Eddie exhaled; she knew Hap Dowell, my agent. A fleshy, hearty, balding man, he had a face the color of rare beef and a voice that carried, even when he wasn't physically present. I laid the receiver on the tea table, just as Hap raised that voice: "... had to get your attention, Alice, you're not listening lately. Your letter to the publisher, it didn't go over real big. You're taking a big risk, delaying pub dates, changing stories, we have a deal — "

I picked up the phone. "We've been *through* this — "

Another tirade.

"Hap." Somehow, I broke through. "Next time you call from another century, be careful. You might get your wires crossed. You wouldn't want to be Lizzie Borden, would you? Or get your call patched through to the Donner boys — *especially* when they're eating."

He hung up on me, while Eddie burst into an uncharacteristic whoop of laughter. I gathered up my research and took one last sip of tea.

"Ready for the check?" I set my cup down with a small, decisive *ching*.

That night, at my desk, I set down my coffee mug with a small, tentative thud. Weatherell's was closed, the building quiet, and I was in my dormered workroom under the eaves. I had looked down at the street, to check on Dinah. I had arranged blank paper into piles. I had sharpened all available pencils. Wistfully, I glanced at phone and fax machine: both silent. I read through my sources one more time. Finally, I switched on my old typewriter, which gave its familiar start-up wheeze. And then, slowly at first, within the borders of white paper, the words began to form in straight black lines, and the images unreeled....

Now, at thirty, the sexton felt old, ancient as his grandmother sitting in her chair, transfixed by the moon as it spilled its silver on her skirts. Nick remembered her and England and, he thought, even his own difficult birth. Wrenched forth into sunlight by a midwife's clumsy forceps, his head was misshapen and his thoughts ran slow. He had grown to be a tiny gnomelike man, slower-limbed as well, of late. It was not so easy now to escape the rowdy lads who chased him up the High Street, their rough jeers striking him like sharp stones. Several times, this past year, the youths had thrown Nick down an old dry well, a dim funnel that appeared to press in upon him till his breath grew scarce. This torment had become more frequent and, the sexton knew, would surely continue. The other servants would not defend him, even Cass, who had been his friend.

And so Nick had started to collect the eyes. He had always felt a tenderness for animals, and a kinship with them, for in these creatures' glowing gaze he had seen that endless Godlike mercy he had seldom seen in men. These dumb creatures drew him, even as they aged and limped and died in lanes and barnyards. There they lay, exposed

*or kicked aside, and this sent pain through Nick's spirit.
He hated to think of their eyes rotting with their carcasses,
for these eyes were miraculous, immaculate, mysteriously
filled with light. And so, in secret, only from the dead
ones, Nick reverently removed the eyes, keeping them in
brine, safe within the glass jars ordered, at some cost, from
England. Precious relics these were to him, this man who
lacked for other treasure, and he found the small globes
oddly beautiful, still points of light. Nick concealed them
with his things, or kept them in vials on his person, for
these relics reminded him of God's protective eye, ever
watching over him, even when he felt alone. God's gaze,
filled with mercy; Nick would feel this as he felt the vial
inside his shirt: God's eye and the eyes of angels,
watching, watching, watching over him, for there was no
one else who did. The Scriptures, which his grandfather
had taught him to read, said the seraphim had many eyes
as well as many wings.*

*Nick thought on this now, for comfort, as he crept
along back lanes. Once more, lads had chased him down
the High Street, so the sexton had returned, unplanned,
leaving errands undone, just to sit a moment in the church
and gather there the courage to go back. He must visit
Evangeline straight off; he had the bad shakes again, and
she mixed him soothing draughts in neat ceramic pots, like
her father's. The old apothecary had been buried in this
church-yard eight years past, Nick remembered. Now the
old man's daughter had become the sexton's friend.*

*Evangeline. For comfort, he said her name as he
entered the sacristy. Just off the chancel, this small room
was plain, dim, and narrow, with but one high window
and a cupboard for vestments and linen. For an instant,
Nick glimpsed his face in the glass, then quickly looked
away. That was the priest's mirror, and no glass for
sextons such as Nick. This priest, the Reverend Jonas*

Drummond, was a holy man, slender, plain-garbed, and much sought for spiritual counsel. Often lost in silent prayer, the pastor tended to forget details. It was the sexton who marked the altar book and noted feast days, sections, collects, and prepared the altar for Holy Communion. These tasks Nick did slowly, painstakingly, but there was such deep sweetness to them, it would make him sing. His mother had done such tasks in their little church in England, keeping her slow son with her, talking to him as she worked. His brothers had of late arrived in Baltimore, but it was not they he thought of. It was their mother, in the old country church, where he sensed holy ground and sacred space, and above all, home.

Home it felt to be now, as he breathed in the good smells of tallow, starch, spiced oils and the polish he used on the silver candlesticks. Nick had a gift for sensing presences, and as he stood very still, he knew someone stood beyond, within the church. It was not a presence he could recognize at once, though it seemed familiar, but he felt its pressure, like a rock displacing water in a bowl. A bright flame of panic spiraled through the sexton as he prayed this was no thief or vandal; the panic burst in orange sparks before his eyes. Seeing no one through the keyhole, Nick slipped outside, around the church, and crept in again through the front door, slipping into a back pew, where he knelt, concealed on the floor.

There he waited, hearing his heart bang against his chest, knowing the church should be empty. No one came here afternoons, except, sometimes, Evangeline, but this was not she, with her scent of herbs and lavender. Nor was this the priest, he knew, for the pastor had said clearly he must be away today, in the next town.

A new set of footsteps sounded in the small church now, down front by the altar rail; steps so soft, so muted,

Nick could hardly make them out. Either someone had slipped past him or come in through the sacristy. Still the sexton waited, bent like an old woman over sewing, in the space between the pews. Sweat began to dampen his shirt as he heard faint rustling, then a whisper. Finally, the sexton raised his head above the pew.

Before the altar, just within the rail, where the gate was open, he made out two figures — naked figures, their flesh pale as moonlight, in the chancel; bodies entwined, pressing together, gasping like some beings from another realm, an enchanted forest. Mouth on mouth now, flesh on flesh, they sank to the floor, and then one was astride the other, rocking, swaying, bucking; faster, faster still, in some wild ecstatic gallop, as a soft wild sound rose from their lips.

Silently, between the pews, Nick began to cry. Pressing his fist to his mouth, he rolled into the aisle and stumbled toward the door. Someone had locked it behind him; he groped for his key, and then he was plunging outside, tripping, running, falling, lunging on. Blinded by his tears, he trampled someone's ground, fell again, and, hearing a harsh voice, ran off. Gasping, clutching his precious vial, he stopped in someone's barn, sinking on a bale of hay, trying to stop his shaking. From his jerkin he drew out his Bible, pressing it to his chest, as if that might still his heart. Then, wiping his eyes, he turned to his most holy passage and pulled out his charcoal stylus, which he'd brought to scribble errands, prices, and the like. In the Holy Book, in the margins, he set down a string of words, hoping they would lose all power there. Write it, set it in the Bible, give it up to God ... his words came out broken, crooked He rose, shaking, knowing he must get to Evangeline....

I looked up from the typewriter. For an instant, my workroom seemed unclear, distant, foreign. I was still moving across the terrain of the story. Running a hand through my hair, I stood and stretched; the room came back into focus. The clock showed eleven fifteen. A breeze stirred the pages I had written. I stacked them on the desk, shut the window, and settled down to read what I'd done.

The pages stirred again. I glanced up at the window, firmly closed. I looked back at my chapter. Very slowly, the pages rippled, edge by edge. As I watched, the top page slithered off the pile; the next page slid to the floor, then another. I got to my feet. Behind me, then, I heard a muffled tap — I swung around. A book had slipped from my shelves to the rug, and now, with that same soft thud, another volume fell; then three. Then eight.

"Red ..." My voice was low as I picked up the cat. More volumes were dropping from the bookcase; Red's ears, had flattened against her head. Snatching up papers, I grabbed a canvas bag and thrust cat and pages within. The room seemed to stretch out, a vast space to cross as I moved to the door, wrenched it open and slammed it behind me. In the hall I paused, listening; for a moment, I felt safe. And then, below me in the shop this time, it came again: one thud, then another; then a dozen, sharper, faster now — the sound of books dropping like stones.

Gripping my bag, I ran down the stairs, flipping on lights. There was a sudden silence. In the shop, now, I edged toward an aisle — and, abruptly, into a hail of falling volumes; the very shelves seemed to be hurling books. I took a step forward and then, from the tumbled books, pages began to fly: pages rose like autumn leaves into the air, swirling in spirals around me — stinging, slapping, a cyclone of paper. I raised an arm over my face and tried to plunge through the shop. The air was white with pages now, dense as a blizzard; blinded, I could not push against it.

Dropping low, I dodged beneath the pale storm, lunging down one aisle and into another, where I paused, gasping. Clear. For just an instant: clear. And then, without warning, I was trapped within a new swirl of white — pages, here, like wild-winged birds, swooping, diving at me, snapping, biting — I felt a series of sharp stings, the odd warmth of blood on my arm. Again, I tried to plunge ahead; it seemed a swarm of ashen hawks descended, slicing my skin and beating my shoulders and stealing my breath — the pale wings caged me. And then, as suddenly as it began, it stopped.

Paper drifted to the floor. Across the shop, the door had opened. Jake stood in the doorway, his key still in the lock. Jake, just in from a flight, coming straight from the airport — I'd forgotten. He stood there motionless, simply staring. Pages wafted down around me, down past empty shelves and tumbled books. Within the canvas bag, the cat was howling; I saw threads of blood crisscross my arm. Slowly, numbly, I walked toward Jake.

"What? *What?*" He was holding me.

"Outta here," was all I could say.

At Jake's place, I told him what had happened and he listened without comment, dabbing at my cuts with his shaving lotion. After I finished, there seemed to be an interminable pause.

"You think I'm insane," I said at last.

"No." He looked up. "I saw it."

"Something's working to block this story, working overtime, big-time...." I tried to keep my voice light, ironic.

"Drop it, quit it, let the story go as is."

"Jake, the right story must matter somehow — otherwise, why this action-reaction cycle? Why the 'special effects'?"

"I don't care, just let it alone."

"I can't."

"Try."

"You sound like Hap."

"I didn't hear that."

There was a silence. I took the shaving lotion from him and capped the bottle. We would not resolve this tonight, I knew, but tonight, at least, we had to resolve the mess in the shop.

"I didn't say it," I conceded, finally.

"I thought so."

And finally, we talked out a temporary plan.

We would return to the shop, survey the damage, gather the books and pages, find a way to sort them . . .

"You'll have to hire someone," Jake said.

"I know, all those pages." My head ached.

We would close the damaged aisles.

We would send the books out for rebinding. "We'll have to make some excuse," I said. "Who'd believe the truth?" Jake looked at me. I hesitated. "Do you?"

He nodded slowly. "Now."

We went back after midnight, carrying Red with us. I tried to think only of concrete plans: I must check my workroom. I must give Jake Xeroxes of all sources and of my manuscript, as it developed, for safekeeping. I must take some inventory of the damaged volumes.... As we neared the shop, I felt my shoulders tighten. We both paused outside. Then we unlocked the door, stepped inside, turned on the light — and stood there, silent.

No paper anywhere.

Not a page, a volume askew.

We checked each shelf, each book.
Everything was perfectly in place.

■

« 7 »

Books, in general, take nine months to emerge, fully embodied, from their publishers.

From typescript to bound copies, there are clear stages, not unlike a pregnancy's trimesters: copy-editing, galleys, page proofs, blue lines, printing, binding — and, of course: hype, sometimes more, sometimes less; depending. Hardbacks have average life spans of four months, unless they're best-sellers. If they go into paper-back, they can live three months more — or, in theory, three hundred years. At most pre-publication parties, despite some omens, a book's life span is unknown. The birth, then, is the occasion, and to my mind, one of the best causes for celebration, to be done up right.

Eddie, bless her, had volunteered to do this one up in her small town house. I had volunteered to assist, unable to face another bash in the bookshop. And now the date had arrived: a party for three of our authors: Brad, Andrew, and Lorna. Triple madness, triple threat. Triple cheers, as well, for Writers' Bloc.

In Eddie's house, that night, books were everywhere:
on tables, on stairs, on windowsills and waiters' trays and
— I'm told — in the powder room. Books were signed and
passed along, opened, closed, and purchased on the tables,
on the stairs, at the windows, from the trays, and, I'm
told, even in the powder room.

" 'All best wishes to — ' " Andrew glanced up at the
attractive blond woman beside him. "Your mother's name
was . . .?"

"Elliot," a tall gray-haired man nearby was saying to
Brad, "I always come to these affairs to decompress.
Make one out to Ginger, will you? 'With ominous regards.'
And, yes, one for Father, his name is — "

"Lisa Beth." A short, breathless woman gazed up
admiringly at Lorna. "A book for my daughter, she writes,
her pen name's New Moon. Could you ... possibly ... sign
it that way? She'd love it, oh, and this one's for — "

"The Pope, let's not forget the Pope." Jake took a crab
puff from a tray. "I mean, just in case he shows. God, I
really hate these things, you know?"

"Nice, I think." I looked around the crowded room.
"Considering that I hate parties."

I caught a glimpse of myself in Eddie's one mirrored
wall. Quickly I looked away. I was all in black, as my
readers, it seems, tend to picture me — long skirt, high
neck, long sleeves. The dress was old and the black made
my fair skin too pale, my face too fey, too fragile-looking.
I looked absurdly like some delicate French widow in a
Lautrec painting: not my role of choice. This was the
only dress that covered the cuts on my arms. I tried not
to think of storms of paper. I tried not to think of pages
flying from books — as it was, I kept dreaming about
them.

I glanced back at the mirror, as if to check on my own
reality; as if to confirm the normal status of the crowd,

the room. In the mirror, beyond my own image, then, I glimpsed something else. "Jake." I touched his sleeve. "Turn around slowly." I inclined my head toward the staircase where, halfway up, a figure perched. At first, it looked as if Gerald was simply surveying the crowd, or analyzing Eddie's house. There was nothing much to analyze in this standard, beige, newish townhouse. Eddie and I had spent part of the afternoon cramming her furniture into a downstairs guest room. We'd left the dining table and upright piano; the caterers had brought chairs. Clearly, the house was not the object of that fixed gaze.

"Gerald worries me," I said.

At first, he had mingled with the guests. I'd seen him request a book of each honored author, only to slip the books back into the boxes at each author's feet. Odd. It worried me. And then Gerald had retreated to the staircase. He sat there drinking; his green gaze raked the guests of honor and Eddie, Jake; perhaps others, too, I didn't note. I was constantly distracted by one guest or another, and the waiters kept on passing trays, and the writers signed their books.

Brad, in a turtleneck, lifted a Flair pen to inscribe *Shadow Mission*, where, for the first time, his recurrent agent Kip teams up with an old nemesis, a boyish Russian spy, for covert action in Beirut. As usual, the novel invalved murder, mayhem, and blackmail. For the first time, however, agent Kip was oddly introspective: angry at "the redundancy of his life," knowing he couldn't keep pace with his young partner; fearing he'd "used up all his moves." The novel ended with a dazzling twist. After a slump, Brad had pulled off his best book, on a deeper plane. The trade grapevine was already signaling "best-seller."

Andrew, nearby, seemed more confident. In pin-striped suit, his fountain pen poised, he was signing *Rituals*: a departure for him as well. The novel focused on the interior crisis of a respected seminary professor, who finds for the first time a hollowness in the rituals he teaches and the school he loves. He feels himself going dry as he watches a gifted young seminarian playing out the rituals afresh. The professor, however, finds renewal in unexpected rituals and relationships; the novel ends with a brilliant resolution. It was Andrew's finest work to date; advance word-of-mouth marked this one as a prize-winner.

Across the room, Lorna, in flowing blue silk, was autographing *End Notes*. In characteristic style, this was a cerebral novel; this time, Lorna's heroine was a middle-aged psychiatrist, losing keenness and interest in her work. For much of her life, she had prized intellect and despised passion. Now, however, she became involved with a young male patient, and through him, she began to change. A deft twist was in the narration, from the patient's point of view; the first time Lorna had written from a male perspective. Early rumors called this book a tour de force, a stunning breakthrough for its author.

Eddie, in green crepe de chine, moved among the authors, coping easily with the cash from buyers. I was glad to see Dinah, in her layers of old clothes, moving about the rooms, stashing food in her pockets; she and I swapped a crab puff for a bacon curl. Her face, like almost every-one's, was animated, pleased; in contrast, Gerald's was immobile as ivory. Sadness, more than anger, filled his eyes, as several toasts were proposed.

"To our three authors," Eddie began, lifting her flute of champagne. "And to their new books, launched tonight."

"To Weatherell's," Brad continued, "for this honor —
and for picking up the tab on three hundred shrimp."

A ripple of laughter.

"To Eddie, for ordering the shrimp, and throwing the
party," I added.

"And to Writers' Bloc," Andrew finished for all. "For
its support to us, and so many writers; your turn, next."

I can't remember the other toasts — my attention was
taken by Gerald again, perched above us. Why did I care
about this difficult, disruptive young man? Maybe
because he stirred us up and disturbed our smugness.
Maybe because he looked like my brother.

"Cheers." Gerald was rising now, lifting his empty
glass. "A toast to a nameless writer, unmentioned in
word or book tonight, who worked hard, trusted; and
believed — " His voice broke; abruptly, tears streaked
his face. Spinning around, he bounded up the stairs.
Somewhere above, a door shut. Around me, there was a
stunned hush, then a hum, a murmur. Eddie, twisting a
long strand of pearls, motioned to the man at her upright
piano.

The music and talk began again, as I followed Gerald
upstairs. For a few minutes, he let me see him cry —
then he was pulling away, wanting to be alone.

I let him be, as I'd often done with my brother, also
difficult, brilliant, uncomfortable with tears. Descending
back into the party, I felt the brush of more than one gaze.
I wish I'd noticed whose; at the time, it didn't seem
important.

More champagne was opened. The man at the piano
played the theme song from *Fame*. Books were being
signed again; music filled the house. Someone kissed me
on both cheeks; who it was, I'd no idea. Passing among
the guests, I felt uneasy. Beneath the music and the
laughter, I sensed some current I could not name.

"What's wrong?" Jake looked at me.

"Nothing." I sighed.

It was nothing but Gerald: Gerald, taking the form of a brother, whose tears I remembered and could not stop — then, or now. Nor could I translate Gerald's urgent whispers, even if I'd wanted to: a slurred tangle of betrayal, sexual innuendo, despair. I must talk with him again.

Jake ran his finger down my cheek, as if to bring me back. I offered my glass for champagne and touched Jake's finger with my lips.

I would find Gerald in the morning.

■

« 8 »

*T*he morning was misty as Evangeline walked home...

I pulled the page out of the typewriter. Crumpling the paper, I tossed it at the wastebasket; a direct hit. I glanced about my dormered workroom. Everything here was muted and serene: a painted Amish chest was the brightest spot of color; the pale-green rug suggested a still, shallow pond. On the oak bookcase, an antique clock showed the time as just past eleven. I paused, listening. All was quiet, except for the rocking chair's faint creak. Jake, reading, sat with me. I reached for fresh paper.

Wearily, Evangeline walked home through a misty...
I wrenched the page out and started again.
Through the mist, through the dawn, through the —
I ripped the third sheet out.
The rocking chair stopped creaking.
"Letting it scare you?" Jake said, not looking up.
A moment later, the typewriter was rapping again.

Evangeline walked home through the morning light. The sun, glinting from windowpanes, hurt her eyes. Her step slowed, her basket trailing from her fingers. A death, and then a difficult birthing there had been, keeping her up all night and past dawn. She still saw the dim, smoky chambers where she had sat, though, at last, the babe's strong cry had come.

Now, on the High Street, the road seemed suddenly too bright, too fast, too noisy: a swirl of cloaks and carts, Market Day's beginnings. Evangeline herself had need of marketing, but was too weary now. All she had the wit for was sleep, and she longed to drop like a stone through her bed's depths, into dreams of her island, its glimmering water, the home where she felt moored.

Sometimes, when weary, she felt childlike again and missed her mother, singing at her spinning, and her father, powdering his sharp-scented herbs. Gone they were from her, and still she could not quite forgive them for the leaving. She saw their faces in the ill, the dying with whom she sat, and again she saw them when she did the laying out. Time it was for her to loose this darkness; she knew she was holding it, and no one else. Evangeline had always known about the Shadow, and the sudden force with which it sundered lives. It was time for her to turn from it, from deathbeds and dark rooms, and marry; yet she feared the loss of someone else, she knew, as well. Strong and sensible for others, managing her shop, caring for so many, she had times like this, where she felt frail. She knew no one would believe her but Luke Arnold, the potter, who would never scorn but comprehend. Sometimes he held her — and she allowed this — till her strength returned. Her hands sometimes grew hot with healing, and now she would seek to heal herself, through sleep and island dreams.

Coming through her door, Evangeline dropped cloak and bonnet on a bench and glanced about, sensing something different from last night. Had she left her shawl there on that stool, when she was called away, first to deathbed, then childbed? She thought not, but uncertain, felt too weary to care. Turning now, she saw her hearth was cold, her fire gone out. She'd not mind it for now, the day was warm enough, and the tinderbox was there to use, once she had some rest. She moved toward the stairs and bed-chamber, feeling still that something was amiss; only weariness, she thought.

Sharp as a rock against a shutter came a sudden rapping at her door. Evangeline paused; she knew of no other birthings due, and no one gravely ill, now that old man Foster had passed on. Harder now the rapping came, louder, proud, imperious, as if it could not be refused. Irked, Evangeline felt tempted to refuse it after all, but with one sharp motion she jerked open the door.

There, outlined by the doorframe, stood four men. The sun behind them turned them into silhouettes, and for a moment they seemed to be one, shoulder melting into shoulder, cloak into cloak, filling the bright space like one solid block of stone. Then, as if on signal, their hands lifted to doff their hats and they seemed to splinter into single forms again. Two church wardens she saw there: pale, reedlike Peagram; massive, rocklike Simms, his proud porcine face and chins quivering with dignity. Beside him, Councilman Cleete, small-boned and elegant as ever, his face etched like a cameo; and the last, the Reverend Drummond himself, balding, slender, with that gentle, nearsighted gaze. All their faces were polite, no more, no less.

Evangeline felt her pulse quicken. She remembered little of the opening pleasantries, only that she stood aside *for the men, and, trades-woman though she was, her voice abandoned her, like a frightened child run off to hide.*

She offered them seats, which they declined. And so Evangeline stood watching the men watch her, while her hand gripped a fold of her gown and her mind recited, as if for protection, healing remedies: Elder leaves for catarrh, lilac leaves for fever, mint tea and hawthorn for the heart ...

"Mistress Smith." They all spoke, then paused. Time seemed to flatten out, wide as a grainfield, and Evangeline surveyed each man. Perry Cleete, surely, would mean her no harm. When she had first arrived in Maidstone, he was newly come as well, and had frequented the shop. After her father had died, he had come more often, and yet seemed to care nothing for courtship, only friendship. Once she recalled him adjusting his sleeves, facing the window, his profile etched sharp against the glass.

"I've got the French disease," he had said then.

"I can dose you for it."

He had turned of a sudden.

"You don't judge me?"

"Nay." She looked direct at him, then smiled. "You're scarce the first to say those words."

And they had laughed; his laugh was like bright juice squeezed from a ripe orange. But after that, and after the dosing, something had changed. Evangeline had expected as much, yet hoped it would not be so. Perry had been her friend; now he was drawing away from her, because she knew. She had grieved over this somewhat, not having a great many friends at that time, but slowly, she had let the grieving go.

Now she looked across at him and knew, somehow, that he was remembering as well. His face tightened; he took a step into the room, and the others, likewise, took a step.

"You'll pardon us, we've come early, so as not to cause delay on Market Day...." The thin warden speaking now, uncomfortable, awkward, clearing his throat.

"Will you take a seat, sirs?" Evangeline's voice returned. "Forgive me, my fire has gone out. I was abroad from dusk last evening until just now." Evangeline saw the men ex-changing glances. "A very long birthing..."

"I didn't know of anyone coming to term." Simms, the large warden, spoke, while Evangeline knelt to the tinder-box and kindling.

Evangeline said nothing, sensing some keen danger now, something hidden from her, as if held within the folds of their great cloaks. The fire in the hearth had begun to catch, the wood snapping and throwing off sparks, and the men began to speak, each a different phrase, as if in anti-phon; standing together, shoulder to shoulder, once again they gave the impression of one massive boulder.

"... some not altogether ... flattering perceptions ... come to our attention ... perceptions that raise our concern for you ... negative perceptions, one could say ... we thought it only fair for you to know...."

Each one took a fragment, voices weaving, low and soft and deep, and Evangeline heard, beneath the voices, the fast rap of her own heart. For a moment, she was not aware that smoke had filtered back into the room.

They were speaking of her lack of regular attendance at Sunday worship, and of her criticism they had heard not only of church, but council.

She tried to explain, but the heavy voice of Warden Simms fell like a weight on her words. Evangeline studied Simms, trying to recall him as a man seen by chance, weeping in a nightshirt in his bedchamber. One evening, she had passed on her way from a birthing, and heard the sound of his cries on the night air; stunned, she had halted, unable to bestir herself for some moments.

Here was a man with a face as stern and merciless as a holy image seen briefly by Evangeline as a child. The image was of a severe prophet — Amos? — and had vanished from the church in Bermuda because the painting made the children cry. Here, then, was this man, this church warden, his face hard, his gaze severe — weeping piteously as a child. Despite herself, Evangeline was moved and did not want to be. She knew certain things about Simms: his harsh treatment of indentured servants and slaves, his neglect of his wife ... and yet, he sobbed before his candle, "No one ... no one ... no one ever ...." And all at once, he had risen to stand before the small looking glass on the table. An instant he stood there, half-dressed, his flesh spilling in folds beneath his nightshirt, weeping in the candlelight. Evangeline's throat had constricted as she moved swiftly, silently, away. Now, however, she could not hold that image in her mind. She could see only the hard face and hear the hard words, crushing hers.

"Now, now, we're not Puritans, this isn't Boston," the priest said gently, coughing a bit at the increase of smoke. "We are simply expressing our concern...."

She knew she must speak about the smoke, now filling the room with bluish mist. Her eyes smarted and she murmured something as she stepped toward the great fireplace, and into it, holding her skirts from the flames and gazing upward. She could see her warming pans, her kettles on their hooks and the dark tunnel of the chimney. Something seemed wedged up there, but she could not quite see; she would have to douse the flames to get a clear look. Her uneasiness increased, for the chimney had drawn properly just yesterday, and there was an odd smell from above.

Somehow, with the water tub and the wardens' help, the fire was put out, and Evangeline stepped into the hearth once more. Her unease was greater, falling like a cloak upon her, for she recognized that odor now; she had smelled it many times before. She took another step deep into the hearth, and forced herself to gaze squarely up the chimney. As she did, something grazed her face. Something human, fleshlike, bonelike, skimmed her hair now as she quickly bent her head. Then, once more, she forced herself to look.

That was when she saw it, hanging in the shadowed recesses just above: a hand, swinging pale and stiff against the chimney's darkness. Evangeline pressed her knuckles to her mouth, unable to look away, and now, she made out a face; it hung upside down, its dark hair drifting on the air as if underwater. The face seemed to stare at her oddly, relentlessly, a dark gaping stare, wide as the dark open mouth.

"Dear God ... " A whisper, blurred; she lacked breath to cry out. Evangeline drew back from the hearth, her knees weak, reaching behind her for a bench, while that dark-cloaked row of men stood watching her. By the table, she sat hard, pointing at the hearth, a strange humming in her ears. The room seemed to fade away, then return, and through the haze before her eyes she saw the men struggling, grunting, wrenching the body from the chimney. When at last they'd laid it on the hearthstone, Evangeline's sight was clear again.

She looked down on him as belay there, legs and torso smudged with soot, and she saw that he was Nick, the sexton; Nick, her friend, stiff and cold and soiled, his blue gray eyes carved out, leaving gaping sockets, dark and blind. She had looked into those eyes just yesterday and touched their tears; now Nick's face swam in her sight.

She sat there unable to move or speak, hearing the commotion build around her, the harsh bark of men's voices, the thud of running boots, the cry for the Town Watch, and then the screams as people pressed in at the door and windows. Dead, the sexton, Lordamercy, killed. *When Evangeline looked up at last, she saw what seemed a thousand eyes through the smoky bluish air.*

The broad, low-beamed room seemed to narrow around the hearthstone, in that smoky light, and into that light, and into the midst of those watchers, the priest moved. Beside the dead man now, he knelt and said the prayer of committal, then called for something to cover the mutilated face. Evangeline dropped her own shawl over Nick's head and as she did, a windlike breath swept through the crowd. Voices rose, fingers jabbed, the priest turned around. On the stool, now revealed, were three glass-stoppered jars, filled with strange colored spheres. Regarding them, the priest drew back; then, with effort, he lifted the largest jar into the light.

Within the vessel now, the spheres shifted like pebbles — but not pebbles. Eyes. Animal eyes, trailing veins and twinelike sinew, drifted in blood-tinged brine, where they rolled and turned; some appeared to stare out crazily, as through a reddish mist, while others, bruised and purplish, were filmed, hardly recognizable.

Behind him, the priest heard a thud: someone had fainted; in the doorway, Cass Tanner was retching. Others crossed themselves and made the circle with thumb and forefinger against evil, for here, across this Market Day, darkness had surely fallen. A breeze touched and turned the spinning wheel; a rush of breath ran through the onlookers again as they looked at Evangeline. She saw them cringe from her and knew they feared her now, dreading that she had blighted them somehow, at sickbed and childbed. The priest was speaking.

"This — " He stared at her. "Your work?"

"Nay." Her voice came strong and clear. "Not mine."

She pointed to the rows of clay jars on her shelves, made for her by Luke the potter; she never used expensive glass, and she had been out all this night past ... She sensed no one was listening. Everyone watched the councilman now as he lifted up a smaller jar, and a wind-like gasp rose again from the onlookers.

"And this?" he asked.

In the light, he looked more closely at the vessel, saw what lay within, and suddenly, it slipped from his hand to the floor. Briny water ran across the boards, and within the spreading red-brown stain lay two more spheres, larger than the others. These were human eyes, blue-gray, staring outward, so it seemed, from a web of veins and fleshy tendrils.

Evangeline heard, as from a distance, a sharp sound in her own throat, and then shrieking from the crowd, followed by a silence. There was a long, slow, rustling slide as another woman fainted. Shaking now, the councilman lifted up another object from the stool: a thing Evangeline had never seen before. His hand shaking, the councilman held aloft, in her own house: a crucifix with the body of the Savior stuck with pins. The townspeople's murmur turned into an odd low growl, and the Town Watch had to shout for order. The priest turned to face Evangeline again.

"That has never been in this house." Her voice held a thread of anger now. She felt her hair, slip from its knot; a hairpin clinked against the Boor. She pointed to the plain wood cross above the hearth. *"This has always been. I demand to know — "*

"Silence." The Town Watch chief looked at Evangeline and then away. A big man, his voice rough and splin-

*tered, his face red as raw beef, he looked at her again and,
despite himself, stepped back a pace. "Mistress Smith, you
may clear yourself of murder ... but this ... this ..." He
gestured at the jars, the crucifix, the mess on the floor.*

*The priest wiped his face and turned back to the restive
crowd. "Thricefold, in the name of God Almighty, all evil
here is bound." Then he turned to Evangeline.*

*"This is fearful, weighty evidence." The priest gazed
around the room, shook his head, then gathered himself
once again. "Evangeline Smith, you stand under suspicion
of murder, occult ritual, and sorcery. May God have
mercy upon your soul"*

*Evangeline stood very still. The room's haze seemed to
deepen like a winter afternoon. Dimly she heard orders
issued: she was confined to home, under guard, till court
and council met; the crowd must now disperse in orderly
fashion. She heard the people leave and then, her blue
gown pooling around her, she knelt by the body till she
was pulled away.*

I looked up, feeling pleased and dubious at once, as
always, with first drafts. Silently, I passed the pages to
Jake, then stared at the rug while he read the new
chapter.

"What do you think?" I addressed the floor.

"Not damn bad." Praise; Jake's version. "What's
next?"

"That's what I was wondering."

We paused, listening. There was perfect stillness in
the room, the house.

"How did you know that stuff about the hairpin?
Make it up?" Jake said, trying for normal conversation.

"Most of it was based on Peagram."

"Where was he? Don't tell me, one of *his* eyes was in
that jar — "

"*Not* funny. He was the second warden, the one who hardly spoke — and the last to leave Evangeline's house."

"And the first to write everything down...."

We paused, listening once more. We listened as we shared a beer and we listened as we turned down the bed. The house remained quiet. We slept with the lights on, anyway.

...

In the morning I woke suddenly, as if I'd been dropped into bed from some great height. Jake was still asleep beside me. Edgy, wary, alert, I rose and glanced around, still listening. Still quiet. I looked at all the lights blazing away. The cat mewed.

"Okay, Red." I turned off the lights. Opening the door into the hall, I snapped off more lights there, and throughout the apartment. With each snap, I felt more childish, foolish — absurd. Two adults sleeping with the lights on. With Red bounding beside me, I went downstairs into the shop.

For the first time in all my years at Weatherell's, I had left all the lights on in the store; the bookshop had been lit like a hotel the whole night. Now I felt guilt as well as absurdity. Out went the track lights. Off went the overheads. Snap went the lamps. The bookshop sank back into a peaceful dimness. Soft morning light filtered through the shutters, and the store took on its customary muted look, like a fading photo from a gentler time.

The vast Civil War desk crouched in comfortable half-shadow; as I scanned it, my sense of foolishness switched to disgust — at myself. The desk was neglected, chaotic. Mail was unopened, messages unanswered. I picked up a loose receipt for a newly arrived shipment. The shipment was still in the cellar, loaded on the dumbwaiter — and left there. This had not been my grandmother's way, nor mine. I'd never let other writing projects take over like this, distracting me from the shop. Muttering, I fed the cat, made coffee, and then moved toward the dumbwaiter.

Mewing, Red rubbed against my legs.

"Okay, babe, just a sec." I opened the square picture-frame door and pulled on the dumbwaiter rope. The books down there were heavy; I pulled harder, feeling the strain in my back. Red began to yowl. Looking down at her, I kept on pulling. "Let you out in a minute."

I turned back to the dumbwaiter, just as it jerked to a halt before me. Staring into it, I felt the room recede, and with the room, soft light, smell of coffee, street sounds, cat's fur, and all memory of restful sleep. Too stunned to scream, I lost my grip on the rope. The dumbwaiter plunged downward as I stood there, paralyzed, gazing at the empty recess in the wall. Below, the dumbwaiter crashed onto the cellar floor.

Leaning forward, I yanked again on the ropes; they burned into my palms. Slowly, the dumbwaiter ascended back to me. I tied it in place, and then, unable to move or make a sound, I stood there, looking into it.

Framed within that squared-off space curled the figure of a man. One arm hung loose, jarred by the motion, the hand stiff and bluish-white, like thin ice. The hair swung forward, the face buried, the body rigid and still.

I seemed to watch it through a haze. Somehow, this could not be real, it wasn't happening — but still I saw that figure, curled within the square. I stood there for what seemed an afternoon, as if before a picture on a wall. I reached into the frame and touched the dead man's sweater. It had texture, fiber, bulk. I had seen it many times. It was real. And this was happening.

Finally I turned. I took one step, then another, moving as if underwater. I watched my hand reach out, slowly, slowly, for the phone. My fingers pressed numbers, pausing after each, and then I sat hard on the desk. I don't remember calling Jake. I don't remember when he got there, or when the police arrived, or how many, or what they said. What I recalled later of that morning was the face of the dead man. I could see it once they'd wrenched him from the wall. It was Gerald's face, the face I'd held between my hands two nights before. Two nights. My hands.

Gerald's face was ashen now, and his blazing green eyes were carved out, as if from a child's jack-o'-lantern. The empty sockets seemed to stare up at the ceiling; trails of blood, like dark tears, stained his cheeks.

The police were asking questions. The police were taking photos of the body. Lights flashed; still, I sat there. That morning formed a harsh bright snapshot in my mind: a Polaroid nightmare, developing as I watched. And past the dumbwaiter, past the shop, the street, I was seeing another picture — a stone hearth, and a woman in a long blue gown, kneeling over a dead sexton.

Fluke. Coincidence.

Words I didn't use again.

They had ceased to serve.

■

PART TWO

NOVEMBER 15, 1991

« 9 »

I am flying — flying over forests, dense and green, sun on my shoulders, air bearing me up. Fields and pastures float beneath me, and then a great brown scar, cutting toward a cluster of roofs; thatch and slate, they catch the light. A church spire stabs the sky, and downhill a river shines; wooden docks thrust at the water like splinters in silk.

Lower now, descending through a flock of plum-colored birds, I see the glint from a well, spots of yellow flowers by the doorsteps, and finally, the ruins of a house: a burned-out blackened square; toppled chimney, flat hearth-stone. On this stone, a woman stands, a woman in a long blue gown. Her face lifts toward mine. Her hand is raised — in greeting, in summons.

I woke abruptly, feeling chilled. I'd felt chilled ever since I'd winched up the dumbwaiter, and now, two days later, I still couldn't seem to get warm. The shop had been closed; the police had temporarily sealed off the cellar, which had been searched and sifted. The books I'd left on the dumbwaiter were gone. A Detective Gonzalez, and partner, promised we could reopen "soon."

I did not have a concept of "soon." I did not have a concept of a great deal, those first muddled days. Eddie and I, like two neurasthenic Victorian ladies, had collapsed in her living room, on opposite ends of her sofa, and pretty much remained there, while Jake brought us dispatches from the outside world:

Everyone with keys to the shop was a suspect.

Everyone with keys had been questioned.

Everyone with keys had an alibi, including us; we, of course, were suspects, too.

Now and then, Eddie and I would call our lawyers, then lurch back to the sofa. Jake could not stay still like that — a definite plus, having someone around who was ambulatory. He brought us fast food and more dispatches, including a major bulletin from the newspapers I could not bear to read:

The medical examiner had determined that Gerald was not killed in the bookshop. In his lungs were traces of river water; Potomac River water.

"How do they know?" I asked Eddie from my end of the sofa.

"They match samples," she said from hers.

"In this case, they must match toxins," Jake commented.

He was pacing as he went on. Most of the water had been forced from Gerald's lungs; still, the cause of death was drowning. The water had no saline content, indicating that he must have drowned upriver: below Key Bridge, the Potomac contains salt; above the bridge, toward Great Falls, the river's saline content disappears.

"However — " Jake turned, as if delivering a closing argument to a jury. *"However,* this was not at all the normal kind of drowning."

We looked at Jake. Was drowning ever normal?

"Gerald," he went on, "was never immersed in water, except for his face. Sweat and grime were found on the body, and splinters were found under the nails of one hand...."

Vaguely, I had an impression of the lawyer Jake might have been; a good one, I thought. It was my fault, this haze, this inability to absorb facts. I was trying not to picture Gerald struggling as he died. Across from me, Eddie looked pale, and even Jake looked sober at the echo of his own words. At least, we knew, the pressure on Weatherell's was less now. Gerald had died somewhere near the river, not in town, not in the shop. Obscurely, absurdly, I felt relief for my grandmother, who would have been horrified by a murder in her store — and would have sprinkled it, top to bottom, with holy water.

That odd relief seemed to raise me from the sofa and, as if the feeling was contagious, Eddie stood up too. Jake, mildly astonished, watched us move around.

"We are going out," he told me, seizing this momentary show of animation. "We are going out to a good restaurant to drink a lot of wine and talk of *nothing* except — "

"Except the murder," Eddie finished for him.

We all laughed: dark, inexplicable laughter.

And, inexplicably, after Jake had left to change clothes and Eddie had left to get groceries, I sank back onto the sofa. I sat there alone, gazing out the window, and once again, the dream unreeled. . . .

Again, I was flying over fields and forests, descending slowly over trees and rooftops and, at last, over the ruins of a burned-out house. I saw the blackened foundations, the spilled chimney, the broad hearthstone. On this stone, a woman stood; I saw her long blue gown, her raised hand. This time, I was close enough to see the sun on her shoulders. This time, I could see her upturned face.

The face I saw was my own.

■

« 10 »

Flying in. Flying low. Flying over treetops, fields, I caught a flash of water from a pond, and then a streak of power lines. There was a broad black scar of highway, the glint of sun from windshields, and now, ahead, a large grayish grid: a crisscross of streets and roofs, the stabs of many spires and a radio tower. Down the hill, I saw a dull brown stretch of river, and beside it, a long warehouse roof, marked in giant letters: MAID-STONE POTTERY.

"Hasn't changed a bit, as I live and breathe." Jake banked his Beechcraft, circling the town. "Beautiful colonial Maidstone. George Washington slept here. Fitfully. And woke up screaming. Sure you want to land?"

"Yes." Leaning forward, I squinted down. Jake and I had had this same interchange four times in the last two hours, but I think we'd known, somehow, we were coming here. No one else knew; we weren't sure the police would like it. The night before, over dinner — where no wine, as it happened, was consumed — we had discussed everything: the parallels between past and present, old story

and current life. They were all too close. I saw that; so
did Jake.

"If there's some way to psych it, beat it, figure it — I
think it's in Maidstone," I said it again, now. "Sorry. I
really am."

"So am I, believe me."

"Don't you have to get clearance to land?"

"In this poky little piece of Maryland? It's uncon-
trolled space."

"Yeah — isn't it, though."

Jake was dropping lower, putting down the flaps as we
neared a small airfield. Another Beechcraft and a few
Cessnas were on the ground. A jeep marked TAXI SER-
VICE waited just beyond the runway; Jake had radioed
ahead. The ground seemed to slant, rising to meet us,
and then we were touching down. As we rolled to a neat
stop on the airstrip, the jeep was already moving toward
us. I remembered the airfield and jeep from before; a year
earlier, when I was last here for research.

Everything was the same.

Everything was different.

This road, unwinding now before the windshield, led
to a town that seemed changed. It could not look the
same to me this time, I knew, though the jeep's driver
was, in fact, different. In the rearview mirror, his eyes
watched us; I looked away. It was nothing: strangers
flying into some small place — curiosity, no more.

Now, as Maidstone opened out around us, I recalled
my first visit: my disappointment in the dingy houses,
few older than fifty years, spliced between massage
parlors, pool halls; and X-rated bookstores. That trip, I
had hoped for a gem-like village, perfectly preserved:
Maidstone as it had been, set down like a star in a
meadow. This trip, I was looking more for shadow than
for stars.

I glanced up. In the rearview mirror, dark eyes glinted; narrowed eyes on us again. All the way to the town's center, that gaze brushed us, searched us. More than curious, I thought.

"Take a lot of people in, this time of year?" My voice sounded unnaturally social, bright.

"Nope." Tight silence.

The jeep stopped short, leaving us in the town square, before the old courthouse. Its faded brick was overarched by sycamores, bare and bone-white in the sun. A bronze statue of a soldier stood, rifle poised, in the square. Spreading out from the monument, the earth was bald and scarred. No one passed the bronze sentry; the courthouse was quiet, the area worn and still. And then, suddenly, from the edge of my sight, I saw a figure, watchful, alert, just beyond the building. Swiftly, then, the figure moved, so fast, so sharp, I stared after it. By then, all I saw was a shadow by the cornerstone: ANNO DOMINI 1867.

I looked at Jake. He had seen it too — the stance, the motion, and before that, the vague figure; nothing more, no face, no sense of height or gender. For some moments, we looked at the stone where it had vanished.

The jeep, I realized, had screeched away. We stood in the center of small, dingy town, and did not speak. Like a pair of children ring an expressway, we touched hands and waded into Maidstone. from that time onward, we felt watched.

"White-Knuckle Tours," Jake drawled. "First stop, the site of Evangeline Smith's apothecary shop and barn. In use till 1738, when it became the setting for Maidstone's very first Hitchcock festival...."

I was trying not to laugh. Jake's light eyes snapped at me; his sandy hair blew in a dirty breeze. Tall, rangy, indefinably Southern, he might have posed for that statue in the square. Now his Virginia-gent accent was thickening.

"Just *look* at this restoration, didn't they do *incredible* work ... re-creating the Smith habitation with *such* attention to period detail ... just smell those herbs, the very same herbs Colonial citizens smoked to make it through the night...."

"I don't *want* to laugh here, you *always* do this to me...."

Jake tapped a Honda's tire and finished off his tour-guide patter. He'd done this another time — our first visit, to tease me out of shock: Evangeline's house was not reconstructed, not even a vaguely atmospheric restoration.

"It's *a damned' parking lot,"* I had yelled here, two years earlier. Then, to my surprise, my eyes had filled.

This time, my vision was clear, my expectations lower. Still, I paced the half-full lot trying to get some sense of Evangeline's presence: a new Evangeline, emerging in my mind. Here, at the lot's center, the hearth-stone might have lain. I paused there, wanting to feel ... something ... and felt only cement beneath my shoes, the swirl of mild November air around my skirt.

I paced off the borders of the house and barn. Here Evangeline had powdered herbs, swept the floor, pinned up her hair. In this space, she had stirred soup and distilled medicinals. In this air, she had listened to others' troubles, and above, she had slept; slept, and dreamed, perhaps, of her island.

And here, two people had died violently. Had the place been so paved over, so parked upon, so streaked with rubber, oil, gas — nothing of that other time was left? "There should be a marker, *something* — " I broke off. Again: that sense of being watched. I looked at the cars, I glanced across the street. A few people moved by but no one glanced our way. I turned to my left, my right. Nothing unusual: a thin tree, devoid of leaves, and the brick wall of the shop next door, Verna's Video. I wheeled around, and caught it — a swatch of dark coat, disappearing past the last car, around a corner.

The manager of the parking lot approached me.

"He'p you?" Tall and rangy, the man had skin the color of strong, rich coffee and large, powerful hands.

"Just looking, thank you," I said. "Someone's house was here once, long ago. We were just ... paying our respects."

He was studying me. I looked up to see his surprising blue-eyed gaze, and a creased, attentive, wise face. "That would be Evangeline Smith," he said. "House burned down, 1738." He stared at me keenly a moment longer, then he smiled.

"Hope you find what you're after." He disappeared into the recesses of a Buick, which screeched into reverse.

"I'm afraid we're closed for renovations."

The gray-haired guide blocked the doorway. "I can only let you look at the front room — *across* the ropes." Her voice was maternal, fierce, protective.

Jake and I looked up. We stood on the steps of an eighteenth-century stone house, meticulously restored. By the door, a bronze plaque read: "Home of William N. Simms, Attorney-at-Law, Senior Warden of All Souls Church, leading citizen of Maidstone, and a tribute to his colony: 1700-1774."

"Buried him in the wall?" Jake muttered.

"Thanks very much," I said, bright and clear, to the woman in the doorway. "That would be fine."

We climbed the rest of the steps. Spacious grounds had once surrounded the warden's house. Now, like a book on a crammed shelf, the house was wedged between Bronson's Bowling Center and Carmine's Pizza. Across the street was a row of run-down shops: faded aqua Laundromat, gray drugstore, Dolly's Hair Design, Pop's Shop. Spliced together with historic images, Maidstone formed an odd, double-take home movie.

Jake and I crossed the warden's threshold and stood just within his front parlor. A gray velvet rope cordoned off the space. The guide, broad-hipped and strong-jawed, did not budge. I remembered her now, remembered this room; its furnishings, for the most part, from a later period — Revolutionary War, I recalled.

"It's the floor that dates to 1738, if I remember ...?" I tried to be mannerly.

"And the writing desk." The guide bristled. "That was Master Simms's *very* own." She gestured toward an object shrouded in a sheet, as was every item in the room. "He did all his legal work there, his church work too. One of Maidstone's pillars, Master Simms was warden of All Souls Church for nearly thirty years...." As if some invisible button were pressed, her guide voice switched on. "A devoted husband and father, he provided a model of Colonial family life. A kind master to his servants, he taught them to sing-hymns...."

"You must be very proud to be one of his descendants." I was guessing.

"That I am." The woman's chins quivered with dignity.

"And ..." My voice was innocent. "You must know ... if Warden Simms had to do with an apothecary?"

"I suppose, if he or his family were ill. But he had a hearty constitution, lived to a fine age."

I let a moment elapse. The wall shuddered. Next door, from the bowling alley, came the crash of falling pins.

"Of course ..." I kept my voice light, curious. "Didn't the warden have something to do with Evangeline Smith's case, the woman who was framed — "

"Certainly *not.*" The woman drew back and squinted at me. "Master Simms was an exemplary man. He had nothing to do with that sordid matter. I fail to understand this sudden interest in it. Someone was here just before you, asking if anyone had come to research that witch. I said certainly not. This was the home of a good man. Good day."

The door slammed behind us.

Doors closing: throughout the day, we heard that sound. At the Historical Society, once the home of matriarch Elizabeth Maidstone:

"Sorry, we close at two."

It was one fifty-nine.

"I should have remembered," I sighed as the great door swung shut.

At the brewery, a restoration of Tom Kemp's place of business, we peered through another doorway, but we only caught the last of the tour guide's patter.

"... and now you've seen the brewing process, we come to the end of our visit to Tom Kemp's brewery. I know he'd enjoy having you as his guests today. Y'all come back, y'hear?"

Kemp appeared in all my sources. The guide was dressed, apparently, as Tom Kemp himself. He wore leather breeches, jerkin, and a homespun shirt. His hair was rumpled and his hose had fallen down around his ankles; I noticed he was wearing jogging shoes.

Herding his group out, the guide kept up a light banter. It broke off as he saw me and Jake.

"Sorry, folks."

The guide leaned against the massive wooden door and lit a cigarette. "That was the last run of the day."

"I was just wondering ..." I found myself edging closer to the guide. "Wondering if you happened to know about an incident in 1738, involving one of the brewer's . . . friends? Another merchant in the town, the apothecary, Evangeline Smith?"

"Evangeline Smith...?" The guide looked at me and dragged on his cigarette.

"Someone was just here, asking if anyone else was asking — right?"

"No." The guide seemed puzzled. "We see lots of people. Sorry, folks, closing time." The brewery door swung shut.

"The only place that didn't shut us out was Conrad's Sub 'N Grub," Jake said as we walked away. "Worst food I've had since flight school, but at least they let us in."

We sat staring into inky cups of coffee in a diner.

"I'm sorry ..." I began. "No leads, bad food ..."

"We'll have a good dinner."

"We're going home? I can't, I have to find *something–*
"

I drained my coffee, turned over my cup, and read the imprint: MAIDSTONE CHINA. "Jake ... ever think about not flying anymore?"

Jake looked at me. "A lot, lately. Why? You thinking about not writing anymore?"

"Don't be insightful. I really hate it when you're insightful. Why do you think about not flying?"

"Because I've done it long enough to make it ordinary, I guess. It used to shine out more when I wasn't supposed to do it. I remember the first time I saw planes, small ones, Carolina beaches, I was five years old — so excited, almost wet my pants. I always knew I'd fly, even with my

Suth'n family of Suth'n lawyers." Jake turned his saucer
in his hands. "I guess flying was my escape, my rebellion
— mission accomplished. I could fly for fun and do something else now. Open a bookstore. Finish my book. Wake
up every morning with this one particular woman who
writes strange novels — am I still being insightful?"

"Yeah, about *yourself,* that's okay." I sighed. "I guess
... I could never stop writing. I love all those words
rattling around in my head, the feel of the story unravel-
ing, but this time it's different, tangled...."

"Time to go back to Real Life." Jake took the cup from
my hands. "Anyplace else we need to stop?"

I sat thinking. Faith Roper's tavern had given way to
a pizza joint. Skip it. Skip the barbershop on the site of
Cleete's house, get out of Dodge ... then something else
came to mind.

"One more place," I told Jake. "This one's not supposed
to close its doors. Ever."

"... that this evening may be holy, good, and peaceful ..."

The old priest's voice was wrinkled as parchment and
fast as an auctioneer's.

"... we entreat you, 0 Lord ..." A handful of worshipers
made soft responses.

"... that your holy angels may lead us in paths of peace
..."

"Amen to that," Jake whispered in the last pew of All
Souls Church: erected to the glory of God, 1721.

"Ssshhhh." Looking around the church, I recalled it as
larger somehow. Last time, I'd walked through it on a
sunny morning, without vices in progress. "Evening
Prayer," Jake whispered now; he'd been raised Anglican.
"Always squirmed through this one. Made the program
into airplanes."

"Ssshhhh." I frowned.

"My family always whispered in church....Proces-
sional to recessional, nonstop. Old established tradition."
He handed me the Book of Common Prayer. "This was too
big, it wouldn't fly."

"... that we may depart this life in faith and fear and
not be condemned ..." The old priest wheezed.

I tried to imagine the Colonial box-pews, painted
white; the sounding board that would have been above the
pulpit. I was distracted by these modern pews and the
runner of gray indoor-outdoor carpeting up the center
aisle; the aisle where Nick, the sexton, would have run. .
. . *Silently, between the pews, Nick began to cry. Pressing
his fist to his mouth, he rolled into the aisle and stumbled
toward the door....*

"Most holy God, the source of all good desires ..."

Past the candles on the altar; past its green frontal
and salt-white linen, I saw the side door to the sacristy
and, behind the altar, a large multicolored Lucite cross.

"... that our minds may be fixed on the doing of your
will, and that we, being delivered from the fear of all
enemies, may live in peace and quietness...."

Through the altar rail, I looked at the stone floor; it
might be the original ... *just within the rail, where the gate
was open, he made out two figures.... Naked figures, flesh
pale as moonlight ... in the chancel's dimness....*

"Be our light in the darkness, O Lord, and in your
great mercy defend us from all perils and dangers of this
night...."

Behind us, we heard the church doors open. Cold air,
in a streak, swept in. The priest glanced up. Whoever
was there remained briefly on the threshold. My head
turned sharply, just as the doors closed again. Footsteps
moved swiftly away outside.

Jake and I slipped from the back pew and moved toward the doors, but by the time we'd reached the church steps, all we saw was an empty flagstone path.

With one motion, we sat on the steps.

"Probably no one," Jake said finally.

"Well, *someone,* but *no one* — "

For a while we didn't speak. Long, low afternoon light slanted over us tawny light spilling across the streets and shops of Maidstone; holding the town in a wash of luminous amber. In that brief radiance, "Maidstone is still ugly," I observed.

"What a relief." Jake stood and pulled me to my feet. "I thought it might go pretty on us." He glanced back at the church. "Indoor-outdoor carpeting. My paternal ancestors would twitch in their graves. Tastefully, of course."

"Graves." I turned toward the churchyard.

Threading past the headstones, I moved to the back of the lot, where the oldest markers were. Bypassing the large monuments to vestry members and town officials, I looked for less conspicuous graves. Under a yew tree, near the fence — somehow, it was not so hard to find: the small stone for Nicholas Rhoades: 'Sexton, Faithful Servant, 1708-1738." We stood looking down on it as the light shifted and changed and faded around us, till we could no longer read the words above Nick's grave.

We left the churchyard, returning briefly, at my request, to the site of Evangeline's house. I didn't know why I wanted to go back; didn't know what I hoped to find, or sense, or see. Jake had a far more practical reason for returning: last visit, we'd gotten a ride there to the airfield.

As we approached the lot, its manager stood: the tall black man we had met that morning. "Find what you were after?" His blue gaze, again, was fixed on me.

"Not ... really, no." I heard the disappointment in my voice. "We were looking for a ride back to the airfield."

"I'm not running rides tonight. Friend of mine could carry you, no trouble."

I hesitated, thinking of this morning's malevolent driver.

"I think you might take to her." The man seemed to weigh his words. "Her inn's easy walking time from here. Got herself a library, private, historical. Name is Jenkins."

His eyes glimmered as he watched the words take effect.

"Even the *mice* date way back, I think. Inbred, slow. Those big ones do the minuet: watch."

The inn's proprietor paused with a spatula upraised like a signal in one hand. "Do sit," she was saying now, pointing with the spatula at kitchen stools. "No other guests tonight, I've time to talk. Always like company in the kitchen. Taste this?" She gave Jake the spatula. "Does it sing? Yeah? Pesto sauce. I do that, seafood pasta — old news in cities, here in Maidstone — revolutionary. I'm Harley."

Jake and I sat in Harley Jenkins's kitchen, at the inn that bore her name. We sat in our jeans at an odd confluence of currents: the quaint, the historic — and the hip, the nouvelle, the off-beat.

Outside, the inn looked utterly traditional: white clapboard, newly painted, with blue shutters and a swinging signboard. Inside, the floor creaked and sloped; the front parlor was furnished with country antiques, and the fireplace was cavernous, glinting with pots and kettles.

Back in the kitchen, however, bistro aprons hung on pegs. Beyond was a circular central stove, with inset chopping block, a food processor, a microwave oven, and a cellular phone. There were herbal teas, zither music, racks of fresh pasta, and, most striking of all, there was Harley Jenkins.

Forty-something, she stood tall and rawboned, laughing in her kitchen. It was a laugh that might have set the floors creaking again — a huge, generous laugh. Her gray eyes were genial, not inquisitive, registering delight at company, and her long-fingered hands were strong; hands that made one think, not of playing a piano, but of boning fish. Now, knife in hand, Harley grinned at us.

"I made silver jewelry for a while, lived in Santa Fe and all over, drifted, went to cooking school, drifted more; now I'm trying to write about it...." Laughter seemed to move beneath her spill of words. "I had my sixties experience in the eighties, I guess. The one thing I always wanted, growing up, was to *get out of Maidstone,* and *I did,* wrong man, wrong choices...." For a moment, the laughter was gone, her face dimmed. "Well, here I am, back again. Six months ago? Eight? Seemed the right time, somehow...." She held out a spoon of something to me.

"Good. Sharp." I was watching Harley. "You have roots here in town?"

"God, yes, roots, bark, trunk. Had a couple of aunts who were heavily into Family Tree *and* branches. One reason I wanted to get out of here." She was pressing bulbs of garlic. "Never was much into that myself."

"That name on the signboard, out front?" I asked. "Jenkins — a big name in town?"

Harley picked some scarlet peppers from a wreath above the steel sink. Now her laugh was lower, almost secretive. "We got some hot pers back there in the old Jenkins tree, my aunts would like to forget that. They'd tell you the family's founder was Ishmael Jenkins: town

councilman, first mayor of Maidstone, *1774, and* represen-
tative to Congress after the Revolution."

"The name certainly sounds familiar." I toyed with a
spoon. "I've been doing some writing, too — about Maidstone's history. Interesting episode in *1738, I* thought...."

Harley Jenkins was whipping cream. "Evangeline
Smith's case?" The cream, under the whisk, rose in
peaks. *"That's* a chapter people happen to forget." Harley
looked up from the cream. "Now *this is* delicious...."

Jake and I watched her, expecting another proffered
spoon, but Harley's hands were on the counter.

"Delicious: the founding father of the Jenkins family
was a mother. Moreover, a *single* mother. Moreover, the
town whore." A tremendous whoop of Harley's laughter
exploded like a sack of flour in the kitchen. "One Lily
Jenkins came from England to Baltimore to Maidstone in
1732." Harley leaned forward. "Ishmael Jenkins was the
bastard child born to her in *1738,* delivered *and* baptized
by midwife Evangeline Smith, the only one in town who
would attend Lily, and the only one in town to be burned
as a sorceress. *Unofficially,* of course: one night, her
house was torched."

"Why, do you think?" I didn't know anymore. "Surely
not for that baptism. *Was* Evangeline a sorceress? Was
Lily?"

Harley glanced at me over a steaming pot; for an
instant, her face seemed to float on the air. "I doubt it,"
she said. "Taste?"

I can't remember what was on the spoon.

"Would you talk about Lily and Evangeline?" I asked
now. "I'm writing about them — any family papers I
might ...?"

"Some are in the house, the rest are in the Historical
Society. You're welcome to poke through my stash; we'll

look after dinner." Harley smiled through the steam again. It was only much later that it all seemed too easy.

After dinner, we were in Harley Jenkins's library: a room of grandeur once, with paneled walls and wing chairs, and antique shelves crammed with books. Now, it was a room of controlled chaos, the upholstery threadbare, the desk and end tables piled with papers, magazines, and correspondence. Cookbooks were stacked on the floor, with issues of *Rolling Stone* and *Mother Jones*. From the walls, a few ancestral portraits gazed — in tactful horror, I thought. One male portrait had a lipsticked mouth and punctured eyes, through which the white wall glowed.

"My handiwork," Harley remarked, following my glance. "I wasn't a real, relaxed kid."

We settled down around the cluttered desk. Without ceremony, Harley swept a pile of mail to the floor and unlocked a drawer. Old papers began to appear before us, shimmering in the green lamplight. Harley was flipping through letters from the illustrious Ishmael Jenkins.

"What I don't quite get," said Jake, "is how a kid from the wrong side of town, born to a ..."

"Whore," Harley supplied.

"... how does he get to be Golden Boy?"

No hesitation: "Elizabeth Maidstone," said Harley.

I looked up, puzzled. We had been to Elizabeth Maidstone's house, now the Historical Society. "The heiress? House-on-the-hill?"

Harley nodded. "Big-time, she owned half the town, kept her independence by staying unmarried." I heard a note of personal relish. "Unusual woman, read a lot, constantly ordered books from England, had a library of sorts. Rare. Also rare: she moved beyond her class. Had a deep affection for Evangeline, who was, after all, in trade. Also had a friendship of sorts with Faith Roper, the tavern-keeper, who was savvy, kind, respected — but well below Elizabeth Maidstone's station. Then. Elizabeth risked scandal, taking Lily Jenkins's kids into that big house. She raised them, left them money, and died in her bed at ninety-one."

"Impressive." I paused. "But something doesn't fit. Why would Lily give up her kids? Or is there something a little grimmer here ...?" I had a sudden sense there was. "Did something happen to Lily?" Again, Harley nodded. "Just before Evangeline's own death." I sighed. "Natural causes?"

"Doesn't look that way to me."

For a moment, there was quiet in the library. I could hear a clock ticking from somewhere behind a stack of *Gourmet* magazines. "Was it because of her association with Evangeline?"

"Hard to say. Looks like Evangeline spoke to the matriarch about Lily's orphaned kids."

"I thought Evangeline was locked in her house by then, under suspicion of — "

"Sorcery, murder; she was," Harley finished for me. "Elizabeth Maidstone, founder, patroness, big shot, visited her often, according to Elizabeth's own journal."

"She left a journal?" For a few seconds, I thought I'd heard wrong. "I never found one."

"That's because I have it." Harley's smile was broad. "It just happened to disappear from the Historical Society a few years ago, when I got this notion of vindicating Lily. The journal means a lot to me, it tells so much of Lily Jenkins's story. No one else bothered. It also records some of Elizabeth Maidstone's meetings with Evangeline...." Harley studied my face an instant. "You *really* want this stuff."

"I *need* this stuff."

"Well ... I made two copies of the journal, I have this fear of fire." Harley grinned. "Maybe I've read too much about Evangeline's death, I don't know. One copy's in my safe, one's here. I couldn't give you the original, but I could *lend* a Xerox. ..." Harley hesitated, studying me again.

I wondered what was in it for her.

"What's in it for me," she said uncannily, "is redeeming Lily Jenkins, a project of mine for a long time." She paused, making some inner decision. "Wait here."

In Harley's car, *all* the way back to the airstrip, I felt the journal's weight in my hands. I had checked this copy against the original, and checked the original for historic authentication. In Harley's lamplight, I had seen the clear, open handwriting of Elizabeth Maidstone, patroness to Evangeline. That writing, in duplicate, in bound Xeroxed sheets, remained in my hands as Jake taxied the Beechcraft and took off. Maidstone receded beneath us. I looked down on the gridwork of streets and saw the floodlit church and courthouse and, before the town sank into the dark, I saw the glowing lot where Evangeline's house and barn had stood.

■

$W_{itch!}$"

Evangeline's house seemed adrift, like a ship, on the currents of the town. Beyond her flowed the street, a brownish stream shifting with figures and colors, but she seldom looked out now. Her windows were too often pelted with stones to be safe and she stayed by the hearth, trying to conserve logs and tallow. In the wide, low-beamed room, the light was aqueous and dim, as if the place had somehow taken on water, and a deep quiet filled the house, like a seaborne mist; strange, for the shop had always been busy.

"Witch!"

Like shrill seabirds, voices flew at the house from outside, then darted off, so no hex could fall upon the speaker. Mostly, though, steady silence washed against the house, and this made Evangeline feel most adrift. Friends and neighbors, those she'd nursed, crossed to the far side of the street. Tom Kemp, once her suitor, did this, and the hired servant, Cass Tanner, and too many others *to think of and this brought her more pain than that sharp cry:*

"Witch!"

Crouching by the hearth, a prisoner in the house, Evangeline glanced up and saw her face reflected dimly in a hanging skillet. It was a face unlike the one she remembered from the glass, for this one was as pinched, as tight, as any she had tended. Somehow, then, the sight of this made her stand and move away from the shadows, back to the window again, though it was still day.

Too long crouching in the shadows, she thought. In the windowpane's reflection, she looked once again for the strong Evangeline, who helped bring new life into the world and touched others with healing. She turned, reaching out to turn her mother's spinning wheel; ever since that long-ago death, Evangeline had tried to forget the sound of her mother's voice, but now, quite clearly, she recalled the lilt of her mother's singing: island tunes — songs of whites and blacks and spinning songs. As Evangeline had done in childhood, she tried to trace the notes with her own voice. Not a fine voice, she knew, but hearing it, she realized that something had shifted. She felt lightened.

At night there were other voices in the dark behind the house, vague figures without lanterns, leaving bread and fruit, eggs and cheese, stopping to offer a word of comfort. These visitors were folk she knew and others she knew slightly; some were slaves, servants and farmers she had dosed or midwifed — the working folk of Maidstone, with an air of their toil about them, a smell of earth and fish and ash, who came in weathered wools to press her hand.

Late each night, Luke Arnold, the potter, came and held Evangeline against him. By the far door to her root cellar, which opened in the barn, he spoke love and rocked her like a child and told her news of friends in town working quietly on her behalf. She listened less to his words than what his hands said, as they touched her face and hair: hard sweet calloused potter's hands, she felt them still in daylight.

Luke had been courting her for a full year now. At first, she had kept the suit slow and he had respected this, only walking out with her of an evening and lingering at the shop. Of late, however, he had grown more intense in his wooing, and she had responded, knowing all the while the danger of this, in her case: a single woman, without family or patronage. Soon, she would answer what he had asked these last weeks, in the dark, with a break in his whisper. She tarried now, for fear of tainting his reputation — she feared, too, that he might not return with her to the island. He would ask again; she must answer. In the meanwhile, she watched for his long stride down the street, and thought of the brush of their hands, the press of their mouths, these last evenings. And she feared for him, associated with her as he was. They had spoken first after her father's death, when Luke had come to the shop to offer his condolences. Through the seasons, he had come again for medicinal draughts: so many, of such varied kinds, one might have thought he had every, malady in 6erard's *Herbal. Of course, Evangeline soon discerned, he was in strong rude health and only came to speak, to gaze, to banter; of this, he made a fine sport. And she, in turn, came to his shop to watch him fashion bowls and plates, and came to love the sight of his long-fingered hands on the clay. Luke was steady, sturdy, amusing, and at times possessed of a temper; this, too, she had seen, and somehow admired. She thought of him most hours each day, and even more so now, waiting for the nights when he would come to the root cellar's far door. Only Luke knew about the root cellar, connected by a passageway to the barn floor, where Evangeline emerged to meet him. Her*

*father had dug the space out by night, and smuggled
runaway slaves to a sailor he knew: seventeen slaves, by
Evangeline's count, four belonging to Warden Simms.
Only Luke knew — and one other, Evangeline discovered.*

*One night, a tall, commanding silhouette appeared just
behind the barn. Etched against a rising amber moon, the
regal figure gave off a scent of peppermint and lavender
and held out a long thin hand. Before any introduction,
Evangeline greeted Elizabeth Maidstone, from the great
house on the hill. She had been a quiet, secret friend of
Evangeline's father, and saw him in this daughter he so
loved, even in the dimness, even in this troubled time. She
would come again, said Mistress Maidstone, and did,
appearing often at dusk, with food and wise counsel. After
her first visit, Evangeline had knelt by her own
hearthstone, as she did each night for Nick, to offer a new
prayer: this one in thanksgiving for Elizabeth..*

"Eggs!" Elizabeth Maidstone said one night.

*In the moonlight, she held them out; they seemed to
glow.*

*"Never did eggs look so rich," said Evangeline, and
startled herself with a laugh, a small one, like the sound
of a dropped spoon. And then there was a silence.*

"Your father ..." Elizabeth said then, and stopped.

"He'd be aggrieved."

"I feel it myself."

*Evangeline noted the curve of the older woman's cheek,
the tilt of her head, the tendrils of whitening hair caught
by the faint light beyond the barn; beyond the door to the
root cellar within. Somehow, in that moment, Evangeline
knew that Elizabeth Maidstone had been beloved of her
father, and he of her, in a secret way; sanctified, all the
same.*

"Could you go back?" Elizabeth asked.

"To Bermuda? I dream of it. Sometimes when I dream things, they come to be."

"What else do you dream, child?"

Evangeline hesitated. "Fire," she said then. "The house ..."

"I pray not. Other dreams?"

"Friends. Thank God. One I've not seen before."

"Perhaps that's yet to be."

Their hands brushed and clasped and Elizabeth swept away; Evangeline vanished into the barn, down the root-cellar steps, and through the underground passage to the house.

On a different evening, Evangeline offered up a prayer in thanks for yet another friend, Lily Jenkins, out of childbed and recovered, come with news that the baby thrived. Lily wished to pass on other news, something secret she had seen, but just then there had been a rustle in th trees behind the fence and, fearing for her safety, Evangeline had urged her off.

She watched Lily go uneasily, and watched for her the next day at the window, just to see her passing by, just to know she was to rights. All at once, then, there she was: fair-haired, fair-skinned Lily, dusted with freckles, her full-blown figure corseted quite low. Lily, with her daring rouged mouth, looked more a poppy than her namesake, ripe as sum-me% an outrageous earthy beauty. Watching her, Evangeline had not noticed a small group of young men massing in the street, hands filled with stones; daring lads who would risk the curse of a sorceress to shatter her windows.

Lily shouldered her way toward the group. "Shame on you," she rounded on them, shouting. "Shame on you, throwing rocks at a defenseless woman. I know you — and you — " She pointed a finger at one face, then another, making them go scarlet. "You'll have no more business in my bed from now on, none of you. And won't you be doubly sorry when you find you're wrong about our Mistress Smith, when you hear about two men" — she jerked a thumb over her shoulder "right here in this house, the night Nick was killed. I saw them, yes I did, on my way home, some other things I saw as well." She spat at them. "I know her — she's far better than the lot of you. Now get away from her house, you bastards — off!"

They turned, shouting as they went, "Whore — slut — bitch — "

"I know all those words." Lily moved off down the street, but after she was gone from sight, Evangeline looked after her, and feared for her, and dreamed of her that night.

I stopped typing.

One again, I glanced at the sources piled beside me on the desk. I knew what they said. Still I sat there, staring at the fresh sheet of paper I'd just fed into the typewriter. I could not bring myself to render what came next:

Midnight, 16 March, 1738, Lily Jenkins, resident of Maidstone, unwed mother of four, found dead from blow to head, on slope before Roper's Tavern....

Once more I checked for corroboration: Maidstone's record of births and deaths; *Peagram's;* Mistress Elizabeth's journal; the priest's diary. And still I sat there looking at those hard words, unable to write or re-create them.

Moments later, when Eddie knocked on my door, she found me before the humming typewriter. I still stared at blank paper; not an uncommon pose for a writer, after all, not worth an explanation.

Downstairs, in the shop's kitchenette, Eddie and I were subdued. We hadn't sat here together since the place had been crowded with police. I didn't mention it and neither did she; nor did she mention my disappearance the day before, which I had left unexplained. It sounded too crazy, too notional, too mystical — I could not explain it, completely, to myself. And so we sat together in silence at my grandmother's wooden table, before her old wood stove. We shared a quick supper, and in the bright room, filled with the safe-child smells of grilled cheese and tomato soup, I found our silence companionable; I found myself returning to this time, this place.

Tomorrow, we would reopen the store. This evening, there would be a special meeting of Writers' Bloc. There, in the warmth, in the light, in the quiet, I felt glad to be back — even with work and a meeting ahead.

The feeling, I recall, lasted about an hour.

■

« 12 »

Blue cigarette smoke filled Weatherell's back room; smoke, and silence. The quiet, I assumed, was due to Gerald's death. His family, traced to San Francisco, had flown his body home. As a group, we were clearly far from home; far from where we'd been just two weeks before.

Eddie and I slipped in, almost late; Jake was out on a flight, due in later. As usual, Eddie sat down front, and as usual, I leaned in the doorway, just behind Dinah, who'd been stubbornly sleeping in her old place in front of the shop, despite everything, these last troubled nights. Before me, the silent, smoke-hazed room seemed oddly distanced, as if seen through old glazed panes.

Then, into the silence, into the smoke, Andrew rose and opened the meeting; opened it with an odd apology, which made me uneasy. He expressed embarrassment, distress, regret over what was to follow: a decision of the group's executive board. And then he stood aside.

Lorna stepped forward, looking hesitant as well. For a moment, she stood creasing a paper in her hands. In that moment, I saw her as she had been twelve years ago,

working on her master's in English: an overweight,
unhappy young woman haunting the shop, escaping here,
escaping into books; too bookish for the men she longed to
meet. I filled the rustle of candy wrappers, back in
ENGLISH LITERATURE, and occasional confessions of
loneliness — then that hard face again. I felt somehow
she hated herself for telling, and hated me for listening.
Somehow I remembered that now. It was the rustling
paper in her hand. It was her face. Almost imperceptibly,
my uneasiness grew.

  With her own apologies, Lorna said that she would
read a letter. It concerned a member of the group; it
concerned us all.

> "Alice" [the letter began]. "A toast to a nameless
> writer, who worked hard, trusted, and believed. I
> am the writer, as you know, and I trusted you,
> admired you. I was thrilled that you wanted to
> help me with my writing. And then you sucked
> the life from my first draft and breathed it into
> your own, plot, characters, everything. I tried to
> confront you, but you wouldn't listen. Now I must
> warn the others. You've fooled them long enough.
> I know my own work and I've seen yours in draft.
> There is only one word for what you've done:
> plagiarism.
>
> > "G."

The letter was written on Gerald's typewriter.

  The signature was one large capital, in orange crayon:
Gerald's trade-mark. The letter, Lorna said, was post-
marked the day of Gerald's death. Its return address,
typed, was his. A copy had been mailed, care Andrew, to
Writers' Bloc, and to my agent and publisher. The copy

mailed to me, I knew, was in a stack of unopened mail on my desk.

The words dropped like small sharp stones, cracking the room's blue haze. In the doorway, I stood very still. Heads turned. My face was hot. Lorna's voice continued.

"... arrived yesterday, while Alice wasn't around, unreachable. Under the circumstances, the executive committee felt it was imperative to share at this meeting. Alice, of course we assumed you'd seen your copy."

"I have not." My voice, thank God, was steady. "The shop was closed, the place in chaos — "

Andrew stepped forward. "I know how upsetting this must be. We're so sorry, all of us; take a minute — "

"I don't need a minute." Somehow, my voice remained even. Only Dinah saw my hands were shaking. "I'm amazed," I began. "Amazed you give this weight. Gerald was upset, that's true, we all knew that. I also know that someone else was distressing him, using him, pretending to help him." Now my voice shook. "I don't know who it was, but I know that letter wasn't meant for me. It's for someone else. This is — God, this — "

I kept standing. For some moments, there was only silence.

"Plagiarism." Andrew sighed. "It's a terrible word, a terrible accusation." He shook his head. "I feel for you, Alice, and I assure you, this didn't go to the police."

"I still think ..." Brad, sweating, looking down, spoke with a hitch in his voice. "I think we have to show it to them, just to be above board; she's cleared of the ... other matter. Anyone want to speak to that?"

Only an oppressive silence.

I waited; surely, I thought, someone would speak, would call this what it was: insane, absurd. Dangerous. The silence continued. I looked at Andrew, his sympathetic eyes. Brad's head was bent again, his shirt damp.

Eddie's face was horrified, while Lorna's hands went on creasing and recreasing the letter. Finally, she spoke again.

"Alice? Did you help Gerald with his work?" Her voice was neutral, legal, official.

"Yes, from time to time," I snapped, my anger rising now. "A lot of us have. Isn't that what this group's *for?*"

"This is upsetting, I know, but let's not get inflammatory — " Andrew began.

"Get inflammatory?" I shot back. "It *is* inflammatory."

"Alice." Brad rose. "It's not generally known that you've delayed publication of your novel. You've told only a few people you're actually rewriting it around a new idea."

"What the *hell* does that mean?" I looked straight at Brad.

"It means a pretty strange intersection here, since Gerald just blew about stolen material. And your novel just got a new lease on life — "

"Just what are you implying, Brad?"

"Had to raise it, Al, it's a concern."

"It's a concern only if the material matches, for God's sake. Has anyone here seen Gerald's drafts?"

"The police have his papers, they can be produced," Lorna said, her voice tight, her face suddenly shut and unreadable.

"They can also be faked." My voice was too sharp, too quick.

Glances were exchanged among Brad, Lorna, and Andrew, and, I saw, around the room. A slow cold sensation came over me, like the onset of illness, one more serious than imagined.

"Does anyone have anything more to say?" Andrew asked the group.

A terrible silence once again. Heads turned to look at me. The silent room seemed eerie to me, as if something held it captive, mute. I looked at the courtly professor, middle row; I'd worked with his essays for years. I looked at the AIDS counselor, a tall sweet woman; I'd known her a long time. I gazed from face to face, and still that terrible silence went on. Were they in shock — or afraid? Suddenly, this seemed a group I didn't know, had never known.

Then there was a tangle of voices, a blur of voices, the words indistinguishable — for a moment, it sounded like a rising babble of foreign tongues. At last, one voice emerged clearly. To my amazement, it came from a figure that had edged forward to stand trembling, twisting a torn glove.

"Ain't right," said Dinah, her pale face flushed, her gingery hair springing out around her head like points of flame. "I know Alice just like you. Slept on her floor winters, I *know* her — "

Andrew stepped forward.

"It's all right," he said.

"*Ain't* right."

Dinah, shoving a grimy fist at the group, swung in a half-circle. "One of you," she spat. "One of you — and the rest, you all keep *mum.*"

Brad and Lorna were beside Dinah now, each with a hand on her shoulders. Abruptly, as if all the strength of the streets welled up within Dinah shook them off and drew herself up into a wild, strong, tattered dignity.

"I *know* her and I know *things.*" Dinah's eyes seemed luminous. "I was here that night the kid died, I was heading for the shop's doorway to sleep, like usual, and I saw two people in the alley here, going in the shop's back door. I *saw* — I *did.* Lights, they went off, then on, downstairs, and all the while, she — " Dinah jerked a finger at me. "She was upstairs, typing, I heard her, and she didn't steal stories from nobody — " She jabbed her finger at the group.

Voices rose again, that disturbed tangle of sound, and then the words came clear and harsh:

"Who the hell does she think she — "

"Rambling, delusional, we can't — "

"Too disruptive, that's enough — "

"Deal with it, Chrissake — "

Something strange and violent seemed to sweep the room; something out of control — people were on their feet, people were shouting. For a moment, under the group's attack, Dinah had frozen like a rabbit trapped in a car's headlights; then, abruptly, she fled, slamming out of the shop. I turned to face the room again, feeling its strange stormy air, hearing that clamor of voices again. Andrew rapped on the table, but even he could not regain control of the meeting. Finally, he stood on a chair in the front row.

"This session is out of order." He spoke clearly. "The matter at hand will be discussed in executive session."

"Adjourned." Brad raised his voice and the gathering broke up; broke into a thousand pieces, it seemed. All I remembered later were fragments — people leaving, buzzing, murmuring. Some stopped to say a word to me, some looked away, walked on; afterward most of it blur ed. I remembered Eddie pressing my hands, and then Jake was there. Soon the room was empty.

Later, I put in a call to my lawyer at home. Then I called the police. Detective Gonzalez listened patiently and took notes; I could hear his pen scratching. He seemed interested in that argument I'd overheard in the shop — a hundred years ago, it seemed. The detective returned to the subject twice, though I'd reported it before; finally, there was nothing more to say.

I hung up the phone. Now that the meeting was past, I couldn't stop shaking; not until Jake had listened to everything and I had finished the whole ugly tale. At last, he drew me onto the couch and I leaned against him thinking.

"It's another parallel," I said finally.

"That's ... how it looks."

"At least it's not a jar of eyes," I tried to joke.

Jake did not smile. "It didn't happen with your other books."

"I wonder why. Maybe I never connected with them this way. Maybe they never dovetailed with my own history like this. But Jake — maybe I'm wrong, maybe I'm literally reading my life into Evangeline's."

There was a pause; I waited for him to agree.

"I'd be the one to tell you," Jake said finally. "That's what I thought at first, that's what I'd *like* to think now, God, yes. But I don't anymore, and I can't talk myself back there. It's a relief, in a way, to admit it. To say, okay, this is strange, now what can we do with it?"

"I'm certainly open to suggestions." A stab at irony.

"Okay." Jake poured himself a Scotch. "We don't know how this is happening, what the damn mechanism is." He turned the glass in his hands. "But we do know other things. Exactly how many people have keys to the shop?"

I thought for a moment. "I do, and you. Violetta, Eddie. Sharon, the new clerk — no, I haven't had one made for her yet. Brad, Lorna, and Andrew, because of Writers' Bloc. That's it, so far as I know. Anyone can have keys copied."

"True. But set that aside for a second — let's scratch you, me, and Violetta. That leaves four keys. And back in the historical mystery ...?"

"Lily Jenkins suspected four people of framing Evangeline. Of course, no one but Elizabeth Maidstone believed her, Lily being persona non grata. A persona non grata who must have known a little too much — " I broke off.

"What's wrong?" Jake sensed my alarm.

"Dinah." I looked out the window, down at the steps.

"Shit. Is she there?"

"'I don't see her. God, after what she said tonight, someone could have thought she saw even more than she did." I was putting on my shoes.

In moments, Jake and I were down the stairs, through the shop and outside. We looked for Dinah in all her likely spots, and then in unlikely ones, and didn't find her. Maybe she'd just wanted to get the hell out of Georgetown, maybe she was meeting a friend. I wished I'd said something, done something before she'd gone.

Now, I called the police again.

There was no sign of Dinah all that night. There was no sign of her the next morning when I opened the shop. And then came the call I had feared, half-expected, and hoped against, even so — a call from Gonzalez.

Dinah Lasko, female Caucasian, early fifties, found dead about one o'clock this morning in a downtown alley, the shop's address in her coat. Gonzalez offered sparse details. Dinah had been found in a well-known drug corridor. She had died, slumped against a wall, of a heroin overdose. When the police had arrived, the syringe was still stuck in her right eye.

∎

«13»

Amazing grace, how sweet the sound ..."

Our voices quavered in the November wind. The words blew back in faces. Before us was a swatch of choppy river, and behind us, a brownish grassy slope, the hum of roadway, and, looming beyond, the white slab-like form of the Kennedy Center.

"... once was lost but now I'm found,
Was blind but now I see...."

We were there, by the Potomac River, there in the November wind, to sing "Amazing Grace" and scatter the ashes of Dinah Lasko. This had been her request, a kind of will, left for me at the shop, one winter evening last year. Sometimes, on cold nights, Dinah had slept inside the store, and on one of those nights, she had written down her final requests, stuffing the paper into my hand. She had specified not only the Potomac, but the part of

the river that flows past the John F. Kennedy Center for
the Performing Arts.

I knew little about Dinah's past, but she'd told me she
would come here often on summer evenings. She liked to
sit outside on the great marble terrace behind the concert
hall, overlooking the river. She liked to watch the con-
cert-goers at intermission; how they'd moved, laughed,
talked. They'd reminded her of a time, long before, when
Dinah herself had gone to Carnegie Hall as a girl in New
York City — before her life had slid, skidded onto the
streets.

"Through many dangers, toils, and snares,
I have already come;
'tis grace that brought me safe thus far
and grace will lead me home...."

My eyes filled. Maybe it was the wind; I knew it was
not. For a moment, I thought of Dinah's gingery hair and
incandescent violet eyes, her face creased and pale as one
of those ancient handkerchiefs she always kept stuffed up
her sleeve; a handkerchief from another life. I wondered
now if Dinah's face was passing through others' thoughts.
Beside me, Jake wiped his eyes; unusual for him, public
emotion. Beyond him I saw bent heads, raised collars,
faces shut and unreadable.

Watching the members of Writers' Bloc, I found my
sight clearing. Two nights before, in the shop's back
room, these people had ridiculed Dinah, or tolerated the
ridicule. Today, by the river, they were singing a hymn in
her honor. One might wonder why they came. Guilt? I
wondered. Perhaps it was fear.

"When we've been there ten thousand years,
bright shining as the sun ..."

I found myself scanning the group and wondering, quite coldly, which of them might hold genuine fear. Which of them might have a memory of this woman's death? What pictures flashed up in which minds? I noted the detectives, up the slope, watching this gathering. Everyone at that last meeting, I knew, had been questioned again.

"... we've no less days to sing Gods praise
than when we'd first begun...."

I turned away sharply, before I could think too much about this water in Gerald's lungs. As I walked up the slope, move into step beside me and a familiar face swung into focus: Dinah's closest friend, who also lived on the streets. Small, black, wiry, Kelina seemed entirely ageless. Straight-spined and graceful, even in her tattered, layered clothes, she moved like a tribal queen. Her explosion of white hair was borne like a crown. Now she gestured royally with her head: a question, a command. She wished to speak with me.

Behind us, the crowd had begun to disperse. Jake joined me and we stood silent, guarded, aware of glances our way. No knots of people formed; it was too chilly today to linger. Still, we waited with Kelina till the last person had disappeared, till we heard the last ignition start up. By that time we were so cold, hot drinks no longer seemed a nice touch but a necessity. And so, in spontaneous memory of Dinah, we passed through the Kennedy Center's great glass doors and up to the rooftop cafeteria.

A small wake. Three mourners and hot cider.

The Kennedy Center, in evening, is all crimson and marble and shine: soaring space, soaring ceilings, chandeliers like a diva's diamond earrings. Music floats from the concert hall, perfume floats on the air. By day however, the whole place is muted. The red carpet isn't quite so red, the chandeliers are dimmed. The sound of vacuum cleaners can be heard. People, perfume, energy are thinned and the place seems vast and hollow. The cafeteria, where we settled, was almost empty on this day without a matinee.

As soon as we sat down, Kelina shifted forward and laid a string of distinct beadlike words on the air before us.

"Dinah never used drugs, maybe you know, maybe you don't, so be clear — never once; we go back ten years."

She lifted her head, proud chin trembling. One hand fished in the recesses of her army jacket. Under the table, an object grazed my knee; my hand closed around it.

"Her notebook?" My voice was low.

Kelina nodded briefly. "The night it happened she left her things with me. She hated to bring her bags to your meetings, shamed her to do that way. She'd just started a new notebook, she said, so this one here, it got left with her stuff. Anyway ..." Kelina's voice was almost a whisper. "She was to meet me later. But she didn't show. I gone to look for her, got my brother. We found her in the alley where she died — and we seen two folks run out the other end."

"You get a look at them?" I asked quietly.

"Huh-uh. Minute sooner, might've. Backs to us, bundled up, they two. White, strangers, for sure, took off in an uptown car. Dinah, she'd never get into a car with strangers, never even with sorta-knowns, 'less there be some strong reason."

"You see the car? The plates?"

"Too fast — just seen it was uptown."

"They see you?"

"Huh–uh. Made sure. I been seen today, had to come anyways. I take her name on me now, so she go on, I be Kelina White Lasko. I can handle myself, be safe. Don't do for me." Her hands lifted as if to bless, as if to decree. "Do for Dinah. *Find out.*" She was gone.

We sat in silence for a minute. I thought of the river again, and the ashes.

"Strange ..." Jake said after a while. "Almost seems the strategy's shifted. First, scare tactics: bookcases, eyes, flying pages — invisible, surreal-type stuff. Now ..." He thought a moment. "All that's stopped, different tactics. Now, seems like ..."

"Seems like it's working right through human beings," I finished for him. I was glancing through the notepad on my lap: the battered pad Dinah had brought to meetings.

"Won't you have to turn that in to the police?"

"Not till I go through it." My voice was grim. I flipped the notebook's pages.

"Anything?"

"Poetry."

"Shit," said Jake.

"Observations ..."

"Dated?"

"Intermittently ..." I kept reading. *"Ah.* The night Gerald died." I looked up. "That night, Brad was seen by Dinah, about nine o'clock, on a bridge over the canal. Minutes later she sees Lorna, standing in an empty parking lot near a church. Dinah keeps walking; stops outside some Georgetown restaurant that gives her food, apparently. And she sees Eddie inside, at a table, alone ... sees her through the kitchen door; the table must have been in the back." I sighed. "Dinah doesn't name the place, just calls it 'my restaurant.' Anyway, an hour or so later she spots Andrew walking on a side street near the university, on the edge of Georgetown."

I reached in my purse for a cigarette. Very occasionally, at bad times, I begged, borrowed — and lit up.

"These are not good alibis." I exhaled. "Everyone was supposed to have a good alibi."

"Iron-clad, I was told." Jake looked irritated; some source, somewhere, had failed him. He took the cigarette from me and dragged on it.

"'Eddie's is almost iron-clad," I said. "She was supposed to be having a drink with her sister that night, maybe she was waiting, and maybe the others ..." I took the cigarette back from Jake. "These are our friends. I hate this, can't do it."

He exhaled, thinking. "Let's go back to the historical mystery. You said Lily Jenkins thought there were four suspects?"

I nodded. "As told to Elizabeth Maidstone. Councilman Cleete, Tom Kemp, the brewer, the sainted Warden Simms, all out in the dark, alone, the! night of Nick's murder..." The journal entry threaded through my mind.

How very peculiar that All were abroad, this night
[Elizabeth had remarked]. Felicitous that poor
Lily observed most of them, even in her Distress.
It pains me to think of her alone, groping her way
to E's House, feeling her Travail commence....

"Lily had been at a tavern," I went on. "She was pregnant, full-term, her labor begin. She went to Evangeline's house for help, but stopped outside." Again, Elizabeth Maidstone's words stitched through the retelling.

There, within, she beheld two Persons moving in
the dark House by one candle's Light. Lily says
she immediately surmised something was amiss,

but just then her Waters broke, and she knew she must get Home. How I wish she had come to me....

"Tough lady, Lily Jenkins," I continued. "She knew she couldn't intervene just then, of course. She managed to get herself home, thought she could get through the childbirth herself, apparently. She went by back lanes, stopping when the pains came on. One of those times, she caught a glimpse of Kemp, another time, Simms. Finally, by some good fortune, on Milne Lane, Lily ran into Evangeline herself, who was coming from a deathbed — natural causes, I've got the name. It was Evangeline who had seen the third man, Perry Cleete, earlier."

"That's only three suspects. By name, that is."

"I know, she didn't name the fourth." I turned the cigarette between my fingers. "I'm sure there's a parallel, I just ... I can't quite put the pieces in the right pattern." I sighed. "The historical mystery's like a jigsaw puzzle in a dark room. And *ours* — ours is a dark room."

"You afraid of the dark?"

"Never," I said, too fast.

"*Never?*"

"No. My brothers tried to make me afraid — I resisted." That wasn't completely true, about the resistance. Of course, in childhood, the stakes had been considerably lower; as far as I knew, neither of my brothers had ever been suspected of murder.

"Well, I was afraid of the dark." Jake took the cigarette and put it out. "Sometimes, even now, I'm not a hundred percent immune. Sometimes it's sensible, fear of the dark." He looked at me. "I wish everyone had it."

■

« 14 »

Long after the cigarette was out, I saw those ashes in the wind the river. Long after I'd returned to the shop, I saw that form in the. dumbwaiter.

And so, that evening, in the dark I said I didn't fear, I set out on a venture of my own. I had decided to conduct a kind of private investigation, from my clanking old car, in the space of a few hours — without telling anyone.

The Chevy started up fine. Then, of course, as soon as I pulled out into the traffic, the old car stalled, then stalled again at a light. The light changed. The car coughed and moved forward. Creaking like a stagecoach, it would run a few blocks, then stall again. Whenever it did, I glanced in the rearview mirror to make sure the car behind me had stopped. Each time, a different car was there. I wasn't being followed. Later, I remembered that.

Now I was nearing my first destination. A parking space appeared. I grabbed it and stepped out into Dupont Circle's European air: its old houses and cafes, its Bohemian urban chic, galleries and dance studios and haircut mills, tossed together with elegant old town houses.

Through the twilight, I walked toward one particular town house I'd known, years before.

Brad looked startled as he opened the door.

"In the neighborhood," I said. "Bad time?"

"No, no ..." He held the door open. The television murmured in the background. Newspapers and empty pizza boxes lay on couch and floor; a Swanson TV Dinner tray gleamed from the coffee table. His wife must be away again with their son. I didn't ask. The house looked much as it had when I'd been Brad's girl — random, littered, easygoing; but what once seemed creative chaos now seemed only chaotic, some sign of inner disarray.

Brad himself looked disarrayed as he stood gazing at me. His shirttail hung over his torn jeans; something like paint had spilled across one shoe. That was Brad, the charmingly rumpled artist — more charming years before, recently arrived from Cambridge, from teaching at Harvard, from living in an artist's loft where he had written poetry instead of spy thrillers. He had dreamed he would live in Paris. Instead, he had moved to Washington to write one money-making novel: just *one*, to get to France. And then, just one more ... Now, as I remembered, I was watching him, watching everything ... even his dishevelment, even the paint on his run-down Gucci loafers; watching as I never had before.

Brad motioned me toward an easy chair, the rushed to clear it of magazines and crumpled packs of cigarettes. He seemed nervous, tongue-tied. Reaction to an old girlfriend? Perhaps, I thought; perhaps not.

"Sorry, dropping in like this...."

He lit a cigarette and ignored my apology. "Get you anything?"

"Thanks, I'm fine." I paused. "I wondered if I could talk to you about something." I began my cover line.

"That last meeting. Writers' Bloc — it seemed so hostile. And that letter..." I looked at him. "I'm wondering, Brad, who would want to frame me."

He sat gazing at me as if I'd dropped from some star, right into his chaos and his chair. "I don't know, Al. Feels like I don't know you anymore. I mean, we've stayed friends, we've tried, but, well, there's Jake and I just can't get past that. Ever since you turned me loose for him, I've wondered if I *ever* knew you."

"Brad. You're the one with the wife."

"Hey: you left *me,* this marriage was a rebound, you know that. And you see where rebound stuff can get you." He waved a hand around the silent room.

"I'm sorry."

"So you said." An edge to his voice. He put the cigarette out. "Would you feel better seeing me screwed over?"

"Shit." He rubbed his knuckles over his eyes.

We sat in silence for a while; his head was bent, I glanced around the room. I saw the familiar bookshelf with its tattered paperbacks; then a row of fine leather spines — some of the bishop's books. I looked over at some object that appeared to watch me: a small stuffed bobcat, orange glass for eyes, staring from a corner. Beside it crouched a stuffed fox, its *eyes* glittering deep green. I looked away. Brad had never had such things before. The silence in the room was growing heavy.

"Well..." I said finally. "It's a terrible time, I know we all feel bad. Gerald, then Dinah. You heard how she died?"

He looked up quickly. Defensive? "I heard."

"Must have been a shock — I remember a scene like that in one of your books. Some other country, some other drug scene — "

"That was a long time ago, my second." His voice was sharp. "Not like it at all."

I let a moment pass. "How's the new book coming?"

"Fine, fine. Could write these in my sleep by now."

I glanced through an archway toward the dining-room table. As I remembered, Brad's computer sat there. Usually, it was surrounded by print-outs and more print-outs, piles of notes, Styrofoam cups of coffee. Now, however, the whole area was barren and clear, the only part of the room that looked unused. There was one neat pile of handwritten pages. Casually I moved toward them, but Brad was behind me in seconds, grabbing my arm. Swiftly he turned me toward him. His grip tightened on my arm. I pulled back; he let go.

"Sorry." He looked at the floor.

I moved away from him. "Maybe I don't know *you*."

"Maybe you don't," he said thickly. "Maybe I don't."

"Good night." My hand was on the door.

"Alice." His voice stopped me. "You know, I used to hope you'd just appear like this. Even thought of coming to you. Spent part of an evening, lately, pacing a bridge, thinking what I'd say. Finally didn't come, figured your Southern gent was with you. Now ... here you are, you came to me. For about ten minutes. And you're leaving, going back to him." Brad's tone shifted. "Just remember, Al. He may be the one you don't really know. Thank about it, think straight. What do you really know about Jake? He flies away. But he's around a lot. He's writing a novel. No one's seen it. He's got this law degree. No one's seen it. He's a charmer. Take care."

"What are you saying, Brad?"

"You think you're being framed. How do you know Jake wasn't stealing from Gerald?"

"That's outrageous."

"Is it? How do you know that Jake didn't just charm his way into the shop, the group, your life. Tries to impress his family, and make it big as a writer. Uses you, uses Gerald, gets blackmailed? Can you swear Jake was asleep that whole night, the night Gerald died?"

"Sounds like one of your spy plots, I think."

"Yeah, well, think what you want. But think, Alice. Think who you really know. And who you don't. And who loves you."

Some lovers take revenge in strange ways." My voice was quiet. "Hope you're not one."

I let myself out.

As I pulled into the traffic, I found I was shaking. I tried not to replay what we'd said but the more I tried, the louder it played back in my mind. Now the car was shaking too; at the next red light, it stalled. I looked in the rearview mirror, signaling for other cars to pass. Directly behind me, one waited while the other went around. I glanced at it again; I hadn't seen it before. Something odd about it — tinted windshields? For a moment I felt uneasy. Than I shifted my eyes to my Chevy, coughing back to life, jerking forward, jolting on.

Lorna's house, a brick Federal, was nestled in the upper northwest quadrant of the District; its neighborhood appeared suburban, prosperous. I felt my pulse tick faster as my heels clicked up the flagstone walk. The door knocker was brass; the wait; interminable. Then, at last, Lorna was there.

"In the neighborhood," I began. "Wondered if I might drop in?"

Lorna looked disturbed, off-guard. Her face seemed to tighten; she seemed to be testing the air, reading the moment. For some moments, I thought she might refuse.

Just before the interval grew long enough to be rude, she held the door wide. "Come in."

A perfect Williamsburg living room opened around me: pewter candlesticks in varying sizes on the mantel, oak dressers, a Queen Anne writing desk, and in the silence, a clock's precise tick. It was the perfect house, the house one dreams around the perfect family, but there was no family, no clutter; only some neatly stacked academic journals. I thought of Lorna struggling with that hot-pink dress, that broken zipper. I looked at her hands and then away. She'd tried red polish on two fingers; the rest were bare.

"Hope I didn't interrupt — "

Lorna waited, saying nothing.

"I wonder," I began again. "Wonder if we could talk about that last meeting. And that letter — "

"I'm not sure that's appropriate." Lorna's voice was baby-soft; her face tight. "It's a group situation. The executive committee is dealing with it."

"I just thought ... as friends..."

"But we're not friends, Alice." Her voice grew more brittle. "We're in this group together. We're colleagues. We've never been friends."

I paused, wondering which way to go. My eyes moved to the mantel, to a row of Indonesian masks, out of place in this American period house — garish, frightening masks, empty slits for eyes. My gaze kept shifting back to them. I recalled that Lorna had been raised all over the *world,* by missionary parents; maybe they'd lived in Asia and brought remembrances home. In Lorna's second, celebrated novel, she had written of a lonely girl in exotic places who had managed to elude her family and had a brief fling as a stripper before she was found and disgraced. The character had become a teacher, I recalled, and celibate, friendless. The book had depressed me. I looked back at Lorna. "Maybe that's been my fault, our not being friends," I said now. "Maybe we — "

"Alice. People take to you, get drawn to you, I've seen it, I admit I've envied that. Maybe that's why I keep my distance, I don't know. But I'd just as soon keep it that way, it's easier for me. Eddie was my friend, now she's yours. Isn't that enough?"

Stung, I rose and moved to go. "I'm sorry you feel that way." My voice was stiff now, almost as self-protective as hers. I could not let this happen. I could not let Lorna cow me, as always. At the door, I turned.

"I guess we're all still upset about Gerald. You must be especially." It was a vague intuition; maybe not so vague, there'd been a rumor I had not quite believed. I looked at Lorna and saw a sweep of fear, like wind, across her face.

"What do you mean?"

"Oh, just that Gerald talked about you so much, these last months. About how close you were — "

Another, clearer, sweep of fear.

"He told you...?" Lorna stopped, realizing she had said too much.

"Does it matter?"

"Good night."

I felt Lorna's gaze upon me as I walked down the path to my car. The lit doorway hung there on the dark, for a moment a bright oblong. In the Chevy, I turned the ignition key, pumped the gas; tried again. Finally the car started. As I pulled out into the quiet residential street, I saw a car pull out behind me. This time, I knew, it was that odd one, behind me before. I accelerated. The other car hung back. Then, just as I neared the corner, it sped forward. I pushed the Chevy faster; it shuddered. The back of my neck felt suddenly cold. The other car was still behind me: a foreign car, with foreign plates and tinted glass. The driver, barely visible, was just a form behind the windshield. The chill at my neck ran like ice water down my back.

I drove faster, the Chevy clanking, protesting, then smoothing out — taking me toward Georgetown and then past it to a different residential area; to a town house on a narrow street of narrow dwellings, a house I knew almost as well as the shop. I knew where the spare key was, and how the teakettle whistled. I'd come here for tea, for lunch for long idle afternoons — for friendship.

And now, Eddie stood in the doorway.

"Saw the car," she said.

"Glad you're home...." Glancing behind me, I saw the odd car was gone. I went in and sat down on the familiar couch and tried to forget cars in general. It was good to be here, in this room where we had talked and drunk endless cups of tea and let hours pass.

"Tea, of course."

"Ed, no, I'm okay. Just wanted to drop in, see if you're still speaking to me. There's been so much ... silence between us since the bad stuff." I wanted to confide; I didn't understand what held me back.

"You just vanished the other day, not a word."

"I know ... sorry."

Eddie shrugged it off and sat quickly in the rocking chair. Her small house was dainty as a shell: lace curtains and English printed wallpaper, but coffee table and dining table were, as always, covered with books, bills, makeup, masking tape, picture wire. In a corner, her computer sat on an antique table with a matchbook under one cracked leg. There was always that odd combination here: perfect lace, perfect chintz, and nicked furniture, broken appliances, islands of odd clutter. Eddie, rocking, seemed to watch me as I took inventory. Why was I thinking that? I was watching her.

"Any news? Developments?" she asked.

"Not that I've heard."

"You must feel wretched about Dinah."

"Yeah, I guess we all do." I tried to focus my gaze on a single point: the coffee table. I needed to clear my mind; I was feeling confused, mistrustful of everyone.

"Saw you talking with that friend of hers by the river — what's her name again?" Eddie asked.

"Kenonah." The first name that came into my head; I realized it was a summer camp I'd attended one year in Massachusetts. For some reason, I felt guarded. Paranoid? I couldn't tell.

Again I tried to fix my gaze on the coffee table. Eddie's usual scattering of mysteries lay there, along with art books, religion books: the big slick one on Monet, the slim one on saints. Between them stood a bottle of hand lotion, a bottle of nail polish; a copy of *Vogue* magazine lay beside a perfume sample, an open carton of cigarettes, a sewing kit, and a thick book titled *Human Anatomy: Dissection*, Vol. II. "Ugh," I said without thinking.

"I know," Eddie said. "Research for the novel. Occupational hazard with mysteries." She lit a cigarette and smiled. *"Vogue's* a relief; people *dressed*."

"How's the novel going? Better?"

"No longer a maze, thank God, really coming. Actually, I might be on the home stretch."

I glanced over at the typewriter. It was flanked by two full ashtrays and surrounded by crumpled paper; no manuscript in sight.

"Great," I said, looking back at the coffee table. "And your ... friend? Less of a maze, too, I hope?"

"Oh, I stopped seeing him." Eddie exhaled blue smoke. "Just broke it off. It's fine, I feel better." She brushed the subject off like dust. "I'm much more concerned about you, the shop — "

"I am too." My gaze was arrested by a round glass bowl on the coffee table. "Wanted to talk to you about that, and Writers' Bloc. That letter, that last meeting..."

The bowl was filled with small glass objects, round, shining, multicolored. Marbles: some special kind, they had some special name — cat's-eyes, that was it.

"Oh, don't worry about that meeting. Terrible for you, I know, but things will calm down, Im sure. People get weird when they're scared. You've got so many supporters, Alice."

I leaned back, and for an instant, just an instant, relaxed. It seemed like all the other times, comfortable times; countless easy afternoons. And yet something almost imperceptible was not like other times: probably, my own inner weather.

"Thanks." I rose. "Look, I've got to run. I just wanted to see you."

Eddie stood up to walk me to the door. I turned, just as always, to give a quick sisterly hug. Over Eddie's shoulder, I saw the rocker, still in motion, and something else, hung over its back, swiftly hidden as Eddie had sat there. It was a man's tie, vaguely familiar but not quite recognizable.

"What's wrong?" Eddie seemed to stiffen.

"Nothing. Dreading my car — worse each day. Take care." Turning, I felt Eddie's eyes on me. I went down the steps, and then I was back in the car; back in the dark once more.

I was cutting across town now, swinging onto Massachusetts Avenue. My last stop: a town house beyond the Capitol. I glanced in my rearview mirror, and suddenly I was pushing the Chevy to accelerate. That car, that same car, was behind me again.

"C'mon, babe, don't stall," I whispered to the Chevy.

It stalled.

I swore.

In the middle of traffic, in the middle of Massachusetts Avenue, I sat muttering, trying to make the engine turn over. Miraculously, it did, on the fourth take. Still muttering, I floored the Chevy and lurched away. The other car was gone.

Behind its wooden fence, the fieldstone house was lit. I heard the doorbell chime within. I paced by the front steps a long while before Andrew, slightly out of breath, unlocked the door — three bolts — and greeted me.

"Sorry, I was in the garden."

"You garden at night, Andrew?"

He laughed and let me in. "My firewood's in the garden. Your coat?"

He hung it on the Victorian coat tree. Everything in Andrew's house was Victorian: the rugs, the horsehair sofas, the dark wood paneling, the dim green-shaded lamps with tassel-pulls. The kitchen, by contrast, was high tech: all black, sleek, complete with gourmet accoutrements.

"Let me guess. You'd like a double martini." Andrew glanced over his shoulder at me. "No; that's what *I'd* like. But with your low blood sugar and my diabetes, we may only fantasize, alas. I'll put olives in club soda, how would that be?"

He opened the onyx-colored refrigerator. Leaning against the onyx counter, I could see artichoke hearts, triple-colored cheese, one trout, caviar. Elegant Andrew. I tried to imagine him as that odd gangly, friendless boy my grandmother had befriended. Maybe onyx and artichokes compensated. For a moment, lit by the refrigerator's glow, Andrew's profile looked wistful, sad. I wondered again about his wife.

"Thanks." I took my glass and followed him into the living room. "I was wondering ... could we talk about the meeting? Kind of hostile, I thought...."

"You mustn't be so sensitive, you know. Defensive." He speared his olive through the pimiento.

"Sensitive? That was pretty serious. Andrew — you don't really think I was plagiarizing, do you?"

"What I think doesn't matter. This is executive-committee stuff. I can't speak for the group, or it shall think me a dictator, you wouldn't want that. We'll all talk with you privately, as friends. Agreed?"

The phone was ringing. Andrew ignored it.

"Fine with me."

"Want to get the whole damn thing over with?" He was still regarding the olive on his toothpick. "Tomorrow night?"

"Sure." I watched him pop the olive in his mouth.

"Good, I'll arrange it." He seemed pleased.

I glanced around his green-hued parlor. Even the paintings looked dim. Several icons hung on the jade-papered walls. A large medieval triptych over the hearth held the faces of three saints. Their eyes, and the eyes of the icons, seemed to scan the room.

"Thanks for taking that off my mind." I sipped my soda. "It's been a terrible time. Multiple murders in the group — "

"Well, of course Mr. Archer wasn't murdered, and Gerald, alas ... Gerald seemed to make enemies."

"Oh, really?"

The phone was ringing again.

"Surely you noticed." He looked sharply at me. There was a pause. "May we speak confidentially?"

"Of course."

Andrew turned his glass in his hand. "I've been concerned about the group. It almost seemed to turn on Gerald, in a very subtle way."

"You suspect someone in the group?"

"I don't really know, I'm just uneasy."

"Aren't you making this sound rather sinister?"

"Isn't it?" He leaned closer. "I'm also concerned about the influence on you, Alice. Forgive me if I'm intruding, I just need to say that."

"Whose influence?"

"I know this may be hard to hear. But I'd be careful around Jake. I don't know what his involvement with Gerald was, but they were reading each other's work. One night I overheard them in the shop after a meeting."

I recalled the half-whispered fight I'd overheard after Mr. Archer's memorial service. "It can't be. I'd know about it."

"Are you sure?" Andrew looked at me. "Jake wants to impress you."

"You actually think — "

"I don't think anything. I'm just concerned. Your grandmother was a friend, I've known you a long time. Sometimes the group puts me in a difficult position with friendships. But I worry about you."

I stood up. "I have to go."

"I've distressed you. I'm sorry."

"Not at all. I've been distressed for weeks."

Andrew took my coat from the coat tree. Watching him, I felt shaken, off-balance, confused; probably just a blood-sugar low. My head full, my hands clumsy, I fumbled with my buttons. Andrew was watching me.

"Careful, driving," he said. "Is eight all right for tomorrow night?"

"Fine."

"I should tell you, Lorna has a call in to me. About you. In confidence, of course."

"Then let's have the meeting at her house." I looked directly at Andrew.

I felt his gaze on me as I walked to my car.

Driving away, I rolled down the windows, and gradually my head seemed to clear. The car ran smoothly. Nothing ominous appeared in the rearview mirror. I was glad to be heading back to Georgetown, expedition completed.

In my mind now, as if on a desk, I tried to lay out all the pieces gleaned this evening. I tried to view them one by one, as I would with written research. Images repeated in my mind. Cat's-eyes. Masks' eyes. Saints' eyes. Glittering glass animal eyes. They could mean something — or nothing. Five faces flashed up before me repeatedly. Had Brad been following me earlier — in a car straight out of one of his own novels? Or Lorna, who took so long to answer the door? But then, so did Andrew; out of breath. Would Jake have followed me? Or even Eddie? Why? I didn't know.

I turned my mind to other pieces. Lorna's flash of fear. Brad's anger: jealousy — or something more? Eddie's questions and evasions — no clear sense of how to judge them. What of Andrew, his wariness, his implications? Not to mention Brad's implications. I kept returning to those, but nothing came clear. There was only one thing I knew now for sure. At least two members of Writers' Bloc indeed *had* writer's block.

I was so preoccupied I didn't quite realize I'd reentered Georgetown; driving slowly, I almost drifted past the bookshop. A man jumped in my way — I slammed on the brakes. Jake stood in the headlights' beams.

In seconds, I was out of the car. "What the hell are you doing?"

"What the hell are *you* doing?" Jake snapped. "I've been waiting forty minutes, no one knew where you were. We were going to dinner, remember?" He looked at me. "No, you didn't."

"I'm sorry." I slid back behind the wheel. Jake got in, not speaking. "I'm sorry," I tried again. "Okay?"

It wasn't. I felt it; he felt it. Even in the restaurant, after cool-down time, we were still silent, stiff. *What do you really know about Jake?* I looked across the table at him.

"I was late," I said, "because I decided to check some people out. .. ."

"People like ... ?"

"Does it matter?"

"People like ... Brad?"

"You weren't following me, were you?" I watched Jake. "In one of your clients' cars?"

"What? Why would I follow you? Why the hell do you think I use their cars? I *fly* them around, you know, in *planes?*"

People at the next table glanced up.

"You don't have to be sarcastic," I said, tight. "You don't have to raise your voice."

Our waiter appeared. "How're we doing tonight?"

"Oh, great," said Jake. "Just peachy."

"I'll give you a little more time." The waiter vanished. Jake and I didn't speak; I glanced around the restaurant. Faintly resembling a French *auberge,* the place was dark and low-beamed, with skillets hanging from the walls. No icons, masks, marbles, stuffed animals. No eyes on me, except Jake's.

"Okay," he said. "Let's start over. How'd it go?"

"Can't talk about it."

"Why?"

"I can't — okay?"

Jake studied me a moment.

"You *did* visit Brad, didn't you? And you don't want to tell me. And I just, happen to wonder — "

"You *were* following me."

"I thought so. Forty minutes late. Acting like I'm a stranger. You and Brad you still — "

"What are you saying?" I set down my water glass.

"What crap did he tell you?" Jake set down his.

"SSshhh."

"You won't talk to me? What did he say?"

"He just wondered ... how much I really know about you. Okay? Am I talking to you now?"

"He said that? What the hell's *that* supposed to mean? You want a résumé? My law degree, my pilot's license? You've got the rest — my history, my rebellions, my journals, my dreams, for Chrissake, including the one about marrying you, which doesn't seem real high on your list."

"Ssshhh."

Jake turned his glass in his hand. "What do I really know about *you*, Alice?" His blue eyes sharpened. "I know a lot of things. I know you're locked into a shadow dance, writing. You want out of that form, but you just can't let go — "

"Ah." I held his gaze. "So much easier to attack *my* writing, isn't it? Easier than talking about yours — and why it's never finished."

"We're not talking about mine." His voice was even. "We're talking about what I really know about you. I really know you're still hooked on your parents' tragedy...."

"Oh." I moved my glass an inch to the left. "I see. You're jealous, so you're coming in low, *really* low, sneak attack, easy target, where you know it could hurt — "

"You know what hurts?" He looked at me. "What else I really know about you. You can't make commitments. To Brad, to me, to anyone. Because you're afraid — "

"Ridiculous."

"Not at all. You're afraid to let anyone get close. Once that happens, you're afraid you'll lose someone again, just like your parents — "

"You sound like a shrink. A cheap shrink. *A vindictive* cheap shrink."

Jake leaned over. "And what does Brad sound like? When he analyzes me, just for you? What does he sound like, when he reaches for you ... ?"

"Could you lower your voice?"

"Sure." He raised it. "Just tell me what he'll sound like next. When he tries to get you into bed."

"I thought Southern gentlemen didn't make scenes in public."

"I thought Yankees didn't make scenes in *private*. With old boyfriends." Jake paused. *"I always* knew they made scenes in public."

"You want to see a Yankee make a scene in public?" I pushed back my chair and stood, letting my own voice rise. "Don't talk to me like this. Don't talk to me again. At all." I dropped my napkin on the table, snatched my purse, and turned to see a hundred eyes on me. I fled.

Screeching from my parking space, I pulled into the street, glancing in the rearview mirror. Swerving out, right behind me — there again: that foreign car with the tinted windshield.

Furious, reckless, not caring anymore, I threw the Chevy into park. Flinging the door open, I rounded on the strange car, running, shouting, as it made a sharp U-turn and started away. Fixing its license number in my mind, I chased it half a block in my high heels, till it was out of

sight. And then I stood, gasping, on the chilly sidewalk.
I leaned back against a wall. Riggs Bank, I realized.

"Lady?" A man, passing, looked at me. "You okay?
Need help?"

"I need ..." I rasped the words out slowly and precisely. "I need ... *to be left alone.*"

I turned and walked up the cold street to my car.

■

« 15 »

I was alone that night and all the next day.
The phone rang. I didn't answer. The fax machine
whirred. I ignored it. Someone knocked. I let it go.
Downstairs, on Eddie's desk, I'd left a note, saying I was
taking some time off. I didn't think there was much need
to explain.

That day, alone, I sat upstairs, perched over the
bookstore, listening to its muted sounds. I felt a great
distance from it; from everyone moving beneath me, and
beyond, on the street. Once, as a child, after some family
explosion, I had climbed an apple tree and sat there for
hours, looking down, feeling this same distance from all
things below.

Now, sitting in the window with Red on my lap, I
wrote many of these pages. The phone kept ringing; I
continued to ignore it. At last, I set all my papers aside
and sat staring out, thinking, trying to make pieces fit. In
my mind, there were a thousand fragments: words, dates,
faces, objects, events; nuances of gesture, voice. They
appeared to me as parts of some strange mosaic; each

particle, set down one by one — always in the wrong configuration.

I recalled being taken, as a schoolgirl, on a tour of Europe by a much-loved history teacher. In Italy, we had visited Ravenna, where we had seen the likeness of an empress in mosaic: a thousand thousand chips of brilliant gem and stone. Now, my own life seemed like that ancient portrait — except, here, an eye was set below the mouth, a hand grew from a knee, a leg from the rib cage: a mosaic in the likeness of a shimmering monster.

Once more, I forced my mind to flex, move, make connections. I tried to arrange my thoughts into orderly lines, setting the mosaic's chips in neat parallels; instead, strange ones emerged: Hap Dowell, my agent, with Johnny Johnson, peddler of Evangeline's potions; Dinah Lasko, an outcast, with Lily Jenkins, another; Gerald Shane with Nick Rhoades, both troubled outsiders; Mr. Archer, perhaps, with Peagram, as gentlemen, scholars, would-be poets.

But Brad Stein with ... Tom Kemp, the brewer? Lorna Mart with ... *Warden Simms?* Or Elizabeth Maidstone? Who was Eddie's parallel? Faith Roper? Andrew could line up with the priest, but as president of Writers' Bloc, he also dovetailed with Matthew Blair, president of Maidstone's council. And Jake — perhaps his parallel was not Luke Arnold, Evangeline's faithful suitor, but Perry Cleete, or ex-suitor Tom Kemp, which meant that Brad ...

The mosaic shattered, its fragments flying in all directions, like so much dust churned by a careless step. I closed my eyes and tried not to think at all. *You're locked into a shadow dance, writing....* Maybe I was. Maybe my dark stories drew the Shadow, conjured it. If so, I'd been summoning it unawares, through thousands of words and three books. My eyes opened. I watched light like water, shifting, receding across the floor. I closed my eyes again.

Other images came. Blueberry-picking, summers, in Maine. Sun on wooden buckets. Smell of berries, ripe and rich. Blue fingers; blue mouth. Sun on my back.... *You're still hooked on your parents' tragedy.* I wasn't angry anymore; at some time, while I wasn't looking, the old fury had left me. Now my eyes opened on my parents' paintings. I had hung them on my walls, for the first time, just this year. My mother's work was abstract, vivid; my father's, a fluid realism. I studied one of his pictures again — I'd watched him paint it. It was a flowing figure of a man, done in layered veils of blue; a man in a field, gazing, pointing just beyond the field, the frame. The painting held my eyes. The phone rang again. I counted twenty rings. *You're afraid to let anyone get close ... afraid it'll happen again....* I waited till the ringing stopped, then took the phone off the hook.

I wrote reflexively in this journal; wrote until the light on the floor had faded. Soon it would be dark. Soon I would leave for my meeting. Perhaps, there, something would clarify. Perhaps I'd get some sense of whom to trust, and get my bearings once again.

After dark, I forced myself to eat: tuna fish, something for strength. I put on a dress, dark green — it had been my grandmother's. Something else for strength. I put the phone back on the hook. I turned out the lights, stepped into the hall, and locked the door behind me.

Just before eight o'clock, my old Chevy pulled up in Lorna's driveway. The ride had been uneventful; only ordinary traffic in the rearview mirror. I scanned the cars parked near this lit house. One was, of all things, a limousine. Another was unfamiliar. Two, at least, I knew.

As I walked up the path, I took a breath. Abruptly the door opened. Lorna stood there, framed by the dark. With few words, she greeted me, took my coat, and led me downstairs. "The family room," Lorna said over her shoulder. "More privacy." It was a warm, wood-paneled room, with a fire on the hearth, deep couches, and Colonial chairs drawn around a trestle table. The sort of room, ordinarily, I would have liked; the sort of room, ordinarily, where I would feel at ease. But then the room seemed to recede before my eyes. I saw only the faces around the table. They stood out as if lit and backed by a photographer's black drapery. My throat tightened; I looked from face to face.

Lorna sat by Andrew at the table. Gravely, formally, together, they regarded me. Brad, his face shining with sweat, looked up. There, beside him, was Eddie; thank God — I hadn't thought to see her here, hadn't seen her car outside. Next to her, however, was a face that sent a shock through me: the face of my publisher, Barton Gold. Dignified, angular, and dark, he sat tapping a pen, his keen eyes appraising as I entered. Across from him, at the table's other end, was someone I hadn't seen in years: Phil Romano, my writing professor from college; now the dean of a university. His dove-colored hair still bristled, his dark eyes still snapped. *I* did not know why he would be here. Again I felt my chest constrict.

Hap Dowell, my agent, hovered in the doorway, intercepting me. "Barton thought this was important, so do I." His voice was low. "Our strategy: *no response,* not here. Take notes — that's all. Alice ..." His voice sank from a rumble to a whisper. "For once: *listen.*"

He pulled out a chair for me. I sat numbly, as if somewhere between the front door and this room I had passed through some invisible cold rain. For a moment, all the faces turned toward me. No one spoke, no one moved. Ranged about the table, the figures seemed a silent frieze, intricately connected. All the faces were fixed on me, faces watching, waiting, absolutely still. And then Andrew, slowly, softly, began to speak. The frieze seemed to break once again into separate figures.

"We're meeting this way," he said, "to be sensitive to Alice, *and* to Writers' Bloc. What happens here matters, for the group's sake, for others' beyond it; we are, after all, a model for writers' groups around the country." He pressed his long fingers together. "What happens to one member affects the whole. It's especially true in a case like this, with such serious charges." Andrew looked at me. "It seemed right to invite Mr. Gold and Mr. Dowell, because they also received copies of the letter concerning this. We invited Dean Romano as a kind of 'process observer,' and as a consultant to writers' workshops all over the East Coast. Gentlemen, we're grateful for your time. As you may imagine, this isn't easy for any of us."

A judicious, polite nodding of heads.

Andrew motioned for Lorna to start. As I watched, her face seemed to snap into sharper focus, as if it had swiftly swung near. And so it began.

". . . deeply concerned about this letter's allegations," Lorna was saying, "and its effect on the group. I don't see a motive for Gerald Shane to write that if it weren't true, and there's no evidence he intended it for someone else. In fact, he had several private 'conferences' with Alice, one very emotional, at a party, the night before he died." Hard voice, dropping words like stones on the air. Hard face, like pale flat slate. Dark eyes, unblinking. My fingers tightened on my pen.

". . . just feel I don't know her anymore, haven't for some time." Brad's voice now. Brad's face, expressionless, ran with sweat. "I was concerned about Alice yesterday, when she..." He glanced down at some notes before him. "When she unexpectedly appeared at my house, on the pretense she was in the neighborhood." Those words did not sound like Brad's. Head down, he continued to read from his notes. "She seemed to play on our past relationship, some years ago, to gain favor before another group meeting." He'd been coached, I knew it; knew it with the small part of me that remained intact, detached, observing. "I wonder how she deals with other people," Brad was going on. "Other people in our workshop, maybe Gerald. I wonder if she's aware of how she..."

I watched my hand take notes. The pen moved reflexively across my yellow pad. The voices were switching once again; the revolving door of witnesses was turning, and I was finding it harder to breathe.

"I'm also concerned about Alice, and about the group, as I've said." Andrew: I knew without looking up. "Writers' Bloc was built slowly, built well. It's important to many people. An incident like this affects the life of a community. It disrupts, rather than builds. I'm deeply concerned for the group's reputation, especially since it's become an inspiration to others. As its president, I feel a special duty here."

He looked directly at me; feeling that strong gaze, I raised my head. "I've felt concern about Alice's effect on the group for some time. She's shown a need to be critical, to challenge leadership unnecessarily, it's become a pattern. Yesterday, she came to my house, where she initiated a very critical conversation about Writers' Bloc. Worse still, she asked for confidentiality, it seemed subversive...."

The room blurred in my sight; the paneled walls seemed to be pressing in upon me. Another voice began to speak.

"Alice and I have been friends, as you know." Eddie, at last; Eddie to the rescue. "This is hard for me to say. But I've been concerned for Alice too, and concerned about the letter, and before that, other things a tendency to make derogatory comments about people in the group...." My hand hung above the paper. I looked up. Eddie's chin had lifted, her jawline taut. "This is something I work hard never to do, something we all work hard at. I've been given permission to say this: Alice has even made disturbing remarks to Lorna, about me. And yesterday, Alice also came to my house, as if to draw out information...."

Under my hand, my writing was smearing, changing, growing illegible. The room seemed very hot. I could smell Hap's sweat beside me. He kept glancing at the publisher, Bart Gold, whose eyes remained fixed on my face.

"The bottom line to all of this is still the letter." Lorna, her voice harsher now, impatient. "If Gerald didn't write it, we need to look at something just as crucial. Someone did, and somehow, Alice elicited it. Somehow, she called out of someone the impulse to frame her. What does this say about her, the way people react to her, the way she can affect a group ... ?"

"What does it say about role-modeling, inspiration...?"

"Even if it's false, the letter casts a shadow...."

Words hurled after words.

"She came yesterday and said, implied — "

"She brings disruption to the fore, on purpose — "

"She spoke recently about an angel putting a book on a shelf for her. As her friend, I feel concerned, again, about such — "

They were all looking at me.

They had asked me a question. Hap nudged me.

I waited; waited for him to say something — anything, in my defense. Hap sat silent. I looked at my former professor. He was gazing at me. His eyebrows and his mustache seemed sharp and animate, as if alive; he looked as if he suddenly saw me stripped, revealed.

The question was put again; Lorna spoke.

"Alice. *Did* you plagiarize Gerald's work?"

"We're not responding at this time," Hap cut in.

"And if you didn't..." Barton Gold said quietly, "why would so many solid people be concerned? These are highly respected men and women, you need to hear them."

"We'll respond at a later time," Hap repeated, low-voiced.

"Is there any truth in what's been said tonight?" Brad's voice was unsteady.

"Truth that's so distorted, it's not truth." I heard my own voice speak. "*Half*-truths. Hearsay. Lies." Hap nudged me again, but I stood.

"I can't defend myself, even if I were allowed to. You've put your answers together, you've made up your minds. There's nothing I can say." My voice shook; my hands shook. I walked toward the door, then turned. The faces were still fixed on me.

"I withdraw. As of now. I don't want to be a part of a group that does this." I don't remember climbing the steps.

Upstairs, I pulled my coat off a hook by the door. Hap, his bald head shining, was behind me. Handkerchief in one hand, mopping his face, he was saying something about "processing the session."

I grabbed my keys, got into my car and pulled away, tires screeching. All the way home, I felt hot, as if fevered. All the way home, even as the Chevy clanked, I broke every speed limit, ran every red light. Back at the bookshop, I dashed up flights of stairs and, still in my coat, sat down at the typewriter. Under my fingers, its keys started rapping.

Through the trees, through the fence-slats, through the darkness came the ripple of torches. Down the dim lanes, the small group moved quickly, Evangeline at its center. By torchlight, by night, the Town Watch was taking her to the house of Warden Simms. She could smell the sweat on the men; they feared her, she knew, and the powers they believed she possessed. A dog whined; a branch snapped under someone's shoe and the men around her exchanged nervous glances. They were almost there now, almost to the tall brick house with its trunklike chimney, its lit windows hanging on the dark.

Here, in this house, there would be a secret meeting; a "hearing" only, she'd been told, to begin investigation of the charge of sorcery against her. This was now imperative, the priest felt, because of the fear within his congregation, a fear that woke people at night and shadowed them inside the church itself. This was urgent, too, the Town Council deemed, due to the disturbances occurring on the High Street, before Evangeline's shop.

And so, wrapped in her cloak, rushed up the steps, she was entering now and led to its back room, where, outside the door, the Watch waited, listening. The room beyond was large, wood paneled and commodious, but as Evangeline entered, the place seemed to recede, and all she saw were the faces around the trestle table, faces that appeared to hang like portraits on a wall of candlelight and air.

There was the heavy, hard-eyed face of Warden Simms, his chins spilling over his collar, and beside him the Reverend Drummond, the light glancing off his balding head; his face, as ever, pale and gentle, with nearsighted squint. Farther down the table sat Councilman Cleete, elegant as always, in a ruffled shirt and waistcoat; his

*fine-boned face was like, sharp-eyed tonight. Evangeline
had expected these, but jumped into clarity. There was
Tom Kemp, the brewer, his plump, pleasant face shining
with sweat, his sandy hair rumpled. At one end of the
table was tall, dignified Matthew Blair, president of the
Town Council, which had licensed Evangeline and given
her leave to practice her trade. Blair's thin face looked like
a whip-pet's, poised and alert, while opposite him was a
face like an ancient cat's, keen and seamed; the face of
Joan Dowd, retired midwife, once Evangeline's teacher,
and still, it was said, gifted with discernment of dark
spirits. Sweating in the doorway was Johnny Johnson, the
scrawny peddler who sold Evangeline's medicinals for her
in other towns.*

*"We don't speak, we've no leave," he hissed. "We only
listen. And don't get me in trouble. "*

*The meeting opened with a prayer for guidance and
protection against perils, and though heads were bowed,
Evangeline felt glances flick at her. Then the priest set
forth the reasons for the gathering and invited Warden
Simms to speak first. Thus, within a weave of candlelight
and shadow, it began.*

*"I remain deeply disturbed by the actual evidence:
those abominations found in Mistress Smith's abode. And
I see no motive for them except sorcery. "*

*The warden spoke bluntly, as if Evangeline were some-
how not present; refusing to look at her, he turned his gaze
only to others and the door. She tried holding his eyes, but
his face was hard, like a Bat pale stone, and his eyes were
dark wells, lightless, unfathomable. Evangeline glanced
toward the one face here that brought some comfort, a face
in the corner, almost overlooked, the face of the second
warden of All Souls, Daniel Peagram. Chair pulled back
beside the fire, he was making notes in a small book, his
face unreadable.*

"... 'tis a sorry thing, but I feel I don't know Mistress Smith at all now, though we once kept company, and were nearly betrothed." Torn Kemp spoke now, sweat streaking his forehead. "I see now how God spared me, though the loss of her seemed unbearable at first. Cruelly, of a sudden, she broke off our courtship, and a cruel streak, indeed, I do believe, is in her. I'd not be surprised if she began with her black arts, her sorcery, about that time, and broke with me simply to conceal it."

His eyes slid away from Evangeline's, as if she might rise up and cast a spell over him, like a net. She pressed her hands together and all eyes followed her gesture. Shadows rippled in the room as logs shifted in the hearth and candles flickered; uneasily the men watched the play of light and dark, as if Evangeline, by a gesture, might shift the balance.

"... great concern for her soul, I fear, in mortal danger." The priest's soft voice was speaking now. "Let her examine her conscience, we shall await this. But I am also much concerned for our church, disrupted by this dread event. Fear follows my parishioners about their work, and even about their prayers, and now our worship is in shadow. Our parish has long been a beacon to others, and, as you know, it has planted missions elsewhere, sorely needed. This beacon must be preserved, protected. Mistress Smith has challenged the church before, she has particularly criticized its leaders, but we are, after all, one body. I fear for her her soul, of course — but I fear for the community."

The room blurred again in Evangeline's sight, and its paneled walls seemed to press in upon her till she found it hard to breathe and sit straight, still listening.

"Mistress Smith and I were friends, confidants almost, at one time," came the cultured voice of Councilman Cleete. "This is difficult for me to speak. But at one time, I was plagued with a variety of ills, and this woman cured me.

*Her arts are like none other, and I've wondered if she does
not work them by sorcery. It was this suspicion that led
me to end our friendship. That, and also my concern with
her loose tongue, her sharp words about her customers,
and church-folk, and her criticisms of the rectors' sermons,
quite repeatedly. She has even spoke of me, and the
council, for what she terms our 'neglect' of these blights on
Maidstone: tramps, whores...."*

On and on it went, and Evangeline found she could no
longer listen, for she saw their pale stonelike faces, and
their eyes, dark and lightless as cavern pools. She saw the
disgust on the face of the council's president, and the old,
respected midwife, and Evangeline knew that she was lost,
along with her father's shop and all his hopes. The gift of
healing, given her, would be lost as well. She looked
around once more, knowing all the secrets in this room,
knowing that, in part, had brought the Shadow down
upon her. She knew of Cleete's private agonies, and of
Warden Simms's sad marriage, the wife and children who
had left him and gone back to Baltimore. She knew of the
priest's great shyness and loneliness, and his rejection by
a prior parish, in England; she knew of Tom Kemp's
thwarted love for her; and she knew of Joan Dowd's
arthritic hands, her failing sight, that had rendered her
bitter, useless. There was pain in this room, pain, somehow offered to the dark, which twisted it, wrenched it
around and recrafted it. Evangeline felt its presence: the
power of the Shadow among them, turning wounds into
woundings, swiftly, endlessly. The room seemed to tighten
in around her, and the faces here became, to her, one face;
a face of stone, with well-like eyes.

They were all looking at her now.

"Are you a sorceress? Will you still deny this?"

Evangeline stood and the men around the table drew
back, as if at last, she would wave a hand and hex them,

blight their lives, their crops, their wives, and, before their very eyes, turn her hair to flame and fly off on the wind.

"Gentlemen." Her knees shook and her hands shook, but somehow her voice stayed steady. *"I have heard what you believe. I doubt there is aught that I can say in my defense, for you have already judged me. Pray you, then, take me home, else I'll go alone and risk disturbance in the street. I withdraw myself from the church here, saving you the trouble. God's presence is vaster than that place."*

I pulled the last page from the typewriter. I had written this rather than cry. Now my tears and anger were imprinted on the paper. I was spent, and the pain was just beginning. I'd seen the looks on the faces of my publisher, agent, teacher, colleagues. There was no more point in sitting at a typewriter. I started to toss the pages out.

And then, suddenly, I stopped. Some small part of me was still a writer and historian. That small part had stayed detached, observing, all throughout the meeting. Now that part stirred, wanting, one last time, to observe one last thing: what had happened, in 1738, to Evangeline at a similar meeting. I could recall the official version now. It placed the gathering in the church, with Evangeline hissing like a cat and shrieking at the sight of consecrated bread. Swiftly, without debate, the priest had pronounced her excommunicate: a "notorious sinner."

But I had not yet read the new sources on this meeting: Elizabeth Maidstone's account, or even Peagram's; I had not worked that far ahead. Now I sorted through my stack of research. As one of the church wardens, Peagram had probably been on the scene, making notes ... perhaps struggling with his conscience. I rummaged through papers, found *Peagram's Journal*. The pertinent pages were stuck together; I slit them open, read them twice. Stunned, I reached for the Maidstone Xeroxes. Elizabeth, too, had an account, and this, too, I read twice. Then I set both accounts side by side and looked at them a long time. After a while, I put them away and sat there, motionless.

Without any research, any prior knowledge, I had just written — as therapy, as parody — an account of Evangeline's 1738 "hearing": an account that almost reproduced the account of Peagram, an on-site witness, and the account by Mistress Maidstone; hers based on a report from her nephew, a member of the Town Watch, and on recollections of Evangeline herself.

I stared down at these papers. I tried to think clearly, in some logical order. Recently, I'd seen new light fall on old events: events in Maidstone, Maryland, in 1738. I had re-created these events in novelistic form — and then watched, half in disbelief, as the same events, in parallel, seemed to play out again, in Washington, D.C., in 1991. Now the reverse had taken place. Something that just happened to me had occurred, in parallel, to Evangeline in Maidstone, two centuries before. Without any prior knowledge, notes, or forethought, I had reenacted a scene from her life — how, I didn't understand.

I only understood that my story was somehow entwined with another. That first story, played out in the 1730s, was in some way playing out again in my own life. And I couldn't seem to stop it.

For a moment longer I sat there. Then, abruptly, I rose. I threw clothes into a suitcase, poured food into Red's dish, and grabbed up my keys once again. There was no one I trusted now. There was no place I felt safe; here, least of all. Groping down the back stairs in the dark, I had one clear thought: run, get out, go anywhere. I had one clear prayer: May the Chevy start.

It started. It ran. I drove across town and downtown, I drove uptown and, at last, out toward the beltway around the city. I had no idea where I was going; still I drove. Rain pelted the roof and fogged the windshield and I drove on, drove till I was almost out of gas, till I was so tired I knew I had to stop. I pulled up to the first motel I saw, a Homeward Inn. Behind the desk in the small lobby, stuffed pink bears were on sale, and numbered keys hung from a rack.

A key was assigned to me; upstairs, in room 303, I put the chain on the door. The walls were pink, the bedspreads floral. In the bathroom, over the toilet, a paper band read: SANITIZED. Small soaps lay in aqua wrappers. The towels were clean. Everything looked magnified and significant. I remember the glowing plastic ice bucket; pink, to match the room. I picked up the bucket but got no ice. Instead, I sat by the window.

Outside, on an expressway, trucks made the wide panes rattle. Rain slanted across the glass and suddenly now, I felt chilled. I pulled a blanket around me and still I could not stop trembling. Once, as a child, I'd gotten lost in the snow. At first the cold had been like this; before numbness had set in. Then, as now, I was too stunned to cry. I just sat there, staring out into the dark.

Gazing past my own reflection, I saw lit rooms across the way: another motel, I thought, but the roof above it was odd, steep, tawny, and the windows were crude. At one window stood a woman in a blue gown. Her windows had a greenish tinge; some of the panes were broken. The woman seemed to be standing guard behind a sheet of water till at last, darkness drew around that window, and I could barely see her: just a faint point of light in her hand.

I sat watching till the rain became a downpour, till I could see nothing but blurred headlights, till my eyes grew heavy and the clock read three-eleven. Then, in that strange bed, between those strange sheets, I fell asleep, my car keys clenched like a talisman in my hand.

■

PART THREE

NOVEMBER 21, 1991

A rustle. Distant; closer now.

Just a moment before, it seemed, I had slid between those sheets, in the motel bed. I thought I'd left the lamp on but now it was out, the room was dim and there were rustlings in the dark. Something gazed my cheek: a hand, a sleeve.

I twisted away. I raised my head — and saw them, all at once. Ranged around the room they stood, a vague frieze of figures, their faces turned toward me; weathered faces, worn by work and sun, with light-filled eyes. Rough shawls swung above long skirts; patched cloaks hung over faded breeches. A smell of toil lingered about these figures; a smell of ash and wood, iron and earth. Their hands held small homely shapes: bread, eggs, cheese, fruit. Now, the figures lifted these to me.

I tried to speak and could not.

The faces appeared to smile. On the air was the fragrance of fresh-baked bread. A grainy loaf seemed to float from hand to hand until, at last, it passed to me. Now the figures drew closer. Their hands lifted once m ore, a gesture of comfort and grace. A shimmering mist gathered in around them then, dazzling, intense, till their faces alone were seen. Their eyes, lit and clear, seemed to send forth strength to me, across the room; down the wordless centuries. I felt this strength and smelled the bread as I drifted back to sleep.

When I woke the next morning in room 303 at the Homeward Inn, I wasn't certain where I was. Then I remembered: the drive, the window, the' dream. The bedside lamp was still on. The chain was still on the door. The clock read seven-sixteen.

I pushed back the covers, rose, and moved across the room. Detaching the chain, I turned the lock and opened the door. No one was in the hall. In front of my room, on the carpet, was a tray; eggs and bread, fruit and cheese.

I took the tray inside, set it down, and called the front desk.

I didn't order breakfast — was there a mix-up?"

There was a pause at the other end of the line.

"We don't offer room service," the clerk said finally.

I stood there, looking at the tray.

■

« 17 »

About nine that morning, I returned to the bookshop.

For a moment, I saw it from a distance, with the heightened clarity of time away. The white clapboard house looked faded and pleated and solid, a great windowed ream of paper: old paper, good paper. Its signboard swung just slightly, glinting red and gold, as I walked up the steps.

I let myself in — and immediately knew that some-one had been there in my absence. Downstairs, two lights were on: lights I had turned out before leaving for the meeting. The display-window lights were off, but I had left them on. Warily, I moved up the stairs. The door to my apartment was closed and I was sure I'd left it ajar, unlocked, in haste. On my desk was a note in Jake's spiky handwriting:

"2 A.M. Where are you?
Worried — dammit —
Flight tomorrow, back by 5 —
Please wait — J.

I looked around the room; nothing seemed disturbed. The cat rubbed my legs. I sat in my rocker, wishing that no one would come, the phone would not ring, and I could just stay very still and think. I had about three minutes of stillness, and then the phone, of course, did ring.

"Detective Gonzalez here."

He, of course, could not know I'd just run away from home and back again; no doubt he assumed that my life, apart from murder, was perfectly normal. Whatever he assumed, he went on talking, his voice so low I strained to hear. The site of Gerald's murder, he was saying, had been tentatively determined: Kelly's Boat House on the District side of the Potomac; did I know of any connection?

"He rowed." I paused. He kept an extra key to Kelly's here, in case he lost his. I decided not to mention that.

"Listen, Ms. Grey." Gonzalez spoke lower still. "This is highly confidential — anyone knows I tipped you, my ass is in a sling. If you remember something, anything, call me. Only me. Don't leave messages. Understood?"

"Understood."

I hung up, thinking in parallels again. Then, intrigued almost against my will, I dialed a number pinned up over my desk. On the third ring, Harley Jenkins's big, cheery voice came through the line from Maidstone. I asked her if she might do further checking at the Historical Society.

"Sure, no problem." She sounded curious.

I told her I was looking for any indications that Nicholas Rhoades, church sexton, circa 1738, had been murdered in a boat house, if such a structure had even existed.

Harley sounded puzzled, unclear.

We'd had some new information, I said rather cryptically. There might be a modern parallel, I'd be checking it out, that was all I could say.

Without pressing further, she said she'd get right on it. There was other pause. To fill it, I told her I wanted to find Nick Rhoades's Bible, possibly passed on through his family — an impossible task.

"Not that one," said Harley, and rang off.

As I hung up, I felt vaguely uneasy, but that was becoming such a familiar sensation. I paid it scant attention. My life, in general, was making me uneasy. I considered closing the store for the day, then forced myself downstairs.

As I reached the first floor, I heard a rustle just beyond, in the shop. Instantly, I halted. Listening, I heard it again: a rustle, and then the click of heels. They formed a repeating pattern — the pattern of someone pacing. I hoped to heaven it was someone from this century. I edged forward.

It was Eddie.

"Oh God — " She jumped. "Alice..."

I stared at her. She looked away, started to speak; could not. Her jawline lacked its usual taut angle, her dark eyes were shadowed. Under her handsome, dusky coloring, there was a pallor. The pin at her collar, I noticed, was askew; an unlit cigarette twisted in her fingers.

"I know ..." She took a fast breath. "I know ... you have every right to tell me ... to ask me to get out of here. I know what we did to you, what I did ... God, I've been up all night." She lifted the cigarette to her lips, remembered it wasn't lit. "I've come to say I'm sorry. I could tell you I got intimidated, afraid, I could blame it on the others, I could say la lot of things." She took another shaky breath. "I guess the only thing that matters is — I was wrong. And I'm sorry." Abruptly, her eyes filled. "I'll get my things."

She turned toward her desk.

Maybe it was the sight of this woman, always composed, always reserved, coming apart. Maybe it was the crack in her voice, maybe it was her respect for the shop; amid her own distress, she did not strike a match here. Maybe it was all those things, but in the end, this was my friend, saying she was sorry.

"Eddie."

She stopped, but didn't turn.

"Ed? Have you had breakfast?"

We had an extremely long one, while the CLOSED sign swung from the door of the shop. We consumed quantities of coffee, fresh fruit and fresh bread, and by the meal's end we both knew a good deal more than before. Most of all, we knew each other once again.

We had also made some decisions.

Eddie would help me draft a letter to Writers' Bloc, and one to my publisher. We would continue at the shop as if nothing had happened, though the workshop might wish to meet elsewhere. Eddie had resolved, early this morning, to resign from the group, and so had I, officially, and in writing. Together, in the sunlight, over fruit and bread and coffee, that resolution seemed less painful.

Fortified, we returned to the shop, opened it, and actually had something resembling a normal day. A great many people came in — concerned regulars, curious tourists, oblivious walk-ins. A great many people wanted to buy books with Weatherell's stamp, and we were so busy I lost track of time and trauma, at least temporarily. I did, briefly, envision a new writers' group, small and informal — just a vision, faint and fleeting, but hopeful. And then, toward closing time, I had another, more concrete vision.

It was a pilot: a pilot in a dark-blue shirt with epaulets, and dark-blue trousers; a tallish, rangy pilot, with sandy hair a little too long, unevenly cut, and long-fingered freckled hands turning a dark-blue hat; a hat never worn. His shirt needed pressing. A gold bar over his breast pocket read: "Captain John Randolph." Jake walked in the front door, through the front room to the front desk. He stood squarely in front of it. His face was creased with fatigue, his eyes pained, clouded. He looked at me and kept on looking and finally he spoke. "Could you ... answer a question?"

I said nothing.

"I'm looking for a book." He cleared his throat. "Can't remember the title but it's a true story. About this flier..." He waited, then went on. "About this flier, he writes a little himself, and he's in love with this woman...." He trailed off. "Anyway, this flier, he gets jealous, he hurts this woman he loves, and he doesn't know the right words ... how sorry he is, how he needs her, it's ... a long story, I'm not sure how it ends."

"And the author? Randolph, I think?"

Jake said nothing.

I looked away; now I lacked the right words. The silence expanded between us, opening like a field.

"Out of print, I guess," Jake said finally. "Well, if it ever comes in ..." He was about to turn away.

"I could ... let you know." I leaned over the blotter. "It ends like this." I touched his mouth with mine, and we were there quite a while, after he slid behind the massive Civil War desk; so long, Eddie had closed the shop and put out some lights before we looked up again.

A half hour later, I was back upstairs in my apartment, looking out the kitchen window. With a smile, Eddie had slipped out. Jake had briefly returned to the airport to get his things. Waiting, suddenly hungry, I rummaged through my kitchen cupboards. What came to hand were simple things: bread and fruit and cheese. For a moment, again, I remembered the motel. This day, begun alone, with a fast, had become a day of feasts and visits. There would be one feast more: a real dinner, tonight, with Jake.

Meanwhile, I had my own plan for ending this day. There would be just enough time. This plan had only to do with visits; one I would make, alone, to the river.

■

« 18 »

*F*lashlight. *Batteries.*
I made hasty preparations.
Car keys; other key.
Jake would be back in an hour.
Rubber-soled shoes.
I'd left him a quick note.
Warm coat, gloves.
Seven o'clock, a brisk November evening.
N Street to Thirty-fourth; Thirty-fourth to M Street ...
Good deep wintry dark, moonlight.
Bear left onto Canal Road.
And now the streetlights were thinning as the road led away from Georgetown. A dimmer stretch of road lay ahead: foliage to my right, an on my left the river, spreading like a silver shawl under the moon. A sharp turn now, onto a gravel road leading to the riverbank — and to Kelly's Boat House. Illuminated by my headlights, the structure rose before me, at the end of a long driveway. My car jolted over gravel, the wheels crunching loud. Ahead, in the dark, was the boat house — a wooden

barn-like structure, with a low roof and peeling blue
paint. Crew teams sped from here, early mornings.
Suitors, for decades, had taken sweethearts out on the
river from this dock. Lone boaters also put out from here,
as Gerald had done since I'd known him. Now, though,
the season for boating was over. The place was closed,
empty, locked.

I pulled the car to a stop and cut the lights. My shoes
crunched across the gravel; my footsteps sounded loud,
powerful, enormous. Around me, all was silent and dark,
the place deserted. I switched on my flash light and took
out my borrowed key. This afternoon, I'd located it in the
Civil War desk's top right drawer — Gerald left a spare
there. The large key, tagged with his trademark orange
"G," was one of Gerald's few effects to escape the police.
Now, in my hand, the long metal shape gave faint, flat
gleam. It was a rarity; Gerald had possessed one only
because the boat-house owner was a friend, and the boat
house itself was Gerald's sacred place.

Ahead of me, the flashlight made a thin stream of
light; light that picked out a door. I fitted the key into the
lock, heard it click, and pushed the door open. The boat
house crouched over me, smelling of wood and dampness.
I remembered how, in summer, the warm wood smelled
like a boardwalk at the beach. Now, beneath my shoes,
the rough floor creaked. Rising beside me were stacked
canoes and racing shells. Piled neatly, one atop the other,
they reminded me of coffins in a mausoleum, but perhaps
this was simply my turn of mind this evening. I had
come, after all, to explore the site of Gerald's murder. If
I could figure out how he had died, I hoped I might figure
out who'd killed him here, in this place that Gerald had
loved.

Now, under the sloping wooden roof, the darkness rose
like walls around me, and the sound of the water was

louder. I played the flashlight over the boat-slips: they reached, finger-like, into the dock beneath these old rafters. At this season, the slips were vacant spaces. I paused by one, running my light over the water before me. It was murky, perhaps five feet deep. The slip's shape was oblong and resembled a parking space or an empty grave. I wondered if Gerald had died here, where there was more seclusion than on the dock by the river's edge. Outside, too, there was a greater drop from dockside to water — unless the Potomac was high.

I tried to remember if the river had been running full when Gerald had died. Not that week, I didn't think; it had been a dry autumn, with little rainfall. Even so, I walked outside to the open dock's edge, beyond the roof's overhang. The river spread its silver before me once again; silver that looked tricky, treacherous, deceptive. The drop between dock and water was more than a foot, I guessed now. I went back inside; back to the boat-slips under the steep-pitched roof.

Standing at a different slip, a different watery oblong, I listened. I heard only the slap of water, the creak of wood, and, now and then, the mild sweep of wind. The boat house itself seemed a ship, riding at anchor on the night — an old ship, frayed and splintering.

I turned my mind again to the detective's words. Gonzalez had said the splinters under Gerald's nails matched this floor's wood, its paint. The paint, probably, had been the strongest tip-off; Kelly's had a distinctive shade of blue. And, I knew, the river water up here, nearer the falls, lacked saline content, like the water found in Gerald's lungs. Who had told me that, about the salt in the river? I paused, thinking. Gerald, I realized; Gerald himself.

Looking down at the slice of water, I recalled Gerald taking me here, last summer, for a boat ride. Jake had come too; I'd worn a straw hat. This had pleased Gerald, he'd taken a picture. I was standing by the slip, thinking of that, when I felt the shock of another body slamming into mine.

An arm locked around my neck — the flashlight fell into the water. A glove covered my mouth as the arm lock tightened, and then I was crushing down against the floorboards. There was a flash of pain in my knees; pinpoints, like embers, sprang up before me. I twisted — I could not move. The flashlight glared from the water, blinding me. I could hear the rasp of my breathing, and the breathing of the figure behind me: a bundled figure, indistinguishable, something silken over its face. Pinned there, held fast, I was forced to kneel. A hand pressed against the back of my head. I tried to jerk, twist away, once again.

No use: the hand was pushing my face down, down toward the water in the slip. The figure pressed against me, on top of me now; I could not kick, slide, roll. Gasping, I snapped my head back and felt it strike my attacker's chin. In that instant, I got one hand free and grabbed, scrabbling, at the dock. Gloved, my hand could not take hold. I jabbed back with an elbow. The attacker's full weight pressed me then; my head was shoved downward — harder, faster now, and the water jumped toward me, water lit by that eerie glow: the flashlight stared like an unblinking white eye. Now the water was nearer, reeking, just beneath my chin — odor of rot, moss, death. I twisted, kicking, and still that water was rising to take me and the slip was blurring — then, suddenly: the sound of tires on the drive, the screech of a car stopping short; gravel spraying wooden walls. Abruptly, I was dropped flat on the boards. I lay there, gripping the edge of the slip, as I heard Jake call my name.

I opened my eyes. The walls were no longer dark but stark white. A bright light shone overhead. The sweep of wind and creak of wood were gone; gone the stench of stagnant water. There was a sharp thin antiseptic smell here, and a rattling sound, like a cart. Beneath me: no hard dock , but something soft. Another sound came now, the metallic slide of a curtain on steel runners.

Jake's face appeared before me. I looked at him and remembered all of it at once. I glanced down at my coat. No coat. An absurd flimsy gown printed with tiny fleurs-de-lis. I knew where I was now, with the white walls and the fluorescent lights: some emergency room's cubicle. I'd not been inside a hospital since my parents' accident, years before; I'd made a point of staying out of emergency rooms after that, and I wasn't about to stay in this one. I sat straight up. There was a vague ache in my knees, my neck, but nothing sharp, nothing to give alarm. Jake was beside me, his face tight, furious, tender, amused. In that light his eyes looked almost navy blue. I could see the faint cleft in his chin, which I had often kissed.

"Hi," I said idiotically. "I'm ready to go."

"Shit," he said in two syllables, maybe three, his drawl strong, as always, with emotion. "You passed out — "

"I certainly did *not.*"

In spite of himself, Jake smiled. A doctor entered the room and asked me if I knew my name. I glared, telling him, in addition to my name and address, who was President, and demanded to go home. Now. There was nothing seriously wrong, he admitted, just some bruises. They were "watching" me. I wondered who else was.

The doctor vanished. Tentatively I stood and took a step. I noticed that the floor felt solid and I felt steady and truly absurd in that gown. I took another step; then several, toward my clothes. Jake was beside me once again.

"I'm *fine.*" I touched his sleeve. "You know, I heard you drive up but no one else. Whoever it was must have parked on grass, down the drive — see anyone?"

He shook his head. "He must have run across the grass, too, through the trees, the way he came. I *heard* someone hightail it out of there pretty damn quick, then I saw you — and that was it. Alice, why in *hell* — "

"Don't say it."

"Soon as I found your note, I got this feeling — "

"Jake. Now I know how Gerald died."

"Terrific. Did you have to reenact it?"

"I didn't exactly plan that part."

"Who knew you were there?"

"You." I tried a smile.

"Not funny. Who else?"

"Detective Gonzalez told me about the boat house, in confidence, he probably didn't tell anyone else." I paused, thinking. "I called Harley Jenkins today, asked her to check on old boat houses in Maidstone.... I mentioned a boat house as a possible murder site here...."

Jake glanced up. For a moment, we were both silent.

"Jake ... we really don't know much about her, do we?" I sat down again. "Only what she told us herself."

Jake looked at me. "We don't know *shit* about Harley."

■

« 19 »

TEMPORARILY CLOSED, read the sign on the door of Jenkins Inn in Maidstone. The sign was neatly and precisely lettered. The inn's shutters were closed. There was a strong, almost palpable silence about the place. Harley's car was gone.

I drove off slowly, watching in my rearview mirror; waiting for a shutter to move, a door to swing ajar. The inn remained absolutely still. As soon as it was out of sight, I accelerated. This trip, the Chevy was running mysteriously well, grumbling just slightly and occasionally. I pulled into the next shopping plaza I saw, found a pay phone, and called Weatherell's, collect. Eddie, accepting the charges, sounded faintly alarmed. She was wondering, I knew, what could have gone wrong so soon.

"You all right?" We both rapped out at once.

"Fine, fine." I was weary of answering that. Two days after my little episode at the boat house, I was only a bit stiff — not that I'd admit it.

"What's happened?" Eddie asked.

I lowered my voice. "Harley Jenkins is gone." I'd briefed Eddie about her. "The inn's closed — 'temporarily,' the sign says. Her car's gone, too. She hasn't called, has she?"

"Not yet."

"You remember how I described her?"

"Yes." Eddie sounded grim. "I'll be watching."

"How's the shop?"

"Busy. Bit of a lull now. I'm reading one of those art books I lent you." Eddie lowered her voice. "Alice, I'm worried about you down there alone."

Without Jake, she meant. He'd left yesterday on a flight to Houston and I wouldn't wait for him; I had to get back to Maidstone, after what had happened at Kelly's. If I couldn't find answers in Washington, I'd look for them here.

"I'm fine," I said again. It was starting to sound like a mantra. "I'm just two hours away, the car's running great — "

"You'll be back ...?"

"Tonight, tomorrow, depending."

"Be careful."

"You be careful. Remember Harley."

We hung up uneasily. Still uneasy, I got back in my car and drove into Maidstone.

Outside the Historical Society, I parked the Chevy and glanced around. I'd been watching in the rearview mirror: no one following. The old house rising before me looked solid, still elegant in the late-morning light. Elizabeth Maidstone's mansion once, its brick walls were ivy-covered now. Its great chimney towered like an ancient tree's trunk, branches and leaves invisible; half lost in time, half planted firmly in the here and now. I thought of tall Elizabeth sweeping through the front door on some wise errand, with a rustle, with a creak of stays. And with a firm step. She must have stepped out into days like this: November — high fast clouds, chilly sunlight; dance of shade and brightness. Now I was moving in reverse: stepping out of the day, slipping through the front door on this odd errand, with a rubber-soled tread and the creak of denim. This time, I was well ahead of the Historical Society's closing hour of two o'clock.

For a moment, after the sharp light outside, the front hall seemed dim. Just inside the door, I stood getting my bearings, letting my eyes adjust. To the left, I recalled, was a room of pottery and silver in tall cases; to the right, a library, run-of-the-mill history. Upstairs were the documents, the collections of family papers, among them, papers that interested me.

Now, the front hall began to clarify. Above the graceful Regency desk at the far end, a face turned toward me. A familiar face; oddly familiar, with eyes like gooseberries, like grapes. Not wanting to be rude, I glanced away, then back. The solid, rumpled woman reminded me of Mrs. Lind, from the library in George-town. Moving toward the desk to ask for directions, I tried to shake off the impression. The face snapped into sharper focus, and with it, the familiar tweed suit, the brooch at the collar.

"It *is* Mrs. Lind." My voice was pleased, amazed. I took one step closer. "Isn't it?"

"Alice." She rose, smiling, holding out a hand.

"Can't believe it."

"You knew I'd left the library ...?"

"Sorry, no — haven't been there myself lately, things have been a little, um, busy."

"Well, I had to take a ... a leave of absence. Right after the tragedy, Mr. Archer ..." Her large eyes filled. "I have family in Maidstone, so I've taken time ... I keep my hand in, volunteering here, part-time, two days a week." She compressed her lips.

"I'm sorry." I didn't know quite what to say. "Must be a hard time for you."

"Well, I'm managing." Mrs. Lind lifted her head. "This place ... it's delightful."

"I wonder, if it's not too much, could you give me a hand with some research here? I'll be down a day, maybe two."

"Why, yes, of course." Mrs. Lind seemed grateful to be asked. "I'd love to, really. Just like old times."

But not quite.

The sources she showed me were from the main collection, the old sources I had used a year ago; sources, I knew now, to be incorrect, probably falsified. And when I asked to go upstairs to the collection of family papers, Mrs. Lind became dim and distant. "That floor's under renovation, I'm so new here, I couldn't let you up, so sorry, not the way it was in Georgetown, I'm afraid...." Her eyes filled once again.

"It's okay." I put a hand on Mrs. Lind's arm, not wanting to provoke more tears. "Really — I'll look somewhere else. Good to see you...."

I tried not to sigh, then swear, till I was outside again. Maybe there was a director of the Society; someone I might find today.... I turned on the front steps, then opened the door again.

By the desk, Mrs. Lind stood facing a back window; one square hand fiddled with the phone cord, one hand held the receiver to her ear.

"... she just left ... research, she said." The librarian's voice was terse. "A day or two." A brief pause. "Yes. I think so. Something."

Swiftly, silently, I shut the front door.

First of all, I moved the car — moved it, without thinking, without planning, to the parking lot where Evangeline's house and barn had stood. The lot's manager smiled at me as if he remembered. I sat in my car and opened a can of tuna fish. Protein. Strength. He let me sit there as I ate, and afterward, as I sat thinking. Now it would have to be done differently. I would think about logistics now — about nothing else till later. I had only two hours to get at the papers I needed.

After about ten minutes, I walked back toward the Historical Society. Harley had mentioned tours coming through; I'd seen tours there myself — I hoped one might arrive to distract Mrs. Lind. Hidden by Elizabeth Maidstone's fence, I waited, watching the front door. It occurred to me that touring this museum was not exactly a national pastime. Church bells rang noon; maybe Mrs. Lind would go to lunch. Maybe there was a back way in and out. I was about to circle the house when a van drove up, stopping at the front door. SUNGATE VILLAGE was printed on its side, the letters enclosed in a yellow circle. From behind the fence, I watched a dozen older women step down from the van. Slowly they streamed up the brick walk. Only after they'd entered the building did their driver pull away. Only after the van had vanished did I try the door myself.

The front hall was empty. The tour was in the room to the left, looking at Maidstone pottery and silver. I could hear Mrs. Lind's voice. Quickly, quietly, I crossed the floor and crept up the stairs. My jogging shoes made no sound; the boards did not creak till I was almost halfway up. I paused. Below me, I could still hear Mrs. Lind's voice, the muted flow of words inaudible. I crept farther up, reached the landing, and the second story of the house opened out around me. I could not allow myself to look in its rooms — not yet, too risky; I might be heard, moving directly above the visitors' heads. The only prudent move to make now was no move at all. I'd simply find a place to hide till closing time, when, I hoped, I'd get locked in. Alone.

I looked at my watch. Almost half past noon; an hour and a half to wait. I stood motionless, letting my gaze shift across this silent floor. There were two open, doorless rooms. One closed door was marked XEROX / SUPPLIES; another, LADIES. No place revealed itself as right or safe, immediately. All that revealed itself, immediately, was one fact: this floor showed no signs of renovation.

It wasn't the first time I'd been locked in a closet. Long ago, my brothers had done it to me and I'd screamed. This time, I had done it myself, and was resolutely mute. Last time, it was a coat closet, where I had crouched beneath drifting forms that smelled, mostly, of wool. Now it was a janitor's closet, where I stood amid brooms and buckets, my back to a steel sink. There was a smell of metal polish and wet mops. The wet-mop smell was dense, but encouraging. It meant the cleaning crew had done its work recently, and probably would not reappear today. A light bulb's string grazed my head. I resisted the temptation to grab it and scan my notes. Instead, I stood in the shadows, thinking out what I needed; which papers I'd hunt first. Dust motes danced in the light from one high window; I heard the tour move from room to room, beneath me, and then, abruptly, on the stairs, I heard the sound of many footsteps. The tour was ascending.

The Colonial lock on the closet door was wrought iron and large, the key, still in it, turned on my side. Slowly, soundlessly now, I removed the key, then peered through the hole, as I had through a modern lock, that day when I was nine and trapped with the coats. That time, I had seen a sliver of wallpaper. This time, I saw slivers of clothing: wool, tweed, polyester. Quite clearly now, I also heard Mrs. Lind's voice; it informed the tour, and me, which room contained eighteenth-century family papers, ledgers, and records. And which held a collection of hats and wigs.

Now the voices and footsteps were retreating. Moments later, below me, the great door was closing. The house grew quiet. I sensed I was alone here — or rather, alone with Mrs. Lind. The librarian's voice murmured vaguely on the first floor. The telephone again? No other voice replied.

I held my watch up to the narrow shaft of light from that high half-window. Only twenty minutes past one. A fit of boldness, or impatience, or stupidity, took hold of me. I reached out, turned the key — and swiftly drew back. Mrs. Lind's footsteps sounded on the stairs. At the top, they paused. In the dimness of the closet, I barely breathed. The steps moved toward the closet door, then turned. There came a series of brief humming sounds, at even intervals. The Xerox machine, I realized. It seemed a long time before the machine fell silent and the footsteps retreated down the hall, down the steps.

After a few moments, I opened the closet and put my head out, listening. I heard lights switch off, then the front door shut firmly, and lock. Standing on the janitor's sink, I saw Mrs. Lind outside, walking swiftly down the brick path and off into town.

The Historical Society of Maidstone had, for unknown reasons, closed early. I'd puzzle that one over later. Now, I went directly to the family papers, then documents, and finally, the. Xerox room. The key was still in the machine. Ninety minutes later, my bag crammed with copied research, I crept down the stairs and out a back door.

The churchyard gate was open; the sacristy unlocked. I slipped into All Souls Church and stood listening again. The place was quiet. Its front doors were bolted, I figured; I'd decided not to try them. Back doors had become increasingly attractive.

The dim sacristy stooped over me, a small, sloping room just off the chancel, its walls the original stone. This was where Nick had stood, the last day he lived. This was how he had entered the church, escaping a town that seemed dangerous. And in this church, he had made his most dangerous discovery. For a moment, I caught a glimpse of myself in the mirror; as Nick had done, I glanced away. Surely, the mirror was different, but standing there, where Nick had stood, I felt suddenly, unpleasantly cold. I looked at the candlesticks on the counter waiting to be polished, and at the basin in the small steel sink. The same morning that Nicholas Rhoades, sexton, had been found dead, other forms of damage had been noted in this church. Odd that the dates coincided. I had found this order with the family papers of Evangeline's suitor, Luke Arnold:

11 March, 1738, ordered by the Wardens of All Souls Church, new ceramic basin for baptismal font. Urgent. Vandalism. Will pay extra.

The words repeated in my mind now, with the report to the church vestry, misfiled, with the potter's papers:

11 March, 1738, sent for repair by the Wardens of All Souls Church, one silver altar candlestick, found damaged this morning. Vandalism suspected.

I stepped out into the chancel. No lights. No lovers, naked on the marble floor. There was the modern altar, hung with a green frontal and set with fair-linen, and behind it, against the wall, the old, original altar, narrow and bare. From its chain, the sanctuary lamp cast a faint amber shire in the church's twilight. I paused. As a girl, I had always felt safe in churches. As a child, I had longed to sit concealed beneath the altar during Mass, at the very center of the Mystery. Now, as a woman, I was behind an altar, at the center of another mystery — in a church where, for the first time, I did not feel safe.

The nave opened out before me: empty pews, dim vaulted space, somber stained glass. Over my blouse, the windows cast deep colors: plum, rust, indigo. At mid-afternoon, here, it was dusk. As I moved into the ave, it seemed I waded into some forgotten evening. I looked more sharply about me — no one here. I scanned the church again, searching no for the baptismal font. To my right, I glimpsed a flash of metal: the font, indeed. Set into a modern wooden stand, the basin was silver, inscribed, I saw, "To the Glory of God and the Memory of Helen S. Crest, 1979." The flimsy stand was undated but recent and smelled of Lemon Pledge.

I sighed. This wasn't doing much for my new theory. I'd developed it sometime after leaving the Maidstone Historical Society and before leaving the Maidstone McDonald's. Leafing through Xeroxes, two bites into a Big Mac, I'd read the records of damage to font and candlestick. The coinciding dates interested me. The misfiling of one interested me as well. Images clustered, then regrouped, in my mind. Gerald, dying face-down in water. Nick — dying how? Perhaps, if I knew that, I'd discover who killed him and framed Evangeline. Perhaps then, I'd find a key to the chaos around me.

Images. Details. Drownings. French fries. Fonts. I
had sat in McDonald's staring into my Diet Coke, as if
some answer might surface from its depths. Parallels —
too many for coincidence. Under that premise, if Gerald's
face was held under water till he died, then Nick's face
was also under water till death occurred. There were
many places along this river where that could have
happened, in the dark, in secret. But then the body would
have had to be carried back into town, through lanes an
roads: a risk, even at night.

How much safer for the murderers to kill Nick indoors
— in a place not much frequented, weekdays, never at
night, and just down the street from Evangeline's house.
A place where water could fill a baptismal font; a font that
might crack during a drowning. I had finished my lunch
with a sense of satisfaction; one I didn't associate with
fast food.

Now, in the church, that sense was evaporating. I
turned from this new font. Baptisms were done differently
now. In recent years, they had become part of the Sunday
service in Anglican and Roman Catholic liturgy, the rite
performed at a font that could be moved, often to the
chancel steps, in sight of all.

Perhaps All Souls had another font: old, disused;
stationary. I had not noticed one before; not at the west
end, within the main doors, nor at the east end, near the
chancel. Now I glanced north and south. Two small transepts gave the church its cruciform shape. The transepts,
though, held chairs — seats, no doubt, that filled up at
Christmas and Easter. Still, behind the chairs, something
could be hidden. Suicides, I recalled, used to be buried on
the cold north side of churchyards. If a font were to be in
a transept, I guessed it would be in the south — the
brighter, warmer side of a church. I was already moving
toward it.

The transept's stone matched the nave's. This small wing was part of the original church, then; not a later addition. Its chairs rose stiffly around me now; I threaded my way among them, pulling out my flashlight. Under its beam, dust appeared: dust on chairs, on prayer books; I sneezed. In this tomblike, windowless space, the sound was somehow reassuring. More chairs, more dust. The light probed beyond, an there, at the center, at the very back — another font.

Sliding past the last chairs, I played light over the stone bowl and stone base, imbedded in the floor. I trained the light on the transept's stone walls, then on the font once more. The old stones matched, as did the masonry and coloration. This, then, was the original font; it would have been here in 1738. A ceramic basin lay within its curved stone cavity: a dusty basin, modern but disused. I lifted it out and turned it over. No dedication. Just the mark: MAIDSTONE POTTERY, 1947.

Carefully, I laid the basin on a chair and, leaning over the font again, trained my light on the exposed bowl-shaped cavity. A dank smell rose toward me. There, under the narrow white beam, a gash showed in the stone — a gash beginning at the font's edge, extending inward to its concave center. *Ordered ... new ceramic basin for baptismal font.... Basin found cracked....* With my finger, I traced the gash: a ragged indentation. No craftsman would leave such a mark. This was no deliberate cut, etched precisely with a tool: this was a crude gash, formed by something heavy, something blunt. *Sent for repair ... one altar candlestick, found damaged....* Something just that size, that weight, brought down hard. I studied the slash again. The mortar in its crevice had eroded, and yet the font had not been repaired, nor even mentioned as damaged. It had only been covered with a new basin and used, reused, until it became a tradition, an antique, a treasure, where generations had been baptized.

Now my light cast waterlike ripples over the whole curving stone cavity. Images flashed in my mind: Nick's small frame, his misshapen head held here. Gerald's small frame, his delicate head, shoved toward the boat-slip, the flashlight rolling from his hand....

I straightened up. The church had faded from me these last minutes. Bending over in this transept, I'd grown less alert. Now I snapped off my flashlight and turned sharply, listening once more. The church still seemed hushed. I replaced the basin in the font's cavity. There was a faint *chink;* I winced, waiting some moments before I inched toward the transept's arch. Peering out into the nave, I could see no change, no danger. Cautious even so, I emerged from this wing, and then I was moving swiftly through the nave, through the chancel, the sacristy, and dodging out *yet* another back door.

The light had changed, lower, reddish, weaker, as it fell across the churchyard. I stood outside the gate, watching to see if anyone else came out of the church. No one did. Minutes later, I saw two elderly women entering the gate, moving slowly around the building to the front. Soon the doors would be open; soon it would be time for Evening Prayer.

I walked away through the rusty light, thinking of other Evening Prayers long before, and of Nicholas Rhoades, preparing for them. If he was killed in the church, as I now believed, his body had been carried by night in this direction. Perhaps I was retracing that furtive journey, following the pattern of old lanes, on the way to Evangeline's lot.

The weather had changed as well; chill had turned to cold. I got in my car and turned on the ignition, then the heat, then spread out my Xeroxes. I scanned them, made notes; missed Jake. *You're afraid to let anyone get close....* He must be on his way back from Houston. If he were here, we'd drive home with his arm around me all the way. Once again, I felt someone's gaze. Startled, I looked up and saw the lot's manager; I recognized his light-blue eyes and broad strong face, his skin the color of rich coffee. He smiled, made a quick gesture. "No sweat — sit tight." For a few minutes, I watched the street beyond the lot: kids in Day-Glo jackets, a woman with a briefcase, a man with a bowling bag. A hooker in a fake-fur jacket, high boots

I looked back at my notes and made one more.

LILY JENKINS, I wrote in the margin. I circled the name. One more place I had to go; I decided to walk.

Four blocks down the main street, one right turn, one block to Herbie's Pizza Parlor. A sign in the window read CARRY-OUT; another, SIT FOR THE SPECIAL. I stepped inside, into the good warm smell of tomato sauce and rising dough. Everything in Herbie's was tomato-colored: red Formica tables, red jukebox in the corner, red Formica counter where kids swung their legs from high red stools. Here, in 1738, Faith Roper's Tavern had stood: a smoke-filled brew-house run by Lily Jenkins's closest friend. According to the Town Council's report, in front of that tavern, down a slope, Lily had been found dead from a blow to the head.

I took a seat in one of Herbie's leatherette booths alongside the picture windows. The kids were playing old rock songs on the jukebox. Again I missed Jake. I thought of us dancing out on that airstrip in the desert. *You're afraid ...* Dancing with him, some old song on the radio, his place, two weeks ago. His hand on the small of my back, drawing me against him; another night we stayed in, forgetting dinner....

Now, looking up at these walls, all I saw were glossy pictures of pizza. White pizza. Red-and-white pizza. Pepperoni. The Works. Sighing, I ordered what would best fuel my blood sugar for the drive home alone: a cheeseburger.

Immediately the manager appeared.

"Herbie." He put out his hand. "No pizza?"

I explained; he understood and sat talking with me. He'd been making pizza in this town since 1951. Before that, his father, before that ... his voice, kindly, soft, ran like a stream of old-fashioned ballroom music. His hair was the soft gray of oysters; he stroked his beard. My cheeseburger arrived.

"Always been a restaurant here?" I took a bite.

"All the way back through my great-grandmother; she had a grocery business."

"Started as a tavern, didn't it?" I glanced up. "Or is this the wrong spot?"

"Faith Roper's joint, that's right. Way back when. Rowdy place, I'd bet. Not what they tell you at the Historical Society."

"They tell you there was a hill here, the tavern on a slope. And someone, about 1738, was found — "

"No hill, no slope. This has always been flat, this lot. Look at those oaks out there." He jerked a thumb toward the window. "They've been here on flat ground over two hundred years. Trees don't lie."

I looked at him.

Another report not quite right; changed? If Lily had been killed here, as the source implied, she wouldn't have been at the bottom of a hill. She must have been murdered elsewhere, on a slope, maybe near her own house, and the two facts had blended. Or perhaps Lily had only been brought here later, to make it appear that she'd died a whore's death — just as Dinah's body, according to Gonzalez, had been brought to a drug corridor....

I looked out the window at the oaks. It was dark out now; street lamps lit them — and the sleek form of a car, just beyond. My napkin crumpled in my hand.

"Something wrong?" Herb asked.

I as watching the car: its tinted windshield, its glossy sheen; the foreign car, with the diplomatic plates, that had tailed me in Washington here, in Maidstone. Just across the street.

"You okay?"

I took a breath. "My boyfriend," I said, low and fast. "He's been hassling me, following me all day, he's out there now — " I didn't look toward the window. "Is it possible — can I go out the back, through the kitchen?"

"You just follow me, hon," Herb said grimly; the voice of a father of daughters.

Slowly, we edged away from the windows and slipped to the back of the restaurant, then down a hall, moving faster through the steamy kitchen; pizza pans, faces, spinning dough, vats of sauce passed in a blur — and then I was at the side door.

I pressed Herb's hand. Before he could speak, I was running, streaking up a back street, dodging in and out of doorways, one block, two, my footsteps loud, breathing strained — turning a corner, I skidded into the parking lot. The manager jumped from a folding chair, alarmed.

"Someone — " I began, as the foreign car sped toward the lot, slowed down as if to scan the place, then edged up the street. " — following me," I finished, out of breath.

"Just hold on." Blue eyes glimmered in the dark face.

I didn't hear his brief words on the phone inside the lot's booth; I was watching the street, I was trying to breathe. All day, I'd been alert, looking for some figure behind me. Somehow, I hadn't expected a car. *This* car.

And I knew it hadn't quit; on the road home, I would see it in the rearview mirror again; that road was long, deserted, poorly lit.

"On the way." The lot's manager stepped from the booth. I didn't ask what he meant. His eyes narrowed; he too was watching the street.

"Behind you," he said then, his voice low. "Look easy."

Slowly, I half-turned. Down the street, through the dark, the strange car was creeping forward like a stalking cat. Its motor was low. Its lights were out. It crept closer.

And then, blazing into the lot, screeching to a stop, blaring music, was a bright-green four-wheel-drive truck. It sat high off the ground on huge wheels. It had four headlights, and over the cab, on a chrome roll bar, five more. The door flew open. "Need a lift?" the driver asked.

I stared at him — a man who looked like my companion's older brother. Dark face, light eyes; flash of grin, graying beard. I glanced over at the strange dimmed car, creeping toward me through the dark.

"Yes," I said, and climbed into the truck.

As it pulled away, I looked back at Evangeline's lot. For a moment, the manager's face looked familiar; I'd seen him, or someone like him, somewhere else.... The truck swerved into the street. Music rocked from the tape deck, and, it seemed, we rode out on that music, high above the ground; big sound, big lights, big wheels. I glanced back. The strange car was right behind us, headlights on now, picking up speed.

The truck's driver winked at me.

"Strapped in?"

I nodded.

"Very fine." He hit the gas. The tires roared, the street's doorways ran together. We moved faster, leaving Maidstone's lights behind. Tires howling, the truck made a sharp turn onto a back road. Behind us, the other car remained, unfazed, following.

"Ah-*right*." The truck's driver glanced into the rear-view mirror. His eye narrowed. "Let's ... get ... busy." He slammed a Tina Turner tape into the deck. He slam-med on the gas. He slammed into another turn — a dirt road this time. He hit all his lights and the road leapt up like day break in July. The truck sprayed dirt; its driver chuckled. The foreign car dropped back a few yards. "Tinted glass," the man beside me uttered, leaving the road now, cutting onto a track through a field. His lights made trees, grass, earth jump out at us, as if some dazzling sun had flashed a pathway through the dark. We were jolting off the track now, cutting across the field itself; the foreign car, farther back, still followed.

But we were flying over rough earth, spraying rocks, scattering weeds, an ahead, the whole land was brilliant, luminous, and Tina Turner was singing "Steamy Windows," as we churned through a shallow stream, water pluming. Behind us now, the lights of the other car had dwindled. It didn't seem to be moving; its headbeams hung like lanterns in that field. Beside me, the truck's driver was laughing softly. So was I.

"Home — too far for you — " I finally managed to get out.

"Naaah. Know where you're going."

I looked at him; for an instant, I thought I knew this man too, or someone like him. Something was familiar; a smell of earth and ash, a look of strength across a room.... Now his hand thrust another tape into the deck; his boot pressed the gas pedal, and we were swinging through that field, back onto main roads and, to my surprise, I saw we were headed for Washington.

When at last I jumped down from the truck, Jake was standing in Weatherell's doorway. From inside, a spill of light caught the sidewalk and the gleaming chrome beyond it. I could hear the driver's chuckle as he pulled away, and all night, I could still hear that rich laughter; I could still see that lit earth, and feel those great wheels fly me free.

■

« 20 »

A bright light snapped on.

A switch flicked, a motor hummed.

My typewriter started rapping; words streaked out across the page. I still saw dark land ablaze with light. I still heard the music, felt the speed.

Half an hour later, the typewriter was silent. Paper was crumpled. Momentum and illumination had ceased.

I looked at a half-filled page:

... Tom Kemp, sweating now, pushed the sexton's head into the font, but Nick, with surprising strength, twisted in the brewer's grasp. Faith Roper, holding the candle, pressed her free hand on Tom's. Her touch gave him strength, even here, in the dim south transept, at this fearful task. Her touch had stirred him that afternoon, till he had to have her again, in broad daylight, and the church had seemed deserted, safe. Nick's gaze had stolen their secret, and Tom had to tear himself from Faith, dressing swiftly, following the sexton. Once he found that Nick has told Evangeline about them, Tom knew they must silence both.

*There was commerce, reputation to protect, and
respectability to win, above all. Now, this was imperiled.
Moreover, he would not be humiliated once again, before
Evangeline; she would be humiliated now. And so, Tom
and Faith had followed Nick back to this place where he
had spied on them; where he struggled with them now in
this dim transept. Faith Roper blew out the light and in
the dark, the candlestick glanced off the font and cracked
against Nick's skull. Still breathing, the sexton slumped
forward into the —*

"Wastebasket," I said aloud, tossing the page.

The writing was bad; the scene was wrong.

Faith Roper, the tavern keeper, had done business
with the brewer, a great deal of business, naturally, all on
record. Perhaps there was more personal business, but I
found no such indication; no record of gifts, no letters, not
a single observation in a journal. Mistress Roper
appeared in various reports as shrewd, kind, prosperous,
with only two questionable friends: Lily Jenkins and
Evangeline Smith. Tom Kemp filtered through the
sources as affable, generous, careless, often late with
orders, sometimes given to "brawling & violent temper,"
and, in 1738, still desolate and angry over his rejection by
Evangeline. It was possible, of course, that he sought
revenge on her; it was also possible that he sought
comfort in some off-the-record dalliance.... I blocked on
him and I knew why: he seemed parallel to Brad. Brad,
who wrote murder so well. I hated to see him in this
scene. Even so, Tom Kemp could have motive.

I started a fresh page.

*Warden Simms, stoic and strong, pressed Nick's head
down toward the water in the font. Holding a candle in
the dim transept, Councilman Cleete averted his eyes.*

Unpleasant, this, but necessary to important reputations, to church and council, to the very town's honor: Who knew what the sexton might rumor about town, after what he had seen here, late this afternoon: the warden himself with one of his own slave girls, a beauty, and ripe for breeding. The church was deserted and safe, especially today, with the councilman there, crouched in the front pew, warring his turn. The sexton had startled them, and Simms had known they must return tonight; after all, Nick was dispensable. Now, before the font, he struggled, gasping, trying to call out. Swiftly, Cleete raised the candlestick and brought —

Another page into the wastebasket.

True, the warden, I had learned, brutally beat his slaves. That fact had come to light in Town Watch reports, Cleete's papers, and the Midstone / Jenkins record. However, there was no indication of sex with slaves on either man's part. True, again, sexual nuance did not always show up in research; still, Cleete had been quite gossipy in his letters about Simms, linking the pious warden with Lily Jenkins.

I sighed, wishing that Detective Gonzalez worked the eighteenth century. Earlier, I'd called him to report last night's chase near Maidstone; I had to confess I'd been followed by the same car before. Gonzalez had promised to run a check on, the license plates, then get back to me. I wished he would interrupt me now. Meanwhile: one more sheet of paper.

One more time-trip to Maidstone's church.

. . . the priest lifted the candle, casting more light on the font. Poor Nick: evil had won him, and now he had been found dabbling in sorcery, with brutal, bizarre relics. It was known that he consorted with Evangeline, who brewed

all manner of potions; perhaps he had corrupted her.
Perhaps, together, they were calling down dark forces on
the town. Shuddering, the priest watched the strong
hands of Joan Dowd, retired midwife, holding Nick's head
down in the font. She had birthed many babies and closed
many eyes and it seemed right that she dispatch this to
tormented, possessed creature. Now with one swift
gesture, she raised the candlestick and murmured —

"Shit."

More paper crumpled. Once again — off the mark.
The sources had described the old midwife as arthritic;
her hands would not be strong enough. And this version
lacked a key element: those Mysterious lovers. Then
there was the Reverend Drummond. I couldn't see a
priest involved in something like this — my own bias, I
knew. And this priest seemed especially unlikely: among
his papers, I had found three letters of adoration to the
Paraclete, the Holy Spirit. This man was a mystic, no a
murderer. The whole thing didn't fit, and till it did, I
knew, the writing would be off.

I leaned my head against my typewriter.

I want a divorce," I whispered into it.

I pulled all the crumpled pages from the wastebasket
and spread them before me on the green rug. Why
couldn't I use a computer like other people? Why did I
write on this old crone of a machine that spat out keys
like bad teeth? Why did every page resemble a dispatch
from prison? I'd had this typewriter since college and all
its keys were slightly off-line. Obviously, this prose would
look better if the letters lined up. Obvious , the sentences
would shine.

And the words would still be wrong.

I was crumpling pages again when the phone rang.

"Gonzalez here." The detective, as always, sounded canny, cagey, quick. "Got a make on that vehicle you forgot to mention last week."

"Okay — who?"

"Not a 'who.' A 'what.' The car traces to the British Embassy. It has a pool of twenty-five vehicles, available to employees. Five of the cars match your description."

"No ..."

"Yeah, well ..." I heard him exhale smoke. "It's tough, dealing with DPLs. Look, until that Jaguar goes out, pulls a hit-and-run ... nothing we can do."

"Swell."

"Hey. Keep looking. Stranger things happen."

Keep looking. The only place to keep looking now was backward — back in time, again, in my Xeroxed sources.

Vehicles: I scanned the 1738 property reports. Carts, drays, wagons, wheelbarrows — and owners.

Thefts: I scanned the 1738 Town Watch report. One mule. Two hogsheads tobacco. A keg of ale. No carts, drays, wagons; not even a wheelbarrow. Not even temporarily misplaced.

I ran a hand through my hair. I had hoped this would be a productive direction. Nick was transported in *something* from the church to Evangeline's. "Something" seemed lost in the shuffle of centuries. This direction looked about as promising as the embassy motor pool.

I glanced at my watch. Time to go downstairs; back to work — real work. I stacked the Xeroxes. A good thing Eddie was pursuing this for me. We'd discussed the whole problem this morning, and decided I could use more information. Eddie had offered to make a research trip to Maidstone; my presence might set off more alarms, while hers would not. She could take a few days and do a thorough job, maybe even locate Harley Jenkins — and

check on my car, left behind in Evangeline's lot. Jake and
I would get it this weekend; meanwhile, he'd taken time
off to help me run the shop. I'd always wondered how this
fantasy of his would play out in reality, in the form of
shipments, invoices, heavy lifting, paper cuts. So far, he
not only seemed to like it, but delight in it. And I could
not quite admit how I delighted in seeing his head bent
over my grandmother's desk.

Still, I couldn't leave him alone down there. I took a
last glance at the Xeroxes and turned off the lamp. In the
window's light, my eyes skipped down the vestry report
once more. Nothing of interest: orders for tallow, paper,
ink; a note of missing linen, a missing crate. Marriage
banns —

I snapped the lamp back on.

> Missing from sacristy, one sheet fair-linen
> one shipping crate
> crate's other contents
>   present & accounted for...

I turned the lamp back off and went downstairs. Jake
said something to me but I didn't quite hear it.
Preoccupied, I opened a small crate, just delivered by
United Parcel. I lifted out one book, then another; then
dropped them back in the box. Moments later, I was
running down the cellar steps. The door slammed shut
behind me.

Weatherell's cellar was well plastered but poorly lit. A
series of naked light bulbs swung above dozens of crates,
sending an intricate shadow-dance across a grid of wood
and cardboard. The place seemed disorderly at first
glance, but was actually well arranged, at least to my
mind. Now, with a sudden loss of inspiration, I scanned

the complex grid. I knew the police had been through the cellar the day Gerald's body was found. All the empty crates from that time were gone; I put them out, each week, for pickup. Still, I wondered, maybe something had been left, over-looked.

I prowled the cellar — half-hopeful, half-expecting to be back upstairs in minutes. I pulled a light cord and the cellar's nearest section sprang into clarity. Here were all the empty crates and cartons from this week; tomorrow morning, I'd set them out in the alley, and by afternoon, they'd be gone.

Unhooking a flashlight from the wall, I examined the stock: every-thin was dated, recent, devoid of interest. I pulled the string to the next bulb. In this section, we kept bulk supplies. Here, again, these cartons were dated, recent, marked — and full. I slit a few open: paper, order forms, nothing more. I moved on to the basement's far end, turning on the last overhead bulb. This, the largest section, held crates of books not yet sorted; books appraised but not yet shelved; books simply in storage, waiting to fill gaps upstairs.

I picked my way through the boxes, playing the flashlight about. Its beam touched a carton marked in my own printing: JUVENILE — STOCK. They had been down here for months. I opened one and saw a series of old Landmark children's books. My light moved more quickly, carelessly now, over my own printing, and Eddie's, marking the crates, identifying contents. One last glance. This time, though, my gaze was cursory, careless. And this time, my light touched something else, returned to it, and stayed.

Only as I'd ceased to strain for something out of the ordinary — only the had the extraordinary registered on me. Now I lifted the flashlight on more, aiming its beam at that last crate in the corner. It sprang back into my vision. The light set off a peculiar double slash on the crate; a slash I recognized. I had made it with my own knife, opening that crate in excitement, in haste, the day of the shop's anniversary. The slash was jagged and cruciform, prominent only now, lit from above in the dark. I recalled my concern at marring the wood; wading toward the crate, I turned it around.

There, on its side, was the ID; I had put it there in heavy black ink, that same day, the day of the party. The mark was small and simple: BP, my shorthand to myself for "Bishop." I had made that mark on all three crates in that shipment. One crate had been sold to Brad, another to an anonymous buyer by proxy, within hours; the third had stayed here a few days while various people bought its contents for the novelty, the camp, the joke. Then, I remembered, I had put this crate out in the alley, with several others. All of them had been taken away, I was certain.

And now, this one was back.

Moving closer, I looked for another mark — a circle, enclosing initials and a shepherd's crook, the bishop's personal crest. I ran my light over the wood and down one side; the small crest seemed to leap out — the circle, the staff, the purple.

Jake? Could you bring something down?" I called up the dumb-waiter shaft: a frequent mode of communication, the damn cellar door was always locking one of us in. "That photo, it ran with the "Style" article about the party here, remember? There was a shot of us with these crates from — " I broke off, not knowing who else might be up stairs. "That file to your left, bottom drawer, by the desk..."

"I'll be right down," he called back, catching the urgency in my voice; normally, we'd send requested items on the dumbwaiter. Over my head, I heard file drawers slide, then footsteps moving toward the cellar steps. The lock clicked; at the top of the stairs, the door opened and Jake came down, a newspaper clipping in his hand. He looked, questioning, at me. I stood like a sentry beside that crate, as if somehow it might vanish once again. Our shadows, thrown against the walls, looked cloudlike, immense as we moved.

Look." I shone my light on the ID marks. "One of the bishop's crates. I put it outside weeks ago, for pickup, I remember noticing it. This crate's been out of here, gone — "

"And now it's back ..." Jake held the newspaper photo under the light bulb. There, in the picture with me, were those three crates, all showing the same pastoral seal.

"Look here ..." I shone the light on the books within the crate: a collection of children's books, inexpensive, a donation — I remembered receiving them, unpacking them; neglecting them.

"Jake." I dropped my voice. "These are the books I loaded on the dumbwaiter the day before Gerald died. Then I got so caught up in my own stuff, Evangeline, I left them there all day. I completely forgot them, never did that before. Next morning, I went to haul them up, *these* books

"When you pulled up the body."

I nodded.

For a moment longer we stood thinking, motionless. Then, without another word, we were kneeling on the cellar floor, pulling those books from the crate. They seemed to fly through our hands, scattering across the cold cement. At last the crate was empty. We took a breath and looked within. I played the light down its sides, across the bottom. "Go back," Jake said. "That way, to the right — stop. There." A small thread-shaped stain: red-brown.

We looked at it for what seemed a long time.

"I think," I said finally, "I think we should call Gonzalez."

"I told you," Gonzalez was saying, hours later, in the bookshop's kitchenette. "Stranger things happen."

He lit a cigarette and sat on a chair's edge. Gonzalez always sat on the edge of chairs. Soon after we'd called, he had come with a partner and two crime-lab cops. Bright lights had gone over the crate. The stain was *tentatively* identified as blood. Minuscule strands, on the crate's underside, were *tentatively* identified as rug fiber. Possibly from a car's rug? we asked. The detectives, now impassive, made no reply. The crate was rapped in plastic for the lab. The alley door was sealed and nailed shut

"Don't hold your breath," Gonzalez told us.

On his way out, we heard him snap, "Rush it."

It was a very long afternoon.

Outside, it grew dark; time to close the shop. We stayed around. We listened for the phone. We wondered where we might go to dinner; some place distracting. There seemed to be no such place. Finally, we started putting out the shop's lights. And then Gonzalez reappeared.

In the kitchenette off the back room, he told us: the lab had rushed. The fiber matched the particular trunk carpeting of British Jaguars of certain years; Jaguars, more specifically, used in the British Embassy motor pool. Gonzalez had pulled "some moves," and managed to pull off a search warrant.

"We check," he went on. "We find the vehicle. We match the fibers from the crate to the carpet in the vehicle's trunk — that's right, a carpeted trunk. Except for this dime-sized spot; it was scraped off."

Jake and I exchanged glances.

"Just to be sure," Gonzalez continued, "I look up in the wheel-well." He exhaled blue smoke. "And what do you think's stuck up there?"

"Weeds," I said.

"Bet your ass."

Now we were waiting for another call; this one from Gonzalez's partner, who was running down a list of embassy personnel with access to that particular car. The wait was growing long.

"She might not get it tonight," I said.

"I might need a Scotch," said Jake.

I rose to take the bottle down from a high shelf. The clink of the bottle an glasses sounded loud. The gurgle of poured liquor seemed a water-fall. Jake and I jumped as the phone rang. I answered; then, in silence, handed the receiver to Gonzalez. He busied himself taking notes. I busied myself opening the freezer for ice.

Gonzalez hung up after what seemed hours.

"Five people have access to the vehicle in question. Employees, mostly on rotation as drivers, one retired. Any of these names mean something?" He began to read them off. "Crockett, Davison, Hunt, Lind, Masefield — "

"Lind." I turned from the freezer. "Lind?"

"Lind, Alberta S.," Gonzalez read out. "Driver since 1966. Retired last year but retained access to vehicle. A reward for twenty-five years' faithful service, why, you know her?"

I turned from the freezer.

"You know her." Gonzalez watched me.

"The librarian, part-time, here in D.C. — "

"Slow down." Gonzalez was taking notes again.

Vapor from the open freezer hung about my head. I turned back to it. "I saw her in Maidstone, at the Historical Society, yesterday; she said — "

"You're saying this Lind woman was in Maidstone? But she works here ...?"

"She said she was on leave, she acted very — " Looking into the freezer, I broke off.

"*Very* what?"

There was something back there, beside the ice tray.

"Ms. Grey? You with us?"

I gazed into the freezer, wanting to slam it shut. Instead, I made elf reach in, past mounds of slush, past the Popsicles from last summer —

"Al?" Jake's voice.

Very slowly, I turned around. In my open palm lay two frozen objects, furred with pale frost. At first glance, they might seem to be large round ice cubes. I held them out to Gonzalez. With his finger he brushed frost away.

The frozen spheres fell like stones to the floor.

Ice

Eyes.

Gerald's green eyes, in our freezer for about two weeks, and now defrosting in the handkerchief of Rafe Gonzalez, in the middle of Weatherell's kitchen. My grandmother would not have been amused.

■

« 21 »

My grandmother once saw a suffragette parade in Washington. A girl herself, she gazed in wonder down Pennsylvania Avenue, as women in white dresses marched twelve abreast, arms linked. They carried signs; they sang. They turned the ordinary avenue into a spill of ivory and pearls. Near the bystanders, a marcher paused; suddenly, a well-dressed man thrust his lit cigar into her arm. The woman gasped but did not turn. Setting her jaw, she simply marched on, that ugly burn stamped into her flesh. Her white dress blended with the others. Watching, my grandmother burst into tears — and remembered, and told me the story.

I remembered it often, throughout these last weeks, and I remembered it again, after that discovery in the kitchen, throughout that following day. That day, for a while, I had the sensation of marching.

The police were looking for Alberta Lind. There might be leads from Maidstone, when Eddie returned. There were possible leads from what we referred to as "Dinah's restaurant;" Jake had located it, and had a call in to a waiter. And then there were the objects from our freezer in the crime lab: further evidence of a frame. Just when I thought we were marching, just when I thought there would be no more burns — fresh burns appeared.

Some came in the form of letters, and even a fax, grinding its way into the peace of my workroom upstairs. These were messages from member of Writers' Bloc: harsh messages, hot words. One came in the form of a Mailgram: a dispatch from my agent informing me that he was terminating our relationship, and that my publishers had abrogated their contract for *The Torching*.

The last came in the form of an article on the front page of a newspaper's feature section: a story on Writers' Bloc — its murder, its move from the bookshop, news to me, and its troubles, all related to Alice Grey, by anonymous sources.

I remember standing there, those papers in my hands. The words seemed to scramble. I could not look away from them. For a moment, it was seven years ago: a group of writers has gone to a wine festival in rolling Virginia countryside. The earth smells of sun and August and childhood, and there is breeze enough to swing a hammock. We are wandering among the vines heavy with grapes, we are wearing old clothes, Lorna in a big straw hat, Brad a farmer in his plaids, Andrew, in his simple denims, almost Amish. He is picking fruit, passing it to Lorna; juice runs down her chin, she laughs, rich and long, and tosses a bunch of grapes to Brad, who catches it, clowning, in his mouth, and then we gather to taste the wine. From hand to hand it passes, shimmering bright as blood, and all I see is the wine, passing from hand to hand....

My mind skipped, skidding like a blunt needle on an old record. Suddenly, stupidly, I remembered one summer when my brother, chopping wood, had accidentally cut my arm with the ax. The gash went white: too deep to bleed right away. I had not cried; at the time, I'd been so proud of that. Now I tasted salt; my eyes filled, my face was wet, and silently, steadily, I cried, feeling the wrench of tears from my very spine. Jake was holding me, I was soaking his shirt and still I could not stop; my shoulders shook and my mouth seemed filled with blood.

After what seemed a long time, Jake wiped my face. With one swift gesture, he took the papers from me. Without a word, he dropped them in a large brass bowl, struck a match, and set the papers on fire. We watched the pages curl and turn brown, till suddenly, we heard a high-pitched shriek: the nearest smoke alarm going off.

On top of a ladder, I was pulling batteries from the alarm as the door opened. Somehow I kept my balance as Andrew and Lorna entered the shop. I remained where I was, forcing the visitors to look up at me. There was a silence.

"We wanted to stop by, see you ..." Lorna's voice trailed off. "We wanted to express concern...."

That word again. I said nothing.

"Concern for your feelings," Andrew added gently. "I thought perhaps we should talk."

I made no reply. In the silence, I heard Jake rise from his chair and move toward them.

"If you ever want to talk ..." Andrew tried again.

"She doesn't," said Jake, and opened the door.

After they left, I stayed on the ladder several moments. A smell of smoke lingered on the air.

Smoke downstairs; smoke upstairs in my apartment that afternoon. Going up to fax a response to my agent, the acrid smell reached me as I neared my workroom. I hesitated. The door was open; I seldom locked it during the day, while I was down in the shop. After a moment I looked in.

Brad stood in my room, smoking; waiting.

"What the hell are you doing here?" I didn't move.

"Nice welcome." Brad exhaled. "Look, sorry to scare you, I just wanted to talk, didn't want it public. I was in the neighborhood — I know these back stairs, this apartment, remember?"

Watching him, I didn't answer.

"Ever since you came by ..." He drew on his cigarette. "I've been thinking, I've ... wanted to talk to you."

"Is that why you're looking at my desk?" My voice was sharp. "What are you really doing here?"

"Couldn't we just — "

"No."

"Alice, I came in good faith."

"I can't quite believe that."

He took a step toward me; his bearlike frame seemed to fill the ring, dormered space.

"You're not letting me — "

"No." I stepped aside from the door.

"All right." His eyes darkened. "Live with it then. Live with the consequences."

"A curse? Or a blessing?"

He threw his cigarette out my window. Turning sharply, he brushed pass me and down the back stairs. I listened to his footfalls. Then I the checked the desk — nothing seemed to be missing. Finally I opened the window to let out the sense of invasion, the smell of smoke. After I'd snapped at a sandwich and faxed my message, I sat down at my desk. Still angry, I turned on the typewriter.

A smell of smoke lingered on the air of Evangeline's house as she burned the notes that came, sometimes, under the door. She could hear them now and then, scraping the floor, before the footfalls outside skittered away. Most of the messages were short, some misspelled, all anonymous, accusing. The letter from the Town Council, signed by many names, revoking her license as midwife, was perfectly written, arrived last and was burned first....

I sighed. This was not what I'd had in mind to write. The sources before referred to these notes; Evangeline's reaction was mentioned in Elizabeth Maidstone's journal. Still, I had not planned to build a scene around this; even before this morning's events, it had been too painful. I took another bite of my sandwich and turned to the typewriter again.

Evangeline did not want to think of letters anymore. Now she must make her mind very keen, and lay plans for leave-taking soon, though that would bring its own pain. Again, she thought of her island, where she had run unafraid as a child, into the welcoming sea. Fine it would be now, to feel unafraid, and to run to the sea, to board a homeward ship. Home, where her mother had died without a word, a look, a reason; where everything had been wrenched into a narrow winding shape. Evangeline sat thinking of her mother's voice. Never had it really ceased, it was threaded through her daughter's own speech. Evangeline must let go her mourning and her anger, else she could not return.

She wished Luke would come away with her. She would wait till the last to ask him, fearing he would not, and this fear became a heaviness, falling like a cloak about her. If only she could talk to a priest; on the island that had been a comfort. Here, of course, it was not possible, though at times, Evangeline had felt drawn to the Reverend Mr. Drummond. She had seen a melancholy in

him that had matched her own, and she had heard some
rumorings of sorrow at his back, pain caused by his last
parishioners. Here she felt in sympathy with him, but
other times he had seemed a hard man, enclosed in a
smooth translucent shell, through which he gazed
pensively at pain. It was true that she had disagreed with
his preaching, his treatment of Lily, and his solemn empty
gestures. Once only had she seen true passion in him, and
that was in a hidden moment, observed at early morning,
as she returned home from another birth. Passing the
church, Evangeline had heard glass shattering. Glancing
in the sacristy, she had seen the priest smashing its small
mirror with his shoe, all the while he gazed into it.
Shocked, she had moved quickly off, but somehow, she had
understood. There had been a time, after her father's
death, when she had felt herself fly apart into a thousand
pieces, and had not willed that feeling away. She would
not call that feeling back again, not now or ever. Once
more, she thought of her island....

This was going absolutely nowhere. Passing observations
from Evangeline as noted in Elizabeth Maidstone's record,
were assuming odd proportions. I was avoiding something, and I knew it. I stacked my sources, turned off the
type-writer, and went down to the shop. For the first
time, Jake looked restless. No customers were in the
store; outside, all I saw were sheets of rain. Inside, I
could still smell smoke.

"Slow afternoon," Jake commented.

I flipped the sign on the door from OPEN to CLOSED.

We needed a new treatment for burns: salve and water.
It occurred to me that we might find them elsewhere — at
the Highwood Health Club. Almost a year before, Jake
and I had bought a joint membership; since then, I think

we'd been there exactly twice. It was one of those his/hers clubs. It was one of those good intentions, one of our few luxuries. It was, that day, exactly what we needed.

We bypassed the exercise bikes and the weight room, ignored a coed aerobics class, and went directly for coddling; some treatment, I hoped, that might lead gently and irrevocably toward amnesia. We went for the softly lit room where attendants hovered over blue vinyl tables. There, separated by a translucent paper screen, we gave ourselves over to be massaged. The walls were painted with a huge soft rainbow: "The colors of each chakra," the attendant murmured. Wind chimes tinkled gently, before a blower. Oils were smoothed into our skin. We were enveloped in modern comfort — and even so, somehow or other, our conversation skidded back to the eighteenth century.

"They used oils for healing in Evangeline's time," I said. "Did she use them, you think?"

"Yes, on babies — and on wounds. She bound up the wounds of Warren Simms's slaves, after he beat them."

"Charming old Southern custom," Jake drawled.

"Simms was chasing a runaway slave the night Nick was killed supposedly, according to official sources. The slave turned up, very conveniently, on the High Street, next morning — just in time for Simms to call on Evangeline with the other worthies."

"Did our friend have uncontrollable rages? Murderous rages?" Jake mused.

"I wonder ..."

"Sometimes," the attendant said, "overwork can cause people to act out."

"What about the brewer, Tom Kemp?" Jake asked.

"Three reports of 'brawling.' Threw ale in someone's face at Faith Roper's tavern. A complaint was registered, he wrote a letter of apology, even so — "

"Stress." The attendant shook her head.

"That was in the latest papers?"

"Yes, but that doesn't make him a killer."

"We don't know that yet."

"Maybe your friend needs a membership." The attendant looked alarmed.

In swimsuits, we moved on to the whirlpool.

"Then there's this servant, Cass Tanner, he keeps turning up everywhere, I don't know what to make of him...." I slid into the pool.

"What about the councilman?" Jake spoke above the bubbling water. "Thy guy on his way up, Perry Cleete."

"Still single at thirty-five. Handsome, ambitious, no indications of bad temper," I said.

A young straw-haired woman shifted near us.

"No betrothals, ladyloves? Someone who might enjoy some hanky-panky in sacred space?" Jake was asking.

The blonde grew even more attentive.

"He'd been friends with Evangeline, but he wrote a letter, breaking the friendship, bidding her silence on the 'confidences he'd entrusted.' Two years later, he was still single."

"Hmmm." Jake frowned. "Unusual."

"Sure is," said the blonde. "Believe me, I know."

"But there's this strange stuff, just came to it," I went on. "Seems he was getting expensive gifts from someone, intimate gifts. Embroidered underdrawers. Silk hose. Ruffled shirts, fancy vests, all ordered from London. Three letters of gratitude are among his papers. The salutation's always 'Beloved Giver.' "

"Could be his mother."

The blonde nodded hopefully.

"I don't know...." I stared at the swirling water. "The clothes show up in his inventory, but the orders don't show up under his name in the agents' ledgers. I traced them by contents. They were ordered by someone else."

"Who?" Jake and the blonde asked in unison.

I took a breath. "The reverend and celibate Jonas Drummond."

"The *priest?*" Jake stared at me. The blonde stared at him.

I nodded. "He only used one agent, one name signs each order. Maybe the agent was paid off, maybe he just thought Drummond liked nice things. After all, they weren't Puritans, these people."

"They weren't innocents, either. Fancy gifts to a politician? Could be a bribe, a way to influence the council, get more land for the church — happened all the time, still does."

"Possible but ... no evidence. Not even of a cover-up." The water jets slowed down. "There's something else. Remember those copies of letters I showed you — the ones the priest wrote to the Paraclete, the Holy Spirit?"

"I remember. I was impressed he used the Greek term."

"I looked back at them again, after I'd seen those orders." Jake, and the blonde, leaned closer. "One of the letters professes devotion to 'my paraclete,' with a hyphen. In another, the beloved is called 'my Periclete.'" I spelled it. "And then he slips, forgets the hyphen, and spells the last part 'c-l-e-e-t-e.'"

Jake sat straight up. *"Perry Cleete,"* he said. The water simmered through our silence. "You think ... the councilman and the priest? Lovers?"

The blonde sighed and got out of the whirlpool.

"Of course that has nothing to do with murder," Jake said,
minutes later, in the sauna. "Neither does the brewer's
temper, or the warden's mistreatment of slaves. Or his
patronage of Lily Jenkins."

"Lily Jenkins ... it all goes back to her account. She
saw *two* people in Evangeline's empty house, the night of
Nick's murder." I paused, thinking. "We only have *her*
word for that. Could *she* have lied? Been in on it with
someone?"

"Nine months pregnant, about to deliver? And she
was Evangeline's friend." Jake shook his head. "What
about Faith Roper, the tavern keeper, and someone?"

"No evidence. Interesting observation, though, by
Mistress Roper, passed on to Lily Jenkins — from her to
Elizabeth Maidstone. Faith noticed a disheveled man,
shirt open, watching Nick from behind a tree, the afternoon of Nick's murder. Nick, on his way to Evangeline's,
was also disheveled. Faith Roper thought the two men
had been brawling."

"Who was watching Nick?"

"She wasn't sure." I sighed. "Perry Cleete, she
thought." Jake looked at me. "Cleete and Nick? The
lovers?"

"I hadn't thought of that...." I paused. "Somehow, I
doubt it. Nick was odd and homely. Cleete, it seemed,
loved beauty, luxury."

"He'd probably love this sauna...."

"Another odd thing." I leaned on an elbow. "The night
Nick died, an old man in the town was gravely ill.
Evangeline was attending him. The old man's daughter
ran all over town, looking for the priest. Never found him.
The family's 'note of complaint' to the church was, curi-
ously, filed with Warden Simms's papers.

"God." Jake turned over. "Nothing more, I hope."

"A scrap about poor Lily Jenkins's death. Faith Roper had some suspicions about where and how — confided them to Mistress Maidstone."

"Don't tell me." Jake spread a towel over his face.

"It's just scraps," I sighed. "Somewhere, I don't know where — there's a missing piece."

We lay there in the sauna, silent then. The hot air rose around us.   And after a while, the warmth, the steam, the unaccustomed luxury — it had so a cumulative effect. After a while we didn't move. We didn't think. We didn't care. About anything.

We'd found missing peace.

Still peaceful, we drifted to Jake's car. Blissfully half-conscious, we went back to the shop. We were speaking meditatively of dinner, when the phone rang, shattering our peace and wiring us into alertness, into action, back into the car. This time, the drive was quite different, as was the destination. Walking swiftly, looking left and right, we entered the shopping mall.

"She said she'd find us." We paced around the central atrium, staring at a window of children's glossy shoes.

"I don't like this," Jake muttered. "You'd think she's the damn CIA."

"God — maybe she is." The smell of caramel popcorn, from a vendor's stand, was nauseating. We passed Jewelry World, Earth Foods, and Cosmic Sound, then turned into a small doorway marked The Corner Bookstore. "This is where she said she'd be."

Warily, we moved through the shelves, pausing to scan the titles in HISTORY.

"Sorry about this," Harley Jenkins whispered.

I looked at her through the books. "Just what — "

"I told you. I was followed back to Maidstone, then here."

"And why would that be?" I snapped.

"You tell me. What's going on?" Her broad freckled face looked pale; hair flowed past a row of Civil War volumes. "You asked me to do some research, right? Okay, I called the Historical Society, got this new person, told her I'm checking facts for a writer, I figured she'd work harder. A writer who runs a famous Georgetown bookstore. The man clammed right up, acted strange, asked your name. Told me nothing. And after that — "

I pushed the Civil War books out of the way. "Wait a minute. What's her name?"

"Lindberg ... no, *Lind*."

"Shit," said Jake, behind me.

"Did you mention my question about the boat house?"

"Yes, you asked — "

I whispered through the books about the attack at Kelly's.

"*Damn,* I blew it, tipped someone off." Harley moved down the book case, placing us in the era of Italian Renaissance. "Who is this Lind person, what's her connection?"

"We're still waiting to find out. She said she had family in Maidstone — "

"I don't know them. I went down to see the woman, didn't recognize her. She looked like some mousy tour guide, then she climbed into this red ports car, floored it out of the Historical Society's parking lot."

Mrs. Lind could not have attacked me at the boat house, I didn't think. Was she speeding to deliver information — and to whom? I looked back at Harley. "You think she's following you?"

"I don't know. Someone is."

For a moment, we were silent. I felt as if today's interlude had never happened. The trouble around me seemed to spread again, like an ugly stain. I thought of

Gerald; I thought of Dinah. I looked at Harley again.
"Someone in a red sports car?"

"No. Foreign car. Black Jaguar."

The fluorescent light above us showed the lines in
Harley's face. My hands, fidgeting among the books,
looked bleached-out, bone-white.

"I'm sorry," I said after a while. "Come back to the
shop — you can follow *us.* "

Harley's smile was thin. "I didn't used to frighten
easily," she said. "I guess that was a while ago." She
looked over at me. "You tell me what's going on, and I'll
give you what I found. You asked me to locate Nicholas
Rhoades's Bible."

"But I never really *thought* — "

"I did. I knew the family, almost married into it.
Think of that gene pool." For an instant, her grin flashed.
"That's where I was. Baltimore. Got the Bible, with some
scribbled notes in it, made with some kind of charcoal
stylus. Carbon lasts better than ink."

"This is wonderful." I stepped around the corner of the
bookcase. Harley looked exhausted, her clothes soaked
with rain. "This is terrible."

"All those things." She hoisted her bag. ■

« 22 »

*M*aidstone lay quiet in the dusk.

It was suppertime. The streets were empty and smelled of wood smoke and the air was the color of plums.

They were waiting for him by the water, in the transept of the church. All was in readiness. Soon, the sexton must return from Evangeline's. The wait grew long and they grew restive; then, at last, they heard his familiar hitching gait.

Nick paused in the sacristy, breathing in again the good safe smells of tallow, starch, and the polish he used on the candlesticks. He stood trying to forget what he had seen, just beyond, just hours before, in the chancel. With effort, he tried not to picture again those two naked figures, pale as moonlight, entwined, pressed together, before the altar. The sexton stopped the images from coming, but then, as he looked into the chancel, he seemed to see them once again: on the floor, before the altar, the priest embracing the councilman, tossing, tumbling, lips nuzzling neck — flash of white buttocks. And then Cleete on hands and knees, with the priest astride him, riding, rocking, and that wild high moan...

Nick had witnessed lovemaking before, in meadows and barnyards, male and female, male and male, and had found its intensity a wonder. It was the church, the priest, he knew, that had made him weep, between the pews. Thinking of it, now, he trembled. What if he had been seen? He pressed his knuckles to his mouth, forcing himself to be calm, allowing Evangeline's potion to work. He wished he were still in her house but she had been called to a sickbed, and Nick had hurried through the lanes to the sacristy, realizing he had missed Evening Prayer.

As he stepped into the nave, he saw the church swimming in shadows, touched with the last colors from the windows, spilling like wine and ink cross the pews. Waiting for him in the south transept was the pastor, calm and tall and gentle-eyed as ever. For a moment, Nick disbelieved what he remembered of that afternoon. This mild man — in black cassock and collar, long hands folded, face sober and kindly, gaze slightly nearsighted — this man could not be the one Nick had seen naked here, this very day.

"Nick ..." The priest's voice, mild as always, called from the transept. "I wonder if you might help me a moment ..."

Obediently, Nick came. Perhaps there would be some kind word excusing his failure of duty, and perhaps now Nick would see for certain, the priest was not that man on the chancel floor.

"I was worried for your sake," Drummond said gently now. "You've not missed a service since I've been here." The pastor's voice was, as always, soft and slightly mannered, as if to control a stammer.

"Sorry, sir ... sorry, I... I wasn't well — " Nick broke off.

"And did you go to the apothecary, for medicinals?"
The priest's tone was patient. *"And stay to chat?"*

Nick hung his head.

"I ask your forgiveness, Master." He hesitated. *"And now, if you would, I pray you excuse me, I'm still not to rights...."*

"Ah, but I'm afraid I am in need.... 'Twill take but a few moments of your time." The priest's voice was still gentle. *"There's a great leak her in the font, and we've a baptism tomorrow. The request came while you were out."* The Reverend Drummond shook his head. *"I saw water dripping, Sunday last, and forgot to mention it."*

Nick's concern for the church caught him, and his guilt over his negligence. He peered at the priest in the dim transept and saw the serene figure moving out of his way. Certainly, Nick thought, what he'd seen this afternoon was wrong, some fevered image; he'd think no more of it, ever.

The sexton bent to the font — and as he did, he felt the shock of another body slamming into his. An arm locked around his neck, a hand covered his mouth, a strong grasp held him. For an instant, Nick heard a match struck, and saw candlelight play over water. Now his face was forced down toward that water in the font's bowl, and he thrashed, twisting to break free, chanting silently his prayer, *"Eye of God, watch over Nick, Eye of God, Eye— "* His face was in the water now, he tasted it and choked, gasped, and once more he thrust back against that strong hand. *"Eye of God — "*

The priest grimaced, feeling a sharp kick in his shins.

"Little bastard," he muttered. Who would guess the simpleton, frail-looking, would have so much strength? *"Damn you."*

Cleete stationed behind a pillar, had locked the sacristy door before lighting the candle. Now, drawing closer with the taper, he added a hand to the one on Nick's head. "The freak — he's fighting."

"Not for long." The priest's voice was grim as Nick twisted in his grasp.

"Best not." Cleete glanced up. "Some woman was outside, calling for you — she's gone now. Still, these people, when they want you — "

"Quite." Under Drummond's hands, Nick's face twisted sideways and he coughed, flailing out with one arm. Shadows played across the walls as the candlestick dipped, flashing silver, and the men struggled. Spewing water, Nick tried to scream. Swiftly then, Cleete blew out the taper and brought the candlestick down through the dark, against the sexton's skull. The blow, a blind one, glanced off the font, and seemed a crash in the quiet church. The priest paused, listening. All remained still outside, and now, beneath him, Drummond felt Nick go slack, though his breathing continued. The priest moved him lower, and the sexton's head fell forward, submerged in the font.

They waited in the dark, hearing now only the faint boiling in the water of Nick's breath. The sounds grew fainter and ceased. Drummond waited some moments.

"He's dead," the priest said at last.

Cleete relit the candle. They saw the crack in the font's basin and, moving quickly, poured its contents into a bucket alongside them. A second water ewer was lifted from the transept floor, along with a small sharp knife.

The priest set the cracked basin aside, and in its place in the font's stone cavity he set the deep bronze offering plate. Over it, he held Nick's head once more, face up this time, as Cleete stepped forward, a cloth over his shoulder. "An eye for an eye," he said quietly. The knife flashed in the candle-light, and waterlike shadows rippled down the transept's wall as the priest lifted the candle high. Perry

Cleete, once a London fishmonger, deftly cut through the translucent membranes around the sexton's eyes, and then the knife was sinking deeper, slicing into veins and sinew. There was blood, though not a great deal, swiftly caught in the offering plate and, just as swiftly, washed with water from the ewer, before the blood congealed. Soon it was done, and the sexton's body, wrapped in new altar-linen, was curled in the crate. Plate and floor were wiped clean with Cleete's towel, as the priest played the candlelight over the transept once again. All seemed perfectly to rights, and soon linen and cracked basin would be sinking swiftly in the river. Drummond had found Nick's prized jars in the sexton's cell-like room, and had gathered the vessels here. Now he lifted the new jar Cleete had filled with fresh brine.

Into this vessel, Cleete deposited one eye, watching as it sank like some sea creature, trailing bloody tendrils through the water.

"Jonas, lift the light?"

The priest raised the candle higher, and Cleete held the other eye up near the flame, turning the moist sphere in his hand, watching its small vein appear and disappear into the dimness. At last, Cleete lowered his hand beyond the candle's light and looked down at his palm, which now seemed to hold only a glistening shadow.

One small candle on the floor to see by, they decided, and that would be all. At Evangeline's house, they must take care and watch, not knowing when she might return. They knew she was at a sickbed, for they'd heard her called, and knowing whose, believed she would be gone much of the night. She had been gone some time already, they saw by the state of her fire, left in haste, not banked, and nearly out. A simple matter it was to spread the coals, then douse them slightly, not enough to have a puddling mess, but to extinguish them.

Cleete watched at the window while Drummond worked in silence by the hearth. The town was slumbering now, for they had waited in the church till the hour had grown later; safer still.

"Now I shall sleep nights," Cleete said, low-voiced, gazing about the low-beamed room. "Years, fearing she'd betray me. Years, remembering how I'd let slip, in loneliness — my secrets."

"She charms people to trust," the priest said, tight.

"Charms, indeed. I'd had enough beatings home, in England, to know ... we can't trust. Anyone. Tricked it out of me, she did. I've dreamed for years I could undo it."

And now you can, love. You did well, Perry. Scarcely marked him, his hair covers all, now 'twill appear as we want. No sign of how he died. They shall think she witched him dead and took his eyes."

The light, cast upward from the floor, sent their shadows across the walls and ceiling, shadows that shifted as one man turned back to the window, and one opened the crate. In that light, the priest saw his lover appear suddenly skeletal, bones lifted into prominence, eyes cavelike. Drummond turned quickly back to the crate, hoisting out the body and, as a father carries a child, he bore Nick to the chimney.

Cleete paced from window to door and back to the window once again. "No one stirring," he said. "Evangeline's having a long visit."

"Too many visits." Drummond's voice was low and sharp. "Too great a following, 'tis unseemly. If it weren't for that, we needn't have feared Nick overmuch. The fool, running off to tell Evangeline what he saw, you watched him. God knows, she in turn could tell half the town — and be as credible as we are. Truly, Perry, midwives can

come to be regarded as priests of sorts, in time. There they
are at the childbeds, the sickbeds, the deathbeds, it
happens. I'd wager she believes she's one — and speaks ill
of me, we've both heard it."

" 'Twill all cease now, dear Jonas." Cleete looked at
the body. "The people do love Evangeline. But that kind
of love can turn hateful rather quickly with the right
tainting."

Suddenly, he drew back from the window, gesturing to
the priest. Cleete moved to stand against the door as
moments passed and their shadows, immense and fluid,
arched over them. The councilman looked at Drummond.
Lit from below, the priest's face was skull-like, chin and
cheekbones seemingly unfleshed, the eyes dark and vacant.
Cleete turned back to the window.

"She's gone."

"Who?"

"Harlot from the docks, I think — drunk."

"No fear." Drummond was brief.

The priest summoned his lover, and now both men
labored to slide Nick up the chimney, wedging him firmly
there with firewood, and high meat hook.

"Head down?" Cleete said. "Makes it harder."

"Makes it better," Drummond said quietly. "I want her
to look up into that face."

Soon this part, most difficult, was finished, and all
refuse was gathered, soon to be dropped with the crate in
the river. There remained but one task more, and this was
easy. From the box now the priest lifted out the jars of eyes
and set them on a hearthside stool. Cleete snatched
Evangeline's shawl down from a peg and stood waiting
while the priest arranged the jars, the crucifix. Just before
he dropped the shawl over the jar the light caught them
and the eyes within, glowing greens and golds and
purples.

The shawl fell over the stool. The candle was snuffed. In the dark, on their way out, they jostled the stool. The last thing they heard as they left was the sound of brine whispering against glass.

They watched her, that next morning, walking home, her step weary. Already, there was a swirl of cloaks and carts, Market Day's beginnings. They watched her go into her house and shut the door, and then, on the High Street, they nabbed Peagram, and Simms, with one of his runaway slaves. The men conferred briefly and soon were rapping on Evangeline's door, which, to Cleete and Drummond, looked remarkably different in daylight. From there on, all went precisely as planned: the polite pastoral reproval, the start of the hearth fire, and at last the sight of Evangeline standing as if frozen, staring up the chimney into Nick's dead face.

The room was filled with bluish smoke from the smothered fire, and into that haze, a crowd had pressed; the town had gathered. The Reverend Jonas Drummond had taken charge. The sexton was down from the chimney, lying on the hearthstone, stiff and cold and soiled, his bluegray eyes carved out, leaving gaping sockets, dark and blind. Evangeline sat there staring, unable to move or speak, hearing the commotion build around her, the harsh bark of men's voices, the thud of running boots, the cry for the Town Watch. When Evangeline looked up at last, she saw through the smoke what seemed a thousand eyes.

The priest was kneeling by the dead man now, saying the prayers, and reaching back, with care, in just the right direction, for the right material. He took the shawl, dropped it over Nick's face, and waited. It was only instants before a windlike breath swept the crowd and voices rose and the priest waited, letting it build another moment. Then, he turned to he stool, where the jars were clustered, just as he had left them in the dark. Regarding them, he drew back, and not only for the show of it, for in daylight they looked different. With effort, Drummond lifted a jar to the window.

Within the vessel, the spheres shifted like pebbles. But not pebbles. Eyes. Animal eyes, trailing veins and twine-like sinew, drifted in blood- tinged brine, where they rolled and turned, some appearing to stare out crazily through a reddish mist, while others, bruised and purplish, were filmed, hardly recognizable.

Behind him now, the priest heard a thud; someone had fainted, and by the door a servant was retching. Others crossed themselves three times, or made the circle with thumb and forefinger, against evil. A breeze touched and turned the spinning wheel, and a rush of breath ran through the crowd again as they drew back from Evangeline. The priest waited, letting the fear and horror mount, till he could practically smell it in the people, and then he turned on Evangeline.

"This — your work?"

"Nay — not mine." Her voice was strong and clear. He hated her for that, thinking she would remain in the daze that had taken her at first.

Now Perry Cleete was stepping forward, lifting other objects from the stool, deliberately dropping the bottle that held Nick's eyes, so they lay on he floor in a spreading crimson stain. He'd waited for that shock to take full effect, and then, from behind the last jar, he lifted the blasphemous crucifix, holding it up until the townspeople roared and the Town Witch shouted for order.

Again, her voice steady, Evangeline denied that she possessed any of these objects, and her gaze held the priest's. He had returned it; he would vanquish her yet, even if it took more time, even if she was cleared of murder.

He turned to the crowd. "Thricefold, in the name of God Almighty, all evil here is bound" Then he turned to Evangeline, his gaze cool, his voice ringing out as hers had done. "Evangeline Smith, you stand under suspicion of murder, occult ritual, and sorcery. May God have mercy upon your soul."

Everything went smoothly, seamlessly, from then on, as Evangeline was confined to her home, until court and council could convene and the sentiment in town turned against her. As Perry Cleete had said, the people's love for Evangeline could turn, and be turned, swiftly. He and the priest, with the help of Warden Simms, worked among the parish and the townsfolk to aid the turning, and it wasn't a difficult piece of work, with fear to play on.

There was one small difficulty with Lily Jenkins, the whore, delivered of boy child by Evangeline on the night of Nick's demise. She must have been the one Cleete had spied from the window, but not quite soon enough. Foolish of her, prattling in the streets of what she'd seen, but if she'd identified the two figures in Evangeline's house, she hadn't prattled that, yet. It was difficult to determine how much she knew, how much she might say. It was easy, however, to be rid of her. There was a hill behind her house, with a stand of trees, where she liked to walk alone at dusk, and it was a simple matter to strike her there, from behind, one swift blow to the head. Drummond had done it while Cleete waited with the wheelbarrow and a pile of burlap sacking for cover. The barrow remained safely in Cleete's barn until that night, and then, very late, it rolled softly down a cow path to the flat meadowland before Roper's Tavern. The priest thought he'd seen Faith glancing out a window, but he'd watched her for days, with Cleete, and then weeks, and nothing came of it.

All that remained now was the discrediting of Evangeline, and that mat ter was not quite so simple. It was exasperating to discover how many people, despite everything, still loved her, remained loyal. The priest knew, however, this was not an insoluble difficulty, and one way or another he would prevail against her, not only now, but in the eyes of history. Drummond cared deeply about history, having loved it ever since he was a clumsy, lonely boy, taking refuge in chronicles, in books. A now he would write a chronicle of his own. With council and vestry to back him, with Cleete and Simms to corroborate, this would be a new history, resounding down the years with his good name.

Everything unfolded according to plan, naught to disrupt it. Every day, in the sacristy mirror, the Reverend Drummond would adjust his stole and study his own face. Once it had borne shame, but one day, in a book, it would be a portrait, showing a priest who rid his church of evil.

Only when he was tired did he see other faces in the sacristy mirror, and those fleetingly. Only once, after a bad night, he looked in the glass and saw no face — only eyes; a thousand eyes, green and gold and purple, holding him in their many pointed gaze.

■

« 23 »

There is a story of a woman who lived long ago, in a simple village, where no one had ever seen a mirror. One day, however, a traveling peddler sold this woman a very odd thing: a small hand-glass. Looking into it, the woman cried out, "That's the face of my mother, dead these many years." And in her apron, she carried the mirror, gazing into it. Soon enough, her husband noticed, and took the mirror. Looking into it, he cried, "That's the face of a handsome man — my wife has taken a lover!" Distressed, the man ran to the village priest, who paid a call on the wife. Standing before her, in collar and cassock, he demanded to see the picture of her lover. Puzzled, the woman laid the mirror in her pastor's hands. Looking into it, he cried out, "That's the face of a parish priest — and he looks *familiar....*"

Detective Gonzalez told us this story the next afternoon, in the bookshop. He had come, it seemed, on a general fishing expedition, and had looked carefully at the names I'd written on a pad of legal paper: names of assorted Maidstone citizens, circa 1738. The priest's

name on the list had prompted Gonzalez's story; an Irish
story, he'd admitted, with "Hispanic touches." I had
heard it from my grandmother.

Gonzalez scanned the pad again. It was a mess of
crossed lines, as I had tried to match Evangeline's
contemporaries with my own. After finishing that last
chapter, I had felt oddly unsatisfied. Always, I thought,
the key to the new story lay nested in the old; now,
however, the old story had spun out, while the new
remained unfinished. My eyes ticked down the list of
parallels again:

Thomas Archer — Daniel Peagram
Gerald Shane — Nicholas Rhoades
Dinah Lasko — Lily Jenkins....

Aside from some peripheral pairings, the victims,
unfortunately, made the surest parallels. None, however,
was neat. Peagram, for example had become a recluse
after the torching of Evangeline's house; he had retired to
a kind of half-life which had ended, like Mr. Archer's, in
his sleep, of unknown causes.... My explanation broke off.
I glanced up at Gonzalez.

"What's the theory?" He tapped the pad. "Reincarna-
tion? Possession? Something else I'm not up on?"

"Oh — possession." Harley didn't sound entirely
humorous.

"Maybe something else we're not up on," I said.

"Interesting." Gonzalez studied the pad. "I don't see
like a writer. But I notice things. I see many people with
faces that don't match the mirrors. People with double
lives. Sometimes they suffer, sometimes they make it.
And sometimes, they're dangerous. Double lives." He
shrugged on his coat. "Me, I make sure I don't have one.
Being a cop's part of who I am. Being Hispanic's a part of
who I am, so's being gay." He glanced at the pad one last

time. "If you're looking for answers here — look for one mirror, two faces."

Double lives.

I went back to work, sorting a new shipment of books. My hands moved capably, deftly, mechanically, while my mind went spinning off to Maidstone again. The eighteenth-century killers were clandestine lovers, with secrets, double lives.

Sometimes they suffer.

Eddie's face came before me, with the pain I'd often seen there. But it couldn't be Eddie. I set more books on the dumbwaiter; I'd forced myself to use it again — forced myself not to think or remember. But suddenly now, by the dumbwaiter, I was remembering anyway: that morning I stood here, hauling up a shipment of books — hauling Gerald's body up instead. Who but Eddie would have known about that shipment, already loaded? If someone had wanted to put a corpse on the dumbwaiter, they would have removed the books and piled them on the cellar floor. Only Eddie would have put them in a crate — only Eddie would have known just how to pack them.

And sometimes they're dangerous.

Anyone with a key would have access to the cellar and crates, but Eddie's access was the most natural. Anyone could get at crates sitting in the alley for pickup, but only Eddie would know exactly when they'd be there. Moreover, for Eddie, carrying a crate into the shop, even at night, would not seem odd. But carrying a crate out again — that could see odd indeed, and it would be a risk; a disposal problem, evidence. Smarter to leave the crate in the cellar — and pack it with the wrong shipment. A packed crate would likely not be searched, but rather, overlooked. And if it *was* searched and found suspicious — after all, it was my shipment, my crate; my shop.

I turned from the dumbwaiter. Upstairs, I grabbed the two art books Eddie had lent me, ages ago; she'd been reading one when I'd called fro Maidstone. Now I took them downstairs and stood before Jake. Behind the Civil War desk, he sat frowning at a bill. Seeing me, he looked up, smiled, then studied my face. "What's wrong?"

"Nothing. Could I borrow your car — an errand?"

Not quite fooled, he handed me the keys.

Eddie's spare house key was, as always, hidden in the eaves of her porch. Now I sprang up to reach it, as I'd done other times, with permission, meeting her here, arriving first. It was unseasonably warm, Indian summer in November. I felt uncomfortable in coat and gloves but kept them on even so: this would not be a normal visit. I glanced around. The street was quiet; the neighbors at work. As I expected, Eddie's car was gone: she was on her way back from Maidstone today. I wondered, now, if she had really been there — and hated wondering; hated sneaking into her house.

Startling, how ordinary it looked. There was the same clutter of books, mail, magazines, and cosmetics on the coffee table; the same bowl of cat's-eye marbles. There was the upright piano, as always with its twin candlesticks. The typing table, in the corner, was clear of paper now, and of course, the tie was gone from the rocking chair. On the couch, I laid down the heavy books: they were an excuse, insurance — just in case; likely not needed. I'd better remember them on my way out.

I stood very still and thought of all the items in a house: all the boots and bowls and bills, the sheer volume of belongings, objects, things — it overwhelmed me. I didn't know where to start, what to look for. In Maidstone, there was something specific. Here, there was a galaxy of things to sift; my friend's things.

In the mirror above the piano, I glimpsed my face. I remembered looking like this before: frozen, pinched, standing in my parents' house, after the accident. I had to sort out all their things; my older brothers, dealing with legalities, had left that task to me. Downstairs I'd glimpsed my face, ashen, in the big hall mirror which had once reflected my parents' parties. In defiance of my own image, I had begun the task; done it all — alone. It was good to remember that now. I looked again in this mirror, in this house. Gonzalez's story came back to me. I was not here to take inventory, to itemize household articles. I was here, quite specifically, to look for the hidden face: the double life. The best place to start was upstairs.

I was moving then. After those frozen moments, everything was going fast. My hands, still gloved, were opening drawers; my eyes scanning, moving. Bedside table. Drawer pulled out quickly; condoms, almost spilling. I paused, feeling another surge of guilt; I tried to remember the dumbwaiter.

I turned to the bureau. On top, a catch-all tray with odds and ends: pennies, safety pins, one earring, two keys, three paper clips, gold pin, more pennies. My eyes returned to the pin. It was shaped like a quill pen, resting on its side; I thought I'd seen it once before. Not on Eddie, on someone else, in a photograph — I couldn't remember, couldn't place it. The earring, too, seemed familiar. Clumsy in my gloves, I reached for it, but it fell back into the nest of pennies. The earring was flat, square. Eddie's? Lorna's? I couldn't remember. For a moment, I paused, thinking. Eddie and Lorna — could they be the lovers?

Downstairs, a clock chimed. Fifteen minutes had passed. I moved to the bathroom. Chaos here — lipsticks, creams, perfumes, powder: everything feminine, everything of a piece, except a pack of cigarettes, Eddie's brand,

and, at the end of a shelf: a heavy, masculine razor. Not hers — a woman's cordless shaver lay on the hamper.

Hating this, taking a breath, I opened the medicine cabinet and scanned the shelves: aspirin, Band-Aids, prescription bottle: Valium. Name on the label: Edwina Cassidy. Tall pump can, Lick Me Love Foam, strawberry flavor; I glanced at it twice. On the top shelf, a plastic packet. I leaned closer. It was a packet of syringes, unmarked; no brand name, just a blue band around each syringe. I stared at them. Drugs? Insulin? Abruptly, the gold pin flashed in my mind; an instant later, I was running down the stairs.

I went straight to the tall, full bookcase, searching the shelves, looking for a particular author: Andrew Hastings. I hadn't noticed his books here before; then again, I hadn't looked for them. Now my practiced eye picked them out of a jammed shelf: one copy each of his first books, three copies of his new one, *Rituals,* with a blank-spined book beside it.   I pulled them all out; another lay on its side at the back of the shelf, hidden by those I'd removed. I snatched it up, but its dusty jacket bore the name and picture of some obscure woman novelist. I dropped it back and dumped the other books onto the couch. The light outside was fading and I didn't dare turn on a lamp. Leaning down in my coat, I turned the first book over and looked at the jacket photo; then the next. Andrew's face, poised and somber, gazed out at me; I saw nothing unusual. Turning to *Rituals,* I looked closer — and heard my own sharp intake of breath. I held the photo to the window.

There, in Andrew's picture, was the gold quill: his tie clasp.

I stood staring at it. Then I flipped the book open to the flyleaf. Perhaps a special, personal inscription ... it was blank. I tried the other copies. Nothing. I stared at the cover of *Rituals,* as if some hidden mark, some scribble, might reveal itself. None did. The title, embossed in gold on a wine-dark ground, reminded me of the bishop's handsome books. Suddenly, then, I was reaching back into the shelf for that one discarded novel. I took off its dusty, feminine jacket and there — yet another copy of *R*^{*i*}*tuals.* Opening it, I saw that this one was inscribed; for a moment, I expected a love note to Eddie. On the flyleaf was small precise hand-writing — not the author's. I recognized it immediately.

Andrew [the inscription began]. How rich to see this luminous story in print, at last. A book to make its author proud.

I hope you enjoy reading this novel as much as I enjoyed writing it: every single word.

— Truly — Gerald

It would have been impossible for anyone to reproduce the flowing, complex signature, distinctively Gerald's. I read the inscription again, thinking of his tears, upstairs, the night of the party, and his halting words ... *A toast to a nameless writer* ... I thought of the argument I'd over-heard in the shop ... *I know my own work....* Gerald must have inscribed this at the party, then tucked it back into Andrew's box of books. Perhaps Andrew had discovered it and brought it here for safekeeping. More likely, Eddie had discovered it and tucked it away, so as not to distress Andrew. The inscription could look like a joke or a mix-up, but why keep this copy at all? As a trophy? Blackmail? Talisman? I'd think it through later. I dropped it into my bag; it wouldn't be missed right away.

Glancing at my watch, I turned to the book with the blank spine. As I'd hoped, it was a journal, and as I'd feared — the wrong kind: not a day book, but a record of

Eddie's feelings and dreams. Flipping pages, I saw my name over and over, and suddenly, again, I felt chilled. I turned a other page, then another, morbidly absorbed. Another page — turning it, I heard the *chink* of some small object against the hardwood floor. Stooping down, I fumbled for what had dropped from the book; then I held it, gleaming, in the palm of my glove--a key.

For a moment, it looked like all other keys: Jake's car keys, Eddie's house key. And then this one looked oddly familiar — like another I'd had recently in my hand. I saw, *on* one side, the small insignia of an anchor; on the other, an orange "G" on a white dot. He'd left me the spare, but this was Gerald's key: his key to Kelly's Boat House.

I was staring at it as I heard a car pull up outside. For a moment, I felt a spiral of panic. I stuck the key back into the journal, thrust journal and books back on the shelf, hoping they were in the right order. Steps came up the path. This house had no back door, so I'd just have to stand here, afraid, feeling foolish — but looking collected, casual. And I had about five seconds to practice.

The lock clicked; the door opened.

"Hi." I leaned, unhurried, against a table. "I was hoping you'd come before I left."

Eddie stared at me.

"Thanks for leaving the key out." I laid hers on the coffee table beside the art books. "Sorry — did I scare you? I was cleaning shelves, wanted to get these back to you."

Still silent, Eddie glanced at them.

"How was Maidstone?" I asked, trying to keep my voice neutral.

"Maidstone was ... a disappointment." Eddie's face was unreadable; in the dim room, her eyes looked dark, fathomless.

"I guess those leads fell through ... ?" Uneasy now, I started moving toward the door. "Well, you must be exhausted, let's talk later, okay? I'll give you a call."

Eddie's gaze was fixed on me. I watched her as my hand found the door knob. I don't remember what I said in the way of good-byes, or if I said anything at all. And then I was outside, walking down the path trying not to run, trying not to look behind me. Driving off, I tried not to speed. It was only as I turned the corner that I realized I was shaking.

By the time I'd returned to Weatherell's, I was pensive; no longer shaken. It was dark out now and the bookshop had closed a few minutes earlier. The lights were still on inside, and I walked up the steps in a spill of amber. Still thoughtful, I let myself in and, without any warning, was grabbed and held fast.

I screamed.

It was, I think, a scream capable of inducing cardiac arrest, a scream that had been coming all afternoon. The cat ran under the desk. Harley came running from the kitchenette. Startled, Jake let me go.

"Oh *God* — " Still shaking, I leaned back against him.

"Okay, let's start again, you've just come in, I *haven't* scared you...." His voice turned serious. "And there's news. They found Mrs. Lind."

"Alive?" I was almost afraid to ask.

"Definitely alive. Gonzalez questioned her."

"And?" My voice was edgy. "Anything?"

"Not much. Just that she was very well-paid, very loyal."

"To *whom*?"

"That's what she wouldn't say."

"Damn it."

"Oh, and she was an ambulance driver for ten years, for the Brits, in Gabon, West Africa. That part checks out."

I felt suddenly tired. It checked out; it solved nothing. I had hoped that Mrs. Lind would somehow solve everything. I had hoped to learn that after all this did not involve a friend; or friends. I took a breath.

"I just broke into Eddie's house," I said.

Jake and Harley looked at me.

"Well ... more or less," I amended. "I know where she keeps her spare key, I've used it before, *with* permission, and ..." I paused. This was harder than I'd expected. "And I used it today. Without permission. I found some things...." Again I paused; then, finally, I told them. The words sounded strange, spoken aloud, and those moments remain a blur in my mind.

The next clear image I have is of a table, the table in the shop's kitchen. We settled around it, with drinks — no ice. It was there that I showed the others the book; it was there that each of us heard what the others had learned.

When I think of that next hour, I hear a blend of voices: quiet voices, each one adding to the whole, setting small odd chips of information into a mosaic — one that now assumed a clear shape. Some of what we set down there came from memory, discovery, search, journals; some was conjectured, based on what we knew of the people in this story. That night, we were all storytellers, but what I remember is not who spoke, or when. What I remember is the story we told in the lamplight, in the bookshop. As we told it, we listened. And as we listened, we saw.

Georgetown lay quiet in the dark.

It was late. It was cold. They were waiting for him by the water.

He had suggested this meeting place because he felt strong here. The boat house reminded him of a church, with its steep roof, its spirelike turret. As a child he had always felt strong in churches, bookstores, and by water. He had drifted from the churches, but never from books; never from the water. Since his boyhood, water had brought him a particular release from inner storms; strength that flowed into him like a current. Wherever he'd drifted, he always sought out rivers, ocean, lakes, and when he'd arrived in Georgetown, he had come to this boat club before he had an apartment.

And so it was here that Gerald had chosen to meet Andrew. It would take strength to break from this man whose approval he craved; this man so like his father — elegant, devious, eccentric. But kind. Here, Gerald had thought, was the kindness his own father lacked, the patience to nurture his writing. For a time, it had seemed so genuine.

Now, Gerald took out his flashlight; he watched the two figures outlined against the boat house. He had counted on Andrew coming alone. Another small betrayal. Gerald tried to summon all the reasons to break from Andrew: the facade of holiness, the rituals, the pretenses. And Eddie; she disliked Gerald, and was permitted to set him aside, put him off, distance him, on Andrew's behalf.

Walking toward them now, Gerald recalled what he had seen, the night of Mr. Archer's memorial service. He had arrived early at Weatherell's. Alice was still upstairs; the meeting room, to his surprise, was locked. Taking the keys from the desk, Gerald had unlocked the room and slid into a chair at the back. The lights were off. Down front, there was a table arranged like an altar, candles lit at either end, Mr. Archer's inkwell set between them, as if in offering. Gerald's eyes had filled, and then, from the front of the room, he had heard a soft sweet moan. Leaning into the aisle, he saw two half-naked figures twining together before the table, their skin flashing in the darkness like fish skimming the surface of a lake. Mouth on mouth, they tumbled and turned and then, with a series of quick sharp bites, her face moved down his chest, his belly, to nuzzle between his legs. His body arched and he was lifting her, turning her onto her hands knees; in the candlelight he was astride her, riding, rocking, his head back in another wild high moan, while above them the inkwell glinted, and in the back of the room, Gerald wept silently, his knuckles against his mouth.

He could not forget it, but did not speak of it; he could not betray Andrew yet. The night of the book party, Gerald had talked of it cryptically to Alice, upstairs, but had veiled the identities, even then. He wasn't ready, earlier, even when he had realized that Andrew had drawn the life, the essence, the juice, from his own work-in-progress. The theft, he guessed, had occurred systematically, chapter by chapter, as Gerald brought each to Andrew for critique: a private workshop with his hero. At first he had not believed it, as he'd stolen glances at Andrew's new novel in galleys; it had seemed coincidence. And then, in the bound book itself, Gerald had read about his own brief affair with Lorna, translated into Andrew's lyrical prose, along with Gerald's other characters, his plot, complete with twists, now immortalized in *Rituals.*

Gerald, that day, had felt abruptly old. He had walked into Andrew's stone house, coming unexpectedly, and had sat waiting while Andrew took a phone call upstairs. Gerald had wandered over to the rolltop desk where Andrew wrote in longhand, in the light of a green-shaded lamp. Flashing across the desk now, as if rising from Andrew's swift, strong handwriting, were the characters of Gerald's own novel, moving, rustling, in a long apologetic line, and finally veering away from him to Andrew. He read more pages. There, within this book, Gerald saw the blue kitchen floor where he had sat as a child in a slice of sun; he saw the water where he had rowed for hours, and the one luminous morning that had turned the river into flowing sacred space.

He read on, seeing Andrew's character take form now; taking over the story, making it his, bending it to him and raping it, chapter by chapter, page by page. Gerald's eyes stung. He shut the book, turning it over. He looked for some time at the jacket photo; at this man who had been teacher, father, guide. And then he had heard Andrew's tread on the stair. Turning, Gerald had seen that tall figure he had strained, most days, to glimpse — the figure he saw now, waiting by the boat house.

Gerald said nothing, only took out his key and let them inside, into his strong place. There, amid the sound of water, the creak of wood, he had confronted Andrew once more, explaining he'd already drafted a letter to inform the others. This time, Andrew had listened, and there was a silence as they stood there by the boat-slip, looking at the water. In the shadows, Andrew had apologized — and then his arm had locked around Gerald's neck. The men crashed to the dock; the flashlight rolled into the water. Briefly, Gerald had twisted free, one hand grabbing at the splintered dock, and then something had struck the back of his head. Points of flame had danced before his eyes, then faded into the water.

Eddie set the oar back in its rack on the wall. Her blow had been careful — enough to stun, not kill, as they had planned. In the dark, by the water, they had waited, listening to the faint boiling sound of Gerald's breathing. Over them, the great raftered roof soared to a steep point, and around them, the boat-slips looked like shimmering graves. Eddie played her own light over the boy, as he lay slumped between Andrew's hands. "No mark, no blood," she noted, glancing up.

"Perfect." Andrew kept his gaze on the water. "No one will know." He grabbed Gerald's wrist and felt the pulse slow, then cease. They waited, listening, for a full twenty minutes, while Eddie kept watch, and en forced the water from Gerald's lungs. Andrew turned him over now, holding him face up, and Eddie, with a boning knife, removed the eyes. Her hands were deft, quick; she had described this procedure in her unfinished novel and had thought through every slice of membrane, every severed tissue.

She wasn't certain how this had come to her, this final twist to the plan. The missing eyes, of course, would tally with Alice's book about Evangeline; the original manuscript, discussed in workshop, was common knowledge. If Gerald was found this way, it would tie his death to Alice — and tie it off from her and Andrew. Then, too, Gerald had seen too much. Perhaps, Eddie thought, that was the real reason. That was the reason, too, in her unfinished novel, for this same mutilation — a scene that came to her, in dreams, until she wrote it down.

"You're amazing." Andrew watched her now.

"Did you think I'd be sick?" She eased the slippery forms into a plastic freezer bag, ignoring a private wave of nausea.

"No, my wife would have been sick. Not you, love."

"I haven't been able to sleep since he saw us."

"It wouldn't matter, except for the divorce."

"That matters."

"It does." He touched her cheek.

"The plagiarism's more damaging, I know." She took the key from Gerald's pocket. "No trouble, getting his letter?"

"None. And he thought that would surprise me. Arrogant, spoiled to the last — playing the writer." Andrew unrolled a cleaner's bag, and together they wrapped the body. Both bags, large and small, were set inside the crate brought earlier, from the car; the crate Eddie had salvaged from the bookshop's alley. The dimensions were exactly right, and the whole thing fit neatly into the trunk of the Jaguar, out tonight on loan from the embassy. Mrs. Lind knew only of a "special reception" that required a special car. She had been flattered, Andrew knew, to do him a favor, and he had paid her well. Beneath her surface dithers, she was shrewd; he knew she understood the need for silence, for her own sake as well. The loan was smooth, and so was the drive back to Georgetown.

They neared the bookstore, entering its alley around the corner. Its lights out, the car moved slowly toward Weatherell's cellar door. No winos slept here tonight, nor had they seen Dinah where she often was, out front. Rolling down a window, Andrew listened, hearing only the faint tap of Alice's typewriter, above. Swiftly, quietly, the door was unlocked, the trunk was opened and shut and the crate was inside. They stood listening again; the cellar was silent, as was the floor above. Eddie played her light over the crates and boxes; briefly, they leapt into brightness then sank away as the long white beam moved on. Last, she illuminated the dumbwaiter, empty now. Just before leaving tonight, she had cleared away those books that Alice had forgotten. Now the volumes lay in neat piles on the floor.

"Ready, love?" Andrew's whisper, in the dark, sounded rough, erotic, aroused. These were the words he whispered, sometimes, in bed, before he filled her, and she knew that somehow this excited him, as it did her.

"Come." Her whisper. She could feel the heat between them; for a moment, they said nothing. Then, together, they lifted the body from the crate and curled it in the dumbwaiter, sliding the plastic wrapping away. Andrew took the smaller bag and, while Eddie began to pack the crate with books, he moved up the cellar stairs and opened the door to the bookshop. Carefully, he let the door click shut; for some moments, Eddie would be locked in down there, but should anything go wrong, they knew she could leave through the alley. Andrew stepped softly into the shop's main room.

All the lights were on. This startled him — he paused, listening again. Overhead, the typing continued and no footsteps made the old floors creak. He turned the lights off, fearing they might draw attention, then turned them on again. Alice had left them that way; they must be found as they had been. Edging past a shelf, he saw the two illuminated bay widows and the backs of all the books arrayed there. He could see his own novels; from its jacket, his own face gazed pensively at him.

For just an instant, he let himself gaze back, and then he was moving soundlessly again, in his old, inelegant rubber-soled shoes. Quickly, he was in the kitchenette, opening the freezer door with a gloved hand. Cold vapor rushed out at his head — a mess in there, he thought, disgusted: Popsicles a year old, freezer never defrosted. He emptied the contents of the small plastic bag beside an ice tray. That, at least, would be used sometime.

Back in the store, moving at a crouch, he edged back toward the window to check again for Dinah. She was there now, huddled in the doorway; wrapped in a blanket, with her hat pulled low over her eyes, she seemed asleep. Andrew glanced away from her. He could never look at her for long, not since the dreams of his father had come back; his father who had ended on the streets. The dreams had begun for Andrew when the writing started to run dry. He had tried, to turn his mind instead to the priests who had taught him, but their faces would not come, in reverie or sleep; only the face of a nameless priest, unknown, distant, misted, somehow promising relief.

Abruptly, Andrew moved back to the cellar door, unlocking it and switching on his flashlight. Behind him, the door shut and locked. Eddie looked up, questioning, as he came down the narrow flight of unrailed step.; he hated these. Alice was careless, Alice would not listen, never had things fixed. Upstairs, she was typing away: he hated her for that — all that lurid stuff just pouring out. Writers' Bloc respected him, but her warmth drew people's affections.

Appalling to think a writer of her quality would challenge him, criticize him and his policies, his style, the whole leadership of the group. She would be a problem, even if Gerald had not told her too much at the party; Andrew was sure he had, as was Eddie, and afterward they had been cautious.

Moving through the cellar now, Andrew made a sign of caution to Eddie, and mouthed Dinah's name. Eddie nodded, playing her light over the area once more. The temporary coffin seemed to have vanished, fading back into the complex gridwork of the cellar floor. Eddie had packed the crate with that shipment of children's books left by Alice on the dumbwaiter. If the books were never found, it would be assumed the killer took them. If they were, they would further incriminate Alice: after all, they were her books, packed into a crate she herself had marked in public. Perfect: now Eddie and Andrew could leave the scene without any suspicious freight; without the risk of carrying the crate, disposing of it — or, worse, getting caught with it. They could simply slip out with two ordinary plastic bags, one from the cleaner's, one from the kitchen; nothing more. Checking everything one last time, they unlocked the alley door.

The alley was clear. The typing continued, above. Headlights out, gears in neutral, the Jaguar rolled down the alley's slight incline and into the street. Soon the car was in gear, moving toward the river again, where the plastic bags, weighted with stones, sank into the dark water. Within half an hour, the Jaguar was left on a prearranged street, and within an hour, Andrew was in his house, Eddie in hers.

But in her house, Eddie could not sleep. She sat smoking in the dim living room, watching the play of headlights on the cat's-eye marbles in the bowl on the table. She went over each step, each scene: freeze-frame, rewind, fast forward. She looked for some mistake; saw none. Her gloves had been discarded on the way home. The car was taken care of, Mrs. Lind was well-paid and, in any case, knew nothing. There were no more loose ends she could find.

Still, somehow, she felt uneasy — not because of Gerald, she knew. He had always seemed demented, dangerous, on the edge of violence. Inevitably, she believed, he would have done grave harm — beyond written threats. Gerald strikingly resembled her ex-husband: the green eyes, the intensity, the brilliance; the rages. He had dimmed her life for too long, and afterward, there had been too many false starts: the wrong men, the wrong jobs. Then she'd come to Weatherell's and at last, she'd sensed an end to the repeating story. She'd liked the store's prestige and her new responsibility; she loved being surrounded by books. Here, she had begun to write, an old dream, and here she had made a new friend in Alice. And then Eddie had met Andrew; another married man, but distant from his wife, close to separating.

Eddie's new story was unfolding quickly, beautifully, when suddenly — Gerald, this terrible business. Andrew, threatened with plagiarism — a literary scandal that could ruin him. It would ruin all their plans, she knew that too, simply because she knew Andrew. Caught in a professional storm, he would back off from a personal one, remaining with his wealthy, well-placed wife, whose money he might need. Eddie did not blame him, only recognized the fact; she would do the same.

But if that happened, she would be abandoned, and she could not let that happen, ever again. Instead, she had devised this plan, which would deal with scandal, ruin, Gerald — and Alice, who could also endanger things with what she might have heard, or learned. If all else failed, Eddie kept that book, signed by Gerald at the party — her insurance policy.

Alice. Eddie thought of her as she sat watching the bowl of marbles on the table. Alice saw things. Alice had a gift for sensing the Shadow in others; Eddie wondered, once again, how much she knew. Alice had a way with others — but others were swayed easily enough, as Eddie had found recently; she had let some rumors, some untruths about Alice to loose in Writers' Bloc. Eddie rose and moved toward her bookcase, pulling out Alice's two books. She took off the jackets and spread them out on the coffee table, studying the face in the photos a long while, until it seemed that Alice looked into the room, at her — at everything. Abruptly, Eddie tipped the coffee table, covering that gaze with a spill of cat's-eye marbles.

The next day, all went seamlessly. The alibis, well-
planned, were well confirmed. Eddie's sister and
Andrew's wife presented perfect stories. Lorn and Brad
also had safe alibis, a drink together in Chevy Chase. No
one knew then that Dinah had seen all of them in
Georgetown: Brad, pacing on a bridge, thinking of
visiting Alice; Lorna, waiting for a date who stood her up;
Andrew, moving down a back street, above the university,
where he'd left his car, and Eddie in a restaurant.

Nothing was found by the detectives at Weatherell's or
at Gerald's apartment, before it was sealed off. The day
before the murder, Andrew had taken Gerald's accusing
letter, first retyping the salutation on Gerald's own
machine — the letter had obligingly opened with the
initial

Everything continued smoothly, though Andrew had
been careful, dispatching Mrs. Lind to watch Alice and
Jake in Maidstone; but again, nothing gave cause for
alarm. Nothing — until that next Writers' Bloc meeting,
and Dinah's outburst. At Eddie's house, afterward, she
and Andrew had conferred.

"How much did she see?" Eddie paced and smoked.

"How the hell do I know?" Andrew exploded.

"She's not a drunk. Not mentally ill. Alice told me.
Never been hospitalized. She could be a credible witness."
Each word seemed vibrant , a note on a lute string.

"She won't be a witness," Andrew said quietly, after a
while.

He had some spare insulin syringes upstairs in the
bathroom; he had a friend, a painter, who used heroin and
knew where it was sold nearby. That in part was fairly
simple; the difficult part was locating Dinah. Eddie
recalled seeing her often, through the back door of a
Georgetown restaurant, where Dinah picked up leftovers
most nights; Andrew's car sped there, arriving as Dinah

left. They had watched her gingery hair catching the streetlights, a plastic bag swinging from one hand. They waited until she was well away from the restaurant, and then Eddie had called out to her. Recognizing a familiar face, Dinah had waved. A waiter, smoking in the doorway, recalled that later — and the car.

Somewhere in the dark, the car had stopped, pulled over; Andrew, deft and practiced from his daily insulin shots, had injected Dinah. The heroin was an overdose; Eddie had held Dinah in the back seat till she died. "She's better off," Andrew had said quietly, in the dark car. "I remember, I know." They had covered her with a blanket and driven downtown, into half-lit streets where broken glass shimmered like ice the sidewalks, and the buildings were abandoned, boarded up. No one seemed near as they propped Dinah in an alley, leaving the syringe where it would be seen and noted; no one was near until they were leaving — there was shouting then, and running feet, but no one had seen them clearly, if at all, and no one down there knew them. Again, everything appeared seamless.

Only one thing worried Eddie now: Dinah's missing bags and notebook — probably lost, long gone. Even so, Eddie dreamed about that notebook repeatedly, the way she used to dream of turning into Dinah. She dreamed, too, of an elegant, fine-boned man, about her age, his features etched like a cameo, his shirt ruffled, quaint. There was a power to these dreams that seemed to give her strength, the shape of new ideas, and the skill to dissemble at Weatherell's after Alice had been discredited.

Soon, however, Eddie would leave the bookshop. It would go on as always, as would Brad and Lorna and the rest. Gerald Shane and Dinah Lasko would become two more unsolved homicides in Washington, D.C. And Eddie would be free.

Late one night, she lay naked with Andrew on her living room rug. He had swept all the debris off the broad glass coffee table and, after making love, the two of them had lain beneath it, looking up through the cleared expanse of glass, as if through a skylight. Laughing, Andrew had reached up and scattered the cat's-eye marbles across the table; across Eddie's body as she lay under the pane of glass. They had watched the play of headlights on the winking spheres above them, as the marbles flashed and rolled and clicked, gaining some momentum of their own; faster, brighter, crazily now — till, abruptly, unnerved, Andrew threw the table over on its side, and they heard the marbles roll all directions in the dark.

Around the table in the bookshop, we sat silent now. In the lamplight, faces looked strained. We had just told a story of people we knew, people who had been our friends — suddenly, they were gone, it seemed, transmuted, unknowable, except, somehow, through history. And now historical parallels stood revealed, as if in harsh light. We wrote out names, lining them up as if in some strange roll call:

Hap Dowell, agent—Johnny Johnson, peddler
Barton Gold, publisher—Matthew Blair, council president
Phil Romano, dean—Joan Dowd, retired midwife
Thomas Archer, librarian—Daniel Peagram, historian
Alberta Lind, servant—Cass Tanner, servant
Kelina White, survivor—Ishmael Jenkins, survivor
Harley Jenkins, innkeeper—Faith Roper, taverner
Jake Randolph, pilot—Luke Arnold, potter
Gerald Shane, witness—Nick Rhoades, witness

Dinah Lasko, witness—Lily Jenkins, witness
Brad Stein, author—Tom Kemp, brewer
Lorna Mart, author—William Simms, warden
Andrew Hastings, author—Rev. Jonas Drummond,
    priest
Edwina Cassidy, writer—Perry Cleete, councilman
Alice Grey, author—Evangeline Smith, midwife
Elizabeth Maidstone, patroness— ?

I thought a moment. Always with me, always in the shop that bore her name — "Kate Ryan Weatherell," I wrote in. The list was complete. It was a long time before we spoke again and when we did, it was perfunctory: talk of logistics, immediate details. None of us could say what we felt.

It as decided that I would call Gonzalez and tell him this story, while the others kept watch on Andrew and Eddie. My visit, this afternoon, might have caused alarm. It was all decided but we delayed, fumbling for keys, as if we did not want this to become too real — as if we did not want this story to come true. Then, with few words, we went off in different directions: Jake in his car, Harley in hers, while I turned toward the stairs. For a moment, I looked back. The bookshop was serene. Its large bay windows were lit, sending pools of amber across the floor. The last thing I saw was the rich, muted glow of books.

■

PART FOUR

NOVEMBER 27, 1991

« 24 »

Idid not plan to write the rest this way.

Everything seemed grimly neat, somber but predictable. The remaining unpleasantness would happen elsewhere, handled and reported by Gonzales: one final chapter to render from notes, as with distant history. There seemed little reason to doubt this; after all, we had traced the pattern, cracked the code.

Actually, there were many reasons to doubt this, but I wasn't paying attention to them at the time. At the time, I was trying to get hold of Gonzalez, who was out of the office. He would call in; I could call back. Somehow, we hadn't factored in the possibility that Gonzalez might be working other cases. Nor had we assumed that Andrew and Eddie might be anywhere except in their houses.

Waiting for the call, I scanned the sources on my desk. I had not probed much into the fates of Evangeline's contemporaries; after her death, that had seemed a foot-note. The official account, I recalled, had stated that most had died peacefully in their beds. Their own beds. The account, an addendum to the original report, had been written by Warden Simms, shortly before he died in his. I glanced at this account again:

Luke Arnold set sail for unknown destination, four months after Evangeline's house was burnt.

Tom Kemp married one year after Evangeline's death, bought farmland , raised a family.

P'erry Cleete eventually went back to England.

The priest eventually went into seclusion.

In he lamplight on my desk, that word "eventually" seemed to grow blacker, bolder, more pronounced. Why, in both cases, no precise measure of time? Why, in both cases, that same vague adverb, used nowhere else in this account?

Now across the green rug, I spread out my other sources, and for some moments I did not hear the tick of the clock or the purr of the cat, nor did I listen for the phone.

Peagram was silent on the fates of priest and councilman; a silence now seemed curious. His last mention of them was in reference to the drafting of a confession to be signed by Evangeline. This had never been signed, never surfaced; I'd known of it from the start. There was nothing more here.

I tilted the lampshade and shifted more papers. The Maidstone/Jenkins Xeroxes came to hand, with a spare, swift description of Evangeline, glimpsed at her upstairs window as a mob hurled torches into her dwelling ... I skipped ahead:

That very night, Priest & Councilman surely slipped away ... 'twas later said that Mr. Cl. returned to London, on pressing Family Matters

... 'twas said also the Rev'd Mr. D. went into Seclusion to pass his life in Prayer, whilst his new Curate assumed his Parish dutyes. However, Servants talk when payd, and those closing up each man's House found disarray, empty Trunks, and Monies, this being rumuored about 'til Mr. Simms took upon hymself both Propertyes....

"Gonzalez," I said aloud. The cat opened one golden eye and looked at me. I reached for the phone — but how to explain a suspicion that the suspects might be leaving the country? In the end, I didn't explain, I just left another message. Gonzalez had not returned.

I scrabbled through the piles of paper, found another reference — one that tossed up new questions. The day after the fatal fire, Faith Roper closed her tavern "from this sory Sunup til next," and wrote a note to "Mistress Elizabeth," which was preserved with the Maidstone family documents:

Mlady [it began], This Day we both Greev — Take this comfort styll — last even I seen Rev & Cl enter E's Howse wyth a Grate Skrole but she neer set a Name to it else twod be told — brave Sole — God Bless E S & you Mlady — Yrs; F. Roper

I sat staring at the letter, comparing it to the other accounts. And then, because I could not call Gonzalez again, quite yet, I began a kind of historical doodling, while I waited:

The two men seemed to stand like dark trees outside the back door of Evangeline's house. The paper in their hands appeared as pale as skin, even after she had let them in, for they permitted no candles to be lit. Their voices were

low as they explained the confession, but their manner was strained, urgent, and Evangeline felt the press of their wills against hers.

"There isn't much time, sign and have done." Cleete looked at her, then toward the window for a moment. "Sign and we'll get you away."

Evangeline held the paper near the hearth and saw that the words professed "witchcraft, sorcery, and other magical arts."

Cleete drew forth pen, inkwell, sandcaster. "You never cared much for what folk thought of you. And you never ceased to care about your island...."

He knew her too well. For an instant, before her, she saw the island's sun-streaked earth, its waters glimmering beyond ... and then she let it slip away. She glanced up at the priest. His countenance appeared to tighten, as if to contain intense strength; some force that coiled within him, waiting, poised, unblinking. Evangeline sensed this as one senses a snake in weeds, before the head rises to sight, and now she kept her gaze fixed on the men. Even if she had believed their promise, she could never set her name to that paper. Not only for truth's sake, but for her father's sake, and Luke's, and even more for the sake of Nick, who had lain dead on his hearth.

"I'll not sign," she said quietly.

"You will, I think." The priest moved closer.

Evangeline turned away, slowly, precisely, and cast the scroll into the fire. For what seemed a long time, no one spoke. She stood listening to the paper burn and the men breathe and the creak of the house in the wind....

I paused, waiting for the next image, and below me, I heard the creak of this house, though there was no wind tonight and no one here. How absurd, I thought — this story was like a tale told late at night when we were children, deliberately trying to frighten one another. I was always quite good at frightening my older brothers; I would watch with satisfaction as they glanced over their shoulders, listening to every odd sound .... just as I was doing now.

Odd sounds, downstairs, I thought. I listened again, annoyed with myself. If I were in a normal frame of mind, I would have said the front door had clicked shut. I would have said I heard a few steps in the shop's main room. For another instant, I discounted this; distinctly, then, I heard another step. It must be Jake, back too soon, or Harley — something had gone wrong. *Damn Gonzalez,* I thought, as I ran down the steps and emerged into the dim shop.

"Jake — ?" I broke off.

In the liquid amber light from the windows, I saw them standing, waiting. They had heard me typing as they came in, or I might have heard them first. They had entered with their own keys and stood listening as I came down the stairs, and perhaps they had exchanged a sm le as I called Jake's name.

They seemed to smile now, watching me, and abruptly, all my theories, all my elaborate stitchery started to unravel. The story I'd constructed appeared to me as some flimsy costume, hemmed with masking tape and spit, the wrong size and style for either figure in this scene. Eddie and Andrew stood there, solid, real, looking as they always had on hundreds of other nights and days, at dinner tables and traffic lights and bookshelves, over coffee cups and reams of paper in this very shop.

"We were hoping you'd be here," said Eddie. In her words, I heard the vague echo of my own, to her, that afternoon. "We came to get a book you borrowed."

I looked at her.

"Let's not dance about." Andrew's tone was brisk. "You took a book that wasn't yours today. You know it, we know it, no need for pretense. It had a humorous inscription from Gerald, a very personal joke — "

Upstairs, the phone began to ring. I turned; Andrew's hand was on my arm. The ringing stopped, then began again. Gonzalez? Jake? Surely they would be alarmed by silence, one of them would come.

"I'd like the book back," Andrew was saying. "It has great sentimental value for me."

"Is that why you kept it hidden? At Eddie's? In someone else's dust jacket?" Suddenly I was angry, brave.

"That was my doing." Eddie stepped in smoothly, too smoothly. "I was afraid it would distress Andrew, so I took it home from the party, stashed it away, silly of me, really."

Silly of me, really ... It sounded like a line from some play; it sounded rehearsed. I imagined them dancing swiftly from Plan A to Plan B, and as I watched them now, I saw again the figures waiting for Gerald by the water. Upstairs, the phone began to ring again.

"Okay, I saw the book — but why would I take it?" I was stalling.

"Alice." Andrew looked at me. "We know each other far too well for this. If you hope to clear your name somehow, using *that* inscription ..." He shook his head. "That's just desperate, very sad." His voice grew gentle. "Don't do this to yourself...."

I studied the floorboards so he couldn't read my face. What an actor he was — that costume wasn't quite so flimsy, after all, it fit him and this scene quite well. "All right," I said, subdued. "The book's in the cellar."

Ignoring an exchange of looks, I led the way; I knew they wouldn't go down first, and going first had some advantages. Firmly, I propped the Cellar door ajar; if it shut, I'd be locked down there with them, since the galley door was still tightly sealed. I flicked a switch, and the cellar stairs sprang into clarity — beyond them, darkness. I planned to run directly down, trap them among the crates, and dodge away, but on the second step down, Andrew's arm locked swiftly around my neck. For a moment, tiny brilliant suns began to burst before my eyes; I saw the murky water in the boat house. With one free hand, I flailed out, groping for the wall, the light switch; darkness snapped down around us once again.

Swearing, Andrew tried to grab my hand — I pulled away from him and we slipped off balance, in some bizarre embrace, crashing against the stairs. Eddie's long nails raked my scalp, gripped my hair, and the three of us thrashed there, skidding down the steps, as we clung like crabs to one another. Halfway down, I felt a sudden, sickening tilt, and we were veering over the stairs' narrow edge. Clinging to a step, I felt some weight lift away from me; below, I heard another crash, a brief low cry, and Eddie's fingers sprang from my hair. In seconds, she was down the steps and in the cellar, pulling on a light bulb's cord.

A patch of floor appeared, shifting in that swinging glare, where Andrew lay dazed, his forehead bloodied; Eddie bent over him. For an instant, caught between an urge to help, an urge to flee, I did not move. But now Eddie was turning toward me — and I was wheeling, climbing, crawling up the stairs. Ahead of me, the steps seemed to fan out and lengthen like a road, and beyond, from the doorway, a vague glow seemed like some remote dawn. Slowly, slowly, one step, one more, closer — something closed around my ankle. Eddie's fingers, strong and hard, gripped my leg as if it were a rope that she would climb. Clinging to the stairs, I tried to shake her loose — she held on; her teeth scraped my skin. I pulled back; sharper now, I felt the edges of her teeth, the wetness of her mouth — I twisted, kicking, and abruptly her grip broke. I was plunging up into the shop then, like a diver breaking water.

For several minutes, I just leaned there, against the cellar door. Then, although I knew it was locked, I wedged an old trunk against it, and called Gonzalez from the desk downstairs. This time, I got through. He was there and I didn't need to say a lot; he'd be on his way. At last, I climbed another flight of stairs; this time to my garret, my safe place, to wait. For good measure, I locked myself in.

Looking around my dormered, peaceful workroom, I felt a sudden wash of gratitude. I was safe, scarcely bruised — and the cycle, finally, was broken. The eaves leaned over me, maternal and protective, and around my chair, the green rug spread, pondlike and serene. I gathered the papers from the floor, glancing at the last page I had written, and realized what must have happened to Evangeline.

She had tried to dart away then, and the men had seized her, dragging her from the window, where she could be seen, and down the cellar steps. Suddenly, she knew, this had been their intention all along. The priest's arm tightened around her as she struggled, and Cleete grabbed her by the hair, the three of them struggling on the narrow stairs; then the were pitching down into the dark. There was a crash — the priest cried out, and Cleete loosed his grip on Evangeline. In that moment, she was up the stairs, bolting the cellar door behind her. As she leaned against it....

I glanced out the window. The dark street was empty and quiet, with few lights on across the way. About five minutes had passed since I'd called Gonzalez; it usually took him twenty minutes to get across town. I was not good at waiting and I was especially bad at it tonight — with two people locked in my cellar. I tried not to think of them; not so easy. Had I bolted the dumbwaiter door? Abruptly, I stood. Yes — I had. I sat down again, glancing from the phone to my papers. Distraction was needed, in the form that worked the best. Once again, I let myself out of this night, as through a back door, and into another one, long before, that could not hurt me now.

Evangeline sat by the window, watching the dark and feeling it shift like water when the wind changes and the air grows heavy. And now, on the dark, she saw the glimmering of distant lights, like a clutch of lanterns. They moved closer, steady and swift — torches, trailing flames against the Sky, coming faster now, streaming like an army's banner on the dark! She was still upstairs as they encircled the house, as the first torch crashed through the window.

I stopped typing and looked up. Sitting on my desk, the cat flicked her tail and knocked a pen to the floor. The room sloped over me, bright and still and warm. The cellar was secure and soon Gonzalez would be here. It was only words on a page making me uneasy.

Another crash of splintering glass below; more torches, hurled into the house. Evangeline opened an upstairs casement, tried to call a warning to the crowd: "The priest is here, and the councilman — " The crowd laughed, mocking her, and her words blew back in her face with the wind. With that wind, she knew, at least it would go fast. She moved quickly toward the bedchamber door, then stopped: the downstairs room was taking flame, filled with

pitch and smoke. The hearthside bench was burning like
a log, flames began to lick along the wooden floor....

Red's ears had flattened against her head; she paced the
desk as I looked up again. I listened; heard nothing. The
cat's fur stood on end.

And then I smelled the smoke, acrid and near. I
listened for the shrill o f smoke alarms, but there was no
sound except the snapping of wood — a series of sharp
cracks, like branches breaking, and the noise jumped from
point to point like a series of relay signals. For an
instant, I stood in disbelief, as if I were caught in the bad
dream that woke me, weeks ago.

Through the house, now, the fire began to send an
eerie roar like a rush of wind, and that roar broke all
sense of unreality. I picked up Red and set her out on the
roof. The cat gave me a reproachful look and waited.
Then, somewhere below, there was a crash — and Red
took off across the shingles, jumped to another roof and
was lost to sight.

I snatched up my last few pages, tossed them in my
bag and, fumbling, unlocked my workroom door. I threw
it open — abruptly, it swung shut. I stared — air
currents shifting, in the heat? Grabbing the doorknob, I
heard the bolt shoot home from the other side. Now, amid
the heat, I felt cold. I rattled the knob, struggled with the
lock. It would not turn. For an instant, I pressed my ear
to the door. No footsteps. No sound but the fire. Picking
up a chair, I smashed it against the door; it didn't even
shudder.

I wheeled around. Three strides took me to the
window; it slid shut. Looking out, I saw people below now
— only a handful, as if they'd just noticed; no fire trucks
yet. If I could just get out on the roof, a ladder could
reach —

The window seemed frozen: it wouldn't open, wouldn't budge. I smashed the chair against it — the glass would not break. Again, again, I swung at the window. Sweat plastered my hair to my forehead; my blouse clung to my back. I lifted the chair one more time — the window might have been made of steel.

Shouting, I pounded on the glass. From below, faces gazed up: faces hard as flat pale stones; eyes dark, fathomless, unblinking — a dim frieze of figures, rustling, whispering, hands upraised in flaring light....

The shutters flew closed across the window.

Sitting at my desk now, I look around at my green rug, the cherry rocker, all my books, as if I have never seen them before. The story is still playing out as it did with Evangeline. Nothing I have done has stopped it.

Somehow, I called it — summoned the story back with my own words, and that old darkness found new cracks to enter, new vessels to fill, new players to exploit. *You're locked into a shadow-dance, writing....* Somewhere, during this month, though, the lock has broken. Was it in that truck, lighting up the fields? Or was it in knowing Evangeline Smith, the healer? Was it in the circle of nameless, forgotten people, offering bread? Or perhaps in the blue gaze of a parking lot manager? Or in another gaze, across this room, from that rocking chair?

As if it matters now. Even the irony doesn't matter: Eddie and Andrew and I, trapped together. Perhaps, somehow, they've broken down the cellar door and slipped away. Perhaps they set this fire only to get caught in it themselves. Perhaps there is no logical answer. Again, it doesn't seem to matter.

My eyes water from the smoke — harder breathing now. It must be like this, drowning. For a moment, I see

Perkins Cove once more: the accident, the ambulance ...
and I let it go, all of it, at last. Dimly now, I hear the wail
of sirens outside. Below, the fire howls like a demon. I
won't listen. I've tried to tell this story, tell it true, and
it's not finished.

I will finish it. Even if the firemen can't get in —
which begins to seem likely. Even so.

The phone works but the connection is hazy; I dial and
hear mostly static. The fax machine, thank God, still
seems to function. Maybe I can get these pages out to
Jake, who will understand them, and put them with the
others he has kept for me. There's a fax machine at his
airline, at the airport; I scrabble through my desk for
Jake's card, for MetroAir's number....

Above the fire's voice, the fax machine begins to whir.
I feed in one page, then another. They go through — odd
how well new tech carries old tales. Downstairs now, I
hear the crash of beams. The bookstore shudders. Soon,
I know, it will start collapsing.

I try not to think of all those bindings, all those pages
turning to ash. I try to think only of this page before me
in the typewriter. Above the keys, my hands tremble.

Now, amid the smoke, there is a streak of cool air on
my face. There is, it seems, the gentle press of hands on
mine. I must be passing out. Perhaps I already have, and
am only dreaming that I write. Light, pure and piercing,
seems to gather in around me and

■

« 25 »

I'm dreaming. I'm flying — flying over forests, dense and green, sun on my back, air bearing me up. Beneath me, I see fields and pastures and a great brown scar of road. Lower, now, descending through a flock of white-winged birds, I see the glint from a well, spots of color at doorsteps. Lower still, gliding face- down on the air, I see, just below, the ruins of a house ... and then it is gone: sky, house, town, all. For a moment, light — only light.

Light glints off the cars parked in this lot, in Maidstone. I left the Chevy here — when was it? Yesterday? A week ago? The man who runs the lot will know. He remembers me, I see that now. I don't tell him how I got here; I'm not sure of that. Blue eyes glimmer in his dark face; I remember him. He asks no questions, just tells me again he's made that phone call; the number I gave him.

I don't remember giving him a phone number but I do remember the fire. It seems just moments ago I was there in the bookstore, typing in the smoke. The last page is

still in my hands. The smell of smoke is still in my
clothes.

Leaning against my car, the lot's manager looks past
me. I follow his gaze. Someone is walking toward us; I
realize it's Jake — Jake, with an odd expression on his
face and a catch in his step and a glimmer in his eyes. He
lifts me into his arms and holds me to him, then away.

"God — what happened?" His voice is quiet.

"I'm not sure," I say slowly.

"You're all right?"

I nod.

"The fire — "

"I remember."

"Al." Jake takes my face in his hands, as if he wants
to make sure I'm real. "Al, the bookshop burned, there's
nothing left. They couldn't get the damn fire out, it was
uncontrollable, they said they'd never seen — " He breaks
off.   His cheek, against mine, feels rough; he hasn't
shaved. "They said you were — "

"I'm not." I touch his hair. "Andrew, Eddie ... ?"

Jake pauses. "Their bodies were found," he said
finally. "Gonzalez came down ... but you, they said you,
the whole upstairs, there was nothing — "

"They were wrong."

"But ... how?"

"I don't know, can't remember. Feels like I was just
there, upstairs.... I tried to fax some pages, then I was
typing again; here's what I wrote."

We look at the pages I hold.

*... the fire howling beneath her now. Evangeline held her
shawl over he face and ran down the stairs toward the root
cellar. Burning sticks fell around her, half the floor had
given way; still she ran, as through a windstorm, to the
cellar door in the back room's floor. Wrenching up the*

doors, she let herself down the earthen steps, pulling the heavy oak panels shut above her; more blazing floorboards crashed into the cellar. The shallow space was filled with smoke, as she looked for the two men. Vaguely, through the hazed air, she saw two forms, half-buried in flaming debris; above her came a splintering rumble: the rest of the floor, sta ting to fall. Dodging through the cellar now, Evangeline felt her way to another door, hidden by shelves, in the far wall. Sweeping the shelves away, she jerked open the door and felt her way once more, this time through the underground passageway to the barn. Around her, the darkness seemed to constrict, dense and tangible. She scarcely breathed, unable to get her bearings; unable to tell if she was moving forward, or moving at all. She smelled earth and damp and death, and in that tunnel, she began to lose a sense of her enclosing skin, her own boundaries, her very presence in time and space. Perhaps she was fainting and only dreamed this flight; perhaps she had died, and her soul was passing ... Vaguely now, ahead, above, she saw a strip of light and, groping overhead, she felt the rough wood of the trapdoor in the barn floor. She waited a moment, listening. Then, carefully, she raised this door. The barn, yards from the house, was in shadow, as on other nights of late, when she'd met Luke here. Now the place was empty, quiet — save for the cows' lowing at the blaze beyond. Evangeline moved toward the barn door. Peering out through a crack, she saw the crowd around the burning house; a silent crowd, transfixed by the fire, as it danced and howled like a demon.

Evangeline drew her shawl over her head again. Slipping out the back of the barn, she moved swiftly down dim lanes, meeting no one. Now the dark seemed soft, permeable, letting her pass to the waterfront, the docks, the boats' web of rigging. And within the dark, within the hour, she sat in a skiff, watching as the river opened out before her, swift and faintly silver, unspooling fast, threading her way home. She listened to the creak of sails and wood; she breathed in the clear night air. Behind her now, the town's lights were fading, and then there were only the water and the sky.

Some, she knew, would say Evangeline, the sorceress, had died in the fire she deserved. Others would say she rose up on the wind and flew. But one day, she hoped, someone would carry the truth of her story to those who knew her and to those who might recall her name....

■

« 26 »

Ibegan this record to tell myself a story, a story I wished to understand. I was seeking what might lie between the lines, what might lie beyond the picture's frame. I understand the story now; I've learned many things. Other things, however, remain out of sight, just beyond logic's narrow borders. And now, that seems right. So be it. I can say this much:

Somehow, as I wrote Evangeline out of the fire, I wrote myself out as well. As my words carried her redemption, they also bore my own — and somehow, she bore me. She and I and all of us, perhaps, are connected in countless ways — but again, I do not pretend to understand. Nor do I need to.

Instead, I understand that moment, years ago, when my grandmother led me deep into the bookshelves and commanded me to listen to the books themselves. *Here, here is where the power is,* she said, *in the words, the stories.* This is the power that Weatherell's taught me. I listen again, anew.

I listen with Jake, in our new shop.

We have great hopes for it.
It sells only contemporary fiction.

■

ACKNOWLEDGMENTS

I wish to thank the old Saville Bookstore and the continuing presence of the Francis Scott Key Bookstore in Georgetown, in Washington, D.C., for the inspiration they provided for Weatherell's Rare Books, my invention.

My gratitude, always, to the late Anne Barrett, my first editor and beloved mentor, who told me the stories of the Boy Scout and the suffragette march, both of which took place during her own Washington girlhood, prior to 1920. I am also grateful for rediscovering the story of the mirror in *The Book of Irish Humor,* edited by John McCarthy, after remembering it in somewhat different form from my childhood.

As ever, my affectionate thanks to my family of loving, steadfast friends, especially during the writing, and rewriting Kathleen Dyke, Nancy Eggert, Hanna Emrich, Shloe Flanagan, Father Thomas P. Gavigan, S.J., Susan Hartt, Art and Margaret Byrne Heimbold, Ellen Holland, Anna Dee Jensen, Sherry Joslin, Leslie Kriewald, Caroline Lalire, Judith Lantz, Elizabeth Leland, Mary Ann Luby, Monica Maxon, Ann O'Donnell, Frances Bailey Shoeninger, Molly Sinclair, Carole LaMarca Steininger, Laura Sessions Stepp, Donna Stirling, Bob and Patty

Strohm, Jean Sweeney, Paul and Elizabeth Valentine, Melanne and Phil Verveer, and the Carmelite nuns of Carmel, California.

Special thanks, again, to Scott Wells, whose creative consultations infused the manuscript with inspiration and laughter, and to Upton Brady, whose perceptive and dedicated editorial guidance was crucial to the early drafts of this novel.

•

Critical Acclaim For Novels By Marcy Heidish

A WOMAN CALLED MOSES

*Award-winning, best-selling novel based on the life of Harriet Tubman, abolitionist and con-ductor on the Underground Railroad.
*Literary Guild Alternate Selec-tion;
*A Bantam paperback.
*TV Movie, starring Cicely Tyson, still available on DVD.
*Houghton Mifflin Co., 1st Pub.

Praise for *A Woman Called Moses*:
Publishers Weekly: "Her story has been told before, but never as eloquently, almost poetically, as here...achingly real...a strong narrative of a totally committed woman, one who speaks directly to our own desperate need to feel committed—and our wish that somewhere in the world there were more people like Harriet Tubman."

Washington Post Book World: "Profoundly rewarding...a daring work of the imagination."

Chicago Sun Times: "Marcy Heidish has, almost uncannily, crawled into the skin and very mind of Harriet Tubman. The dialogue sings with poetic beauty."

Houghton Mifflin Co.: "As events build toward a stunning climax, we are drawn into the spellbinding narrative of an extraordinary life, and a portion of our American past." ♦♦♦

WITNESSES

WITNESSES

A Novel By Marcy Heidish

* Award-winning novel based on the life of lay minister Anne Hutchinson, <u>America's first female advocate of religious freedom</u>.
* Citations: Society for Colonial Wars; laudatory reviews; large-print, hard-cover and paperback versions.
* Houghton Mifflin Co., 1ˢᵗPub.

Praise for *Witnesses:*

The New York Times Book Review: " .nothing ordinary about her creation of this remarkable woman. The novel abounds in literary grace. It employs the voices of the times as though heard this minute."

The New Yorker Magazine: "A striking novel...a compelling portrait."

The Washington Post: "Pure pleasure. Anne Hutchinson is real; thanks to *Witnesses,* she at last assumes her proper place in American history." —Jonathan Yardley, Pulitzer Prize-winning critic.

Ballantine Books: "This fearless woman, mother of fifteen, a leader in medicine and politics, comes to vivid life in these pages. A true believe in religious freedom who paid dearly for her principles in two trials for heresy. In the tradition of Arthur Miller's *The Crucible*, Witnesses is the deeply felt portrait of a woman in the paranoid climate of 17ᵗʰ century Boston." ◆◆◆

THE SECRET ANNIE OAKLEY

* Acclaimed novel based on the life of the legendary sharp-shooter.
* Hard- and Paperback versions
* A *Readers Digest* Condensed Novel.
* Optioned for film.
*Translated into several languages, laudatory reviews.
*New American Library, 1st Pub.

Praise for *The Secret Annie Oakley:*

Kirkus Reviews: "An immensely touching and cohesive fictional biography of the legendary sharp-shooter.builds from exemplary research to a fresh portrait of a talented woman in crisis.a class act—as Heidish reconstructs. with color and drama, the choreography of the shows, the tone of the period, and the textures of a haunting past."

The Arizona Daily Star: "...an imaginative, amaz-ing writer.a magician with words. Each character has been brought to life with a mere pen stroke; flesh and blood beings that are more than fiction. A master-piece of creative writing."

The Kansas City Star: "An unforgettable story."
Christian Science Monitor: "...Marcy Heidish weaves historical facts into a novel so moving that there will be many times in the years to come that I'll take pleasure in remembering that stout-hearted woman. 'Annie Oakley' hits the bull's eye every time." ♦♦♦

MIRACLES

A Novel About Mother Seton,
The First American Saint

MIRACLES

A Novel By Marcy Heidish

* Historical novel based on the life of **Mother Elizabeth Seton**, first American-born canonized saint.

* Main selection, *The Catholic Book Club*.

*New American Library, 1ˢᵗ Pub.

Praise for *Miracles*:

The New York Times Book Review: "This appealing book, told from the point of view of a skeptical modern priest, moves swiftly through tragedy to triumph."

Kirkus Reviews: "Working delicately with a balance of Church hagiography and psychological insight, Ms. Heidish provides another strong focus on the root dilemma of female saints and achievers."

New American Library: "*Miracles* is the story of an unforgettable woman's life and love. It is a novel charged with the vitality of a life that saw many changes, and with the power of a love that took many forms.[whether] as a lonely daughter of a wealthy, indifferent man; a searching young woman; a contented matron embracing a marriage that produced five beloved children; a widow searching for new meaning to life." ♦♦♦

DEADLINE

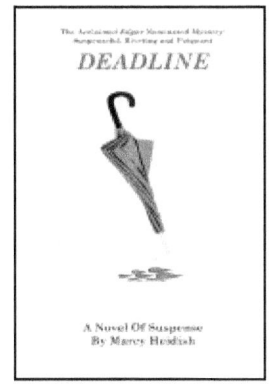

* Contemporary psychological novel with a "mystery" as a narrative line.
* Nominee for prestigious na-tional "Edgar" Award; fine reviews.
* St. Martin's Press, 1ˢᵗ Pub.

Praise for *Deadline*:

Washington Post: "*Deadline* is a tense, well-turned tale, filled with authentic police and newspaper people. Heidish's taut, punchy style moves the story at lightning speed."

Kirkus Reviews: "The high-tension plot is enhanced by sharply etched pictures, by many vivid characters, and by a crisp, clean, first-person style. Heidish imbues her haunting story and her gutsy heroine with a rare sense of tenderness and poignancy. An impressive mystery by a gifted writer."

St. Martin's Press: "This wire-tight novel probes re-lentlessly, driving deep into psychological darkness and violent death. As the riveting story reaches its stunning conclusion, we see a complex woman forced to meet the ultimate deadline." ◆◆◆

A Dangerous Woman: Mother Jones, An Unsung American Heroine

*A compelling, inspiring new historical novel, another powerful "profile in courage" American-style novel based on the life of Mary Harris Jones, a self-proclaimed Hell Raiser, daring labor leader, and colorful, quirky humanitarian.

*The arresting novel of an indomitable force, dressed demurely in widow's weeds and lace collars who:

> As an Irish immigrant—lost her homeland to the Great Famine.

> As a wife and mother—lost her whole family to yellow fever.

> As a dressmaker—lost home and business to the Chicago Fire

> As a survivor—turned from sorrow to help others survive.

Follow one of America's most feisty, fearless.and forgotten heroines whose rallying cry was:

"PRAY FOR THE DEAD—AND FIGHT LIKE HELL FOR THE LIVING!" ♦♦♦

DESTINED TO DANCE: A Novel About Martha Graham

> They called her a genius.
> They called her a goddess.
> They called her a monster.

Which title best fits Martha Graham, iconic Mother of Modern Dance? Find out—in the <u>first historical novel about this great American diva</u>.

DESTINED TO DANCE is a creative portrait of the legendary dancer and choreographer. Heidish offers another remarkable account of an American heroine: her successes, her sorrows, and her struggles.

Here is a masterful portrait of Graham, on stage, backstage, offstage. We see Graham's break-through brilliance, often compared to Picasso's or Stravinsky.

We also witness Graham's triumph over alcoholism, despair, and a failed marriage. Set against the intriguing world of dance, Martha Graham's story offers us a close-up on a complex and compelling overcomer.

Martha Graham (1894-1991) invented a new "language of movement," still taught around the world and exemplified in such classic works as *Appalachian Spring*, among 180 others.

As always, Heidish's research is thorough and her sense of her subject is magical. For all who love the arts, all who seek inspiration, and all who like to read between history's lines, *DESTINED TO DANCE* is a must-read book.   ◆◆◆

Scene Through A Window
A Historical Romance

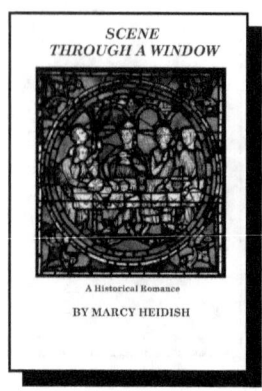

Travel through the centuries to watch a timeless love unfold around a timeless masterpiece: the fabled cathedral of Chartres, France. In 1194, an unthinkable disaster struck that sacred site. In one June night, a firestorm devastated the cathedral, its artwork, and parts of its surrounding town.

Immediately, the finest artists converged on Chartres to plan a new and innovative structure, built to endure and to surpass all that went before. Inevitably, these plans led to plots and rivalry, threatening the realization of a daring and demanding dream.

Against this backdrop, two lovers struggle to conceive the new cathedral's stained glass windows, still regarded as marvels today. This quest centers on discovering new gem-like colors: unique, precious, and incomparable. The pair, under increasing pressure, embarks on an intense search for the mysterious but elusive answers

Deftly weaving fact with fiction, Marcy Heidish sets an inspirational love story against a thoroughly researched Medieval backdrop. With her proven attention to detail, Heidish transports us to the winding streets of Chartres: its sounds and smells, its interiors and intrigues. Suspenseful, engrossing, and imaginative, *Scene Through A Window* creates a magical space where the impossible can happen. ◆◆◆

<u>NON-FICTION BOOKS</u>:
Soul and the City
WaterBrook Press, Random House imprint

<u>Praise for *Soul and the City*</u>:

*"I actually started reading Marcy Heidish's *Soul and the City* on a subway train. I must say it had exactly the effect she writes about: it gave me peace in the middle of the hurry, the rush, the loud noise of the city."

—Rick Hamlin, executive editor, Guideposts; author of *Finding God on the A Train*

* "Marcy Heidish has compiled a rich and nuanced touring companion to rival any Michelin or Eye-witness guide—usable in any city of the world. Keep it close and.you will meet beauty and holiness no matter where you pause to look."

— Leigh McLeroy, author of *The Beautiful Ache* and *The Sacred Ordinary*

* "*Soul and the City* is a deeply inspiring call to awareness to connection with God and with others, and ultimately to soulful worship through so many aspects of life in the city that we find mundane, undesirable, or that even go unnoticed. Almost instantly, upon delving into its pages, you find your perspective changed."

— Sarah Zacharias Davis, author of *Confessions from an Honest Wife, Transparent, and The Friends We Keep*.

Defiant Daughters
Liguori Publications.

A Candle At Midnight
Ave Maria Press

Prase for *A Candle At Midnight*:

   * "Heidish honors modern medicine and spiritual healing in this compelling work."

   — Alen J. Salerian, M.D., Medical Director of the Washing-ton Psychiatric Center

   * "This is not a book of abstractions. I recommend this book to anyone who is caught in the darkness of mid-night."

   — Martha Manning, Author of *Undercurrents: A Life Beneath the Surface*:

   * "A masterpiece!"

   — Rev. Nancy Eggert, Spiritual Director ◆◆◆

Who Cares? Simple Ways YOU Can Reach Out

Ave Maria Press

<u>Praise for *Who Cares?*</u>:

A lonely neighbor, a colleague in distress, a friend in difficulty. In situations like these we want to reach out and help, yet so often we feel unsure about our response.

What to do?
What to say?
What is enough?
Too much?
Too little?

This practical book is designed to bring out the caring person in each of us. Marcy Heidish offers simple, specific ways to practice the art of caring, especially within our immediate circle of concern: family, friends, neighbors, and coworkers.

Heidish reminds us of the many little things we can do to open the door to a caring relationship.

— **Ave Maria Press**

"Contains savvy insights and wisdom about service. This is an ideal resource for anyone interested in engaged spirituality."

— *Cultural Information Service*: ◆◆◆

Too Late To Be A Fortune Cookie Writer

"A novelist has a specific poetic license which also applies to his own life."
~ Jerzi Kosinski

Marcy Heidish, award-winning author of fourteen books, fiction and non-fiction, is just such a novelist with a "specific poetic license."

Her work has been praised for its "lyrical grace" and so it is a special joy to present her first book of poetry. Ms. Heidish has written poems for decades.

With humor and humanity, this collection spans a broad range of subjects. Insight, wit and depth enliven these poems. They address universal concerns: maturity, mortality, memory and much more.

Ms. Heidish gives us an intimate glimpse into a writer's soul. Adept at varied verse forms, she amuses, reflects, recalls, and rejoices:

• "A watched pot never boils unless you're boiling vodka."

• "Houses crowd my life like chairs on a Novem-ber beach."

• "The sun is a peach, half ripened, at hand."

And the poet brings us with her. ♦♦♦

POEMS FOR JOAN OF ARC

"Joan was a being so uplifted from the ordinary run of mankind that she finds no equal in a thousand years....Her story would be beyond belief if it were not true."
—Winston Churchill

"She is the Wonder of the Ages. And when we consider her origin, her early circumstances, her sex, and that she did all the things upon which her renown rests while she was a young girl, we recognize that while our race continues, she will also be the Riddle of the Ages."
—Mark Twain

Here, in poetry, is a fresh approach to Joan of Arc, that famous heroine-for-all-seasons. Almost six hundred years after she was burned at the stake, Joan's story still compels, fascinates and challenges us.

Credited with saving France, that famous warrior-maid leaps from a new poetry collection by Marcy Heidish, a gifted specialist in historical fiction (*A Woman Called Moses, Destined to Dance,* etc). Heidish's poetic reflections on Joan are riveting, imaginative, and beautifully crafted.

Whether you know a little or a lot about Joan of Arc, this original and elegant collection will invite you to see "The Maid of Orleans" from a wealth of insightful perspectives. If you approach Joan as a role model, a puzzle, or a poem herself, you will find this book an impressive and inspiring read. ♦♦♦

Short Pieces:

Articles and book reviews published in *Ms.* Magazine, *GEO* Magazine, *The Washington Post*, *The Washington Star*, and various in-flight periodicals.
Two of these pieces are:

* ***The Pilgrim Who Stayed***, *GEO* Magazine, about Chartres Cathedral, widely translated.

* ***The Grand Dame of the Harbor***, about the Statue of Liberty, was a highly acclaimed cover story for *GEO* Magazine. This article is included in a textbook anthology designed to teach writing to college students. Winner of coveted Apex Award. ♦♦♦

See Marcy Heidish page at:
www.Amazon.com

www.marcyheidishbooks.com

[AND Kindle] *

* Marcy Heidish Books are printed by Lightning Source and distributed by Ingram of Ingram Content Group Inc., the world's largest distributor of physical and digital content, providing books, music and media content to over 38,000 retailers, libraries, schools and distribution partners in 195 countries. More than 25,000 publishers use Ingram's . ♦♦♦